JAMES HADLEY CHASE

Also by James Hadley Chase

James Hadley Chase

Tiger by the Tail

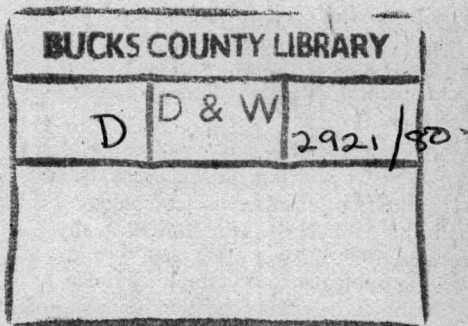

A PANTHER BOOK

GRANADA
London Toronto Sydney New York

Published by Granada Publishing Limited in 1966
Reprinted 1966, 1968, 1969, 1974, 1975, 1977, 1980

ISBN 0 586 02652 5

First published in Great Britain by
Robert Hale Ltd 1954
Copyright © James Hadley Chase 1954

Granada Publishing Limited
Frogmore, St Albans, Herts AL2 2NF
and
3 Upper James Street, London W1R 4BP
866 United Nations Plaza, New York, NY 10017, USA
117 York Street, Sydney, NSW 2000, Australia
100 Skyway Avenue, Rexdale, Ontario, M9W 3A6, Canada
PO Box 84165, Greenside, 2034 Johannesburg, South Africa
61 Beach Road, Auckland, New Zealand

Made and printed in Great Britain by
C. Nicholls & Company Ltd
The Philips Park Press, Manchester
Set in Monotype Plantin

Granada ®
Granada Publishing ®

*Tiger by
the Tail*

PART ONE

CHAPTER I

A TALL slim blonde in a white summer frock, walking just ahead of him, caught Ken Holland's eye. He studied her, watching her gentle undulations as she walked. He quickly shifted his eyes. He hadn't looked at a woman like this since he had first met Ann.

What's the matter with me? he asked himself. I'm getting as bad as Parker.

He looked again at the blonde. An evening out with her, he thought, would be sensational.

What the eye doesn't see, Parker was always saying, the heart doesn't grieve about. That was true. Ann would never know. After all, other married men did it. Why shouldn't he?

But when the girl crossed the road and he lost sight of her, he jerked his mind back with an effort to the letter he had received that morning from Ann.

She had been away now for five weeks, and she wrote to say her mother was no better, and she had no idea when she was coming back.

Why did her mother have to live miles away from anywhere and be so cussedly independent? Ken asked himself as he walked briskly towards the bank. No one over seventy should be allowed to live alone. When they got ill, their long-suffering daughters had to go and look after them, and their still more long-suffering sons-in-law had to fend for themselves.

Five weeks was too long, and Ken was sick of looking after himself; sicker still of being without Ann.

He ran down the steps leading to the staff cloakroom where he found Parker adjusting his tie in the mirror over the toilet basins.

"Hello," Parker said, grinning. "How's the bachelor this morning? When's Ann coming home?"

"I wish I knew," Ken said, washing his hands. "The old

girl's still bad. Ann doesn't know when she'll get away."

Parker sighed.

"I wish to heck my wife would take a month off. I haven't had her out of my hair for fourteen years." He inspected his chin in the mirror. "You're a damn lucky guy, but you don't seem to know it. Why you haven't painted the town red beats me. I don't know; some guys don't know what they're here for."

"Oh, shut up!" Ken growled. He was sick of Parker's continual jibes. Ever since Ann went away, Parker had been on at him to kick over the traces. Not a day passed but Parker was nagging at him to have a night out.

Parker was forty-five, inclined to fat and going bald. He was always resurrecting the past, remembering what a rake he had been, and how all women had found him irresistible, and still found him irresistible for that matter.

"You're edgy," Parker said, looking intently at Ken. "And I don't blame you. You want to let off a little steam. I was talking to old Hemmingway on the way up. He says you can't do better than have a night out at the Cigale. Haven't been myself, worse luck, but he goes regularly, and he was telling me it's the spot. It sounds swell: good food, cheap drinks and plenty of willing wantons. It'd do you a power of good. A change of women now and then is good for us all."

"You go ahead and change women," Ken snapped. "I'm satisfied with what I've got."

But during the morning he became aware of an increasing restlessness: something he had been experiencing in a milder degree for the past week. Ever since he had married he had looked forward to going home opening the front door and seeing with a sense of satisfied pleasure Ann appear to greet him. But these past five weeks had changed all that: the thought of returning each evening to the empty bungalow irritated him now.

His mind shifted to the conversation he had had with Parker. The Cigale. He had seen the nightclub several times from the outside. It was down a side turning off Main Street: a gaudy place, decorated with neon lights and chromium. He recollected the glossy pictures of show girls that he had glanced at as he had passed.

It was not a place for a respectably married bank official to go to. As he closed his till before going to lunch, he decided firmly against the Cigale. He would go home as usual and be bored.

He went down to the cloakroom for his hat.

Parker was washing his hands, as Ken came in.

"There you are," Parker said, reaching for a towel. "Well, have you made up your mind what you are going to do tonight? What's it going to be – wine, women and song or just a nice, friendly woman?"

"I'm going home. The lawn wants cutting."

Parker grimaced.

"Hell! You must be in a worse rut than I am. Imagine cutting the lawn when the wife's away! Seriously, Holland, you have a duty to yourself. What the eye doesn't see, the heart doesn't grieve about. It may be your last chance before you get old and useless."

"Oh dry up!" Ken exclaimed, exasperated. "The trouble with you is that you've never grown up."

"Thank the Lord I haven't." Parker said. "When my idea of fun is cutting the goddam lawn, I'll know it's time I was buried."

Ken left him, still talking, and climbed the steps that led to the staff exit.

Parker's continual suggestions irritated him, and he was frowning as he walked along the hot sidewalk to the restaurant where he always took his meals.

He was thinking: of course he's right. I am in a rut. I've been in a rut ever since I married. I don't suppose I'll get another chance to kick the can around. Ann won't leave me again: anyway, not for years. But do I want to kick the can around? If only I knew when Ann was coming back. This might go on for weeks.

It may be your last chance before you get old and useless, Parker had said. That was true. Ann would never know. Why not have a night out tonight? Why not?

He suddenly felt excited and reckless. He would do it! It would probably turn out to be a flop, but anything was better than returning to the empty bungalow.

He would go to the Cigale and have a couple of drinks. Maybe some blonde would be willing to share his company without making any complications.

That's it, he said to himself, as he walked on towards the restaurant; a final night out; a swan song.

9

The afternoon dragged for Ken. For the first time since he could remember, his work bored him and he caught himself continually looking at the wall clock.

The stale, baked air coming in from the street, the roar of the traffic and the hot, sweating faces of his customers irritated him.

"A perfect evening to cut a lawn," Parker said with a grin as the messenger closed the doors of the bank. "You'll sweat like a horse."

Ken didn't say anything. He began to check his cash.

"You want to get organized, Holland," Parker went on. "There are plenty of able-bodied men who'll cut your lawn while you go out and enjoy yourself."

"Skip it, will you?" Ken said shortly. "You're not even being funny."

Parker eyed him thoughtfully, sighed and shook his head. "You poor guy! You don't know what you're missing."

They worked in silence until both had checked their cash, then Parker said, "If you've brought your car, you can drive me home."

Parker lived in a road next to Ken's; and although Ken didn't want any more of his company, he couldn't refuse.

"Okay," he said, gathering up his cash-box and books. "Make it snappy. I've had about enough of this place for today."

As they drove through the heavy traffic, Parker glanced at the evening papers and gave out the more interesting items of news.

Ken scarcely listened.

Away from the bank now, and heading for home, his natural caution reasserted itself.

He would cut the lawn, he told himself, and he would spend the rest of the evening at home. He must have been nuts even to contemplate having a night out. If he slipped up, was seen or got himself into a mess, he might not only ruin his marriage, but he might end his career.

"Don't bother to take me right home," Parker said suddenly. "I want to stretch my legs. Take me to your place and I'll walk the rest of the way."

"I don't mind taking you home."

"I'll walk. Maybe you'll offer me a drink. I'm right out of whisky."

Ken was tempted to say he was too. He wanted to be rid of Parker, but he checked the impulse and, now he was clear of the heavy traffic, he accelerated and in a few minutes pulled up outside the neat little bungalow in line with a number of similar bungalows.

"My word! Your lawn does need cutting," Parker said as they got out of the car. "That's going to be quite a job."

"It won't take long," Ken returned, leading the way up the path. He unlocked the front door and they entered the small hall.

The air was hot and close, and Ken hurried into the lounge to throw open the windows.

"Phew! Been shut up all day, hasn't it?" Parker said, following him.

"All the afternoon," Ken returned, taking off his coat and dropping it on to a chair. "Our help only comes in during the morning."

He went over and mixed two large highballs. The two men lit cigarettes and raised their glasses.

"Mud in your eye," Parker said. "I can't stay long; my wife will be wondering where I am. You know, Holland, I sometimes wonder if I was wise to get married. It has a lot of advantages, of course, but women are so damned exacting. They don't seem to realize a guy wants a little freedom now and then."

"Now don't start that all over again," Ken said sharply.

"It's a fact," Parker said. He finished his highball, sighed and looked expectantly at Ken. "That was pretty good."

"Want another?"

"I wouldn't say no."

Ken finished his drink, got up and made two more.

"How long has Ann been away?" Parker asked, taking the glass Ken handed to him.

"Five weeks."

"That's too long. What's the matter with the old girl?"

"I don't know. Old age, I guess. This could go on for another month."

"How would you like to step out tonight?" Parker asked, looking at Ken with a little leer.

"What do you mean?"

"Well, strictly between you and me and the bedpost, I have

a little arrangement that works pretty well. I wouldn't mind putting you in the way of some fun too."

"Arrangement? What's that mean?"

"I have an outlet that the wife doesn't know about. It's not always easy to fix, but I manage to have a fling every once in a while when the wife goes to see her mother."

Ken looked at him.

"You mean some woman?"

"Some woman! How right you are. Old Hemmingway put me on to this dish. Everything's very discreet; no danger of being seen, and everything taken care of. She's a hostess. You needn't be more than friendly if you don't want to. She takes care of lonely guys like you. You pay her, of course. You can take her out for the evening and leave her at her apartment if you feel like it, or if you don't you can go in. She's a damn convenient and very safe outlet." He took out his billfold, scribbled something on one of his cards and put it on the table. "That's her phone number. Her name's Fay Carson. All you have to do is call her, tell her you want to see her, and she'll give you an appointment. She rates a little high, but she's worth it."

"No, thank you," Ken said sharply.

"Take it and don't be a mug," Parker finished his drink and stood up. "I'd like to do her a good turn. I promised her I'd recommend her to my friends. I always keep a promise."

Ken flicked the card off the table towards the fireplace.

"No, thanks," he said again.

"Keep it by you. Take her out. She's fun. She's just what a lonely guy needs. Take her out tonight to a show. What's the matter with that? She's really something. I wouldn't put you on to a cheap floosie. This girl's got everything."

"I'm sure of that," Ken said curtly. "But I'm not interested."

"Well, it's your funeral. See you tomorrow. Thanks for the drink." Parker nodded to the card lying in the hearth. "Don't leave that about. Lock it up somewhere for future reference."

"You better take it," Ken said, moving towards the hearth. "I don't want it."

"Keep it. You never know. So long now. I'll let myself out."

As Ken picked up the card, Parker crossed the hall, opened the front door and went off down the path.

Ken glanced at the telephone number written on the card. *Riverside* 33344. He hesitated for a moment, then tore the card in half and dropped it into his trash basket.

12

He picked up his coat and went along the passage to the bedroom. He stood in the doorway, looking into the big, airy room. It looked horribly neat and unlived-in and forsaken. He tossed his coat on the bed and began to strip off his clothes. He felt hot and sticky. Through the curtained window he could see the evening sun blazing down on the thick grass of the lawn.

Too early to start pushing a mower yet, he told himself, and went into the bathroom and took a shower.

He felt better when he had put on an open-necked shirt and a pair of old slacks. He wandered into the lounge and stood looking around.

The time was twenty minutes past six: a long time before he went to bed, and already he felt lonely.

He crossed to the table and splashed whisky into his glass, carried the glass to an armchair near the radio and sat down. He turned on the radio, lit a cigarette and stared emptily at the opposite wall.

So Parker had found himself a girl. That surprised Ken. He had always regarded Parker as a man who talked a lot and did nothing.

As some speaker began a lecture on the horrors of the H-bomb, Ken impatiently snapped off the radio. He got up and walked over to the window to stare out at the garden. He had no inclination to cut the lawn or go out and weed the rose bed, which was in need of attention.

He remained looking out of the window for some minutes; his face darkened by a frown. Then he glanced at his wrist-watch, lifted his shoulders in a resigned shrug and went across the room to the hall. He opened the front door and walked out on to the porch.

The atmosphere was hot and close.

Probably a storm blowing up, he thought. It's too damned hot to cut the lawn. I'll skip it for tonight. Might be cooler tomorrow.

The moment he had made the decision he felt more relaxed in mind. How quiet and empty the bungalow felt, he thought, returning to the hall. He wandered into the lounge and finished the whisky in his glass, and without thinking, splashed more whisky into the empty glass and carried it into the kitchen.

This was going to be another dull evening, he thought as he opened the refrigerator to see what Carrie, the coloured help, had left him for supper. A glance at the empty shelves told him she had forgotten to prepare anything, and he slammed the door shut. There were cans of food in the pantry, but he didn't feel like eating out of a can.

Shrugging impatiently, he went back to the lounge and put on the television.

The prancing blonde in a frilly little skirt who appeared on the screen held his attention. He sat down and watched her. She reminded him of the slim blonde he had seen on the street that morning. He watched an indifferent programme for half an hour or so and during that time he twice got up to refill his glass. At the end of the programme, and before a new one began, he snapped off the television, got to his feet and began to pace slowly up and down.

Parker's flat-footed cliché kept going through his mind: what the eye doesn't see, the heart doesn't grieve about.

He looked at his watch. In another hour it would be dusk. He went over to the whisky bottle. There was only a little left now, and he emptied what there was into the glass. The previous drinks he had had were now affecting him, and he felt in an increasingly reckless mood.

Why stay in tonight? he asked himself. Why not give Parker's girl a trial? She takes care of lonely guys, Parker had said. That's what he was, wasn't he?

He carried his drink into the bedroom, set it down on the dressing-table, pulled off his shirt and took a new one from a drawer.

What was her telephone number?

He closed his eyes while he tried to think, and discovered he had drunk more whisky than he had thought.

Riverside 33344.

Everything depends on her voice he said to himself and what she says. If she sounds awful, I can always hang up. If no one answers, then I will cut the lawn. That's a bet.

Buttoning up his shirt, he went into the lounge and dialled the number. He listened to the burr-burr-burr on the line, aware that his heart was now beating rapidly.

She's not there, he said to himself after a few moments and he felt both relieved and disappointed. Well, this lets me out. I'll skip it and cut the lawn; but he was reluctant to replace the receiver.

Then suddenly there was a click over the line, and his heart missed a beat and then raced.

A girl's voice said, "Hello?"

"Is that Miss Carson?" he asked cautiously.

"That's right. Who's calling?"

He could almost hear a smile in her bright, gay voice.

"I guess you wouldn't know me. A friend of mine . . ." He broke off, floundering.

"Oh." The girl laughed. It was a nice, friendly laugh and Ken felt suddenly at ease. "Well, don't be shy. Do you want to come on over?"

"That was the idea, but perhaps you are tied up?"

"I'm not. How long will you be?"

"I don't know where you are."

The girl laughed again.

"25 Lessington Avenue. Do you know it?"

"That's off Cranbourne Street, isn't it?"

"That's right. I'm on the top floor; only heaven is higher. Have you a car?"

"Yes."

"Don't leave it outside. There's a parking lot at the corner."

Lessington Avenue was on the other side of the town to where Ken lived. It would take him twenty minutes to get there.

"I could get over by nine," he said.

"I'll be waiting. You'll find the front door open. Just walk up."

"I'll do that."

"Until nine o'clock then. Good-bye for now."

The line went dead, and he slowly replaced the receiver.

He took out his handkerchief and wiped his face. Even now he hadn't committed himself, he thought. I needn't go. I have still time to make up my mind.

He returned to the bedroom and finished dressing. As he knotted his tie, he recalled the sound of her voice. He tried to create a mental picture of her. Was she blonde? Was she tall? She sounded young. Parker said she had everything. She must be pretty good for Parker to say that.

He slipped on his coat. Then leaving the bedroom he went into the lounge. For a long moment, he stood, hesitating.

At least I can look at the place he thought. If it isn't much I needn't go in. Damn it! I needn't feel so shifty about this. It's not as if I'm going to misbehave myself with the girl. I'll take her to a show or a night-club.

He took out his billfold and checked his money. He noticed

his hands were shaking and he grinned.

As he looked across the room to the front door, he found he couldn't look at the silver-framed photograph of Ann which stood on the desk.

CHAPTER II

I

THERE were only four cars in the big parking lot at the corner of Lessington Avenue.

The attendant, an elderly man wearing a white overall, came out of his little hut and waved Ken to park beside a glittering Buick.

As Ken cut the engine and got out of his car, the attendant said, "Going to be long, mister?"

"I may be. I don't know. Depends if my friend happens to be in," Ken said cautiously. "How long can I keep it here?"

The attendant gave him a knowing little smile.

"All night if you want to. Lots of guys leave their cars here all night."

Ken wondered uneasily if the old man guessed where he was going. He paid for the parking ticket.

"I bet I don't see those four guys tonight," the attendant went on, waving his hand towards the four cars. "This is a proper night-out district."

Ken forced an uneasy smile.

"Is it? I didn't know."

The attendant gave him a wink.

"Nor did the other guys," he said, and walked back to his hut.

By now dusk had fallen, and Ken felt fairly secure as he walked along Lessington Avenue.

It was a quiet street, bordered on either side by shady trees that acted as a screen. The houses looked neat and respectable and he met no one during the short walk to No. 25.

Parker had said it was very discreet, no danger of being seen, and everything taken care of.

So far he was right.

Ken paused to look up and down the street before mounting the steps that led to No. 25. Satisfied no one was watching him, he climbed the steps, turned the door handle and pushed open the door. He stepped quickly into the hall.

Facing him was a flight of stairs. On the wall, by the stairs, was a row of mail boxes. He paused to look at them. Above each was a card, carrying the owner's name.

He read: May Christie, Gay Hordern. Eve Barclay. Glorie Gold. Fay Carson.

Birds of a feather, he thought uneasily. What was he walking into?

He stood hesitating at the foot of the stairs. For a long moment his nerve failed, and he almost decided to retreat back to his car.

He was nuts to come to this house, he told himself, not knowing what this girl even looked like.

If it hadn't been for the whisky he had drunk, he would have turned back, but the whisky still had charge of him and urged him on.

Parker said she was all right. Parker came to see her regularly. She must be all right.

He began to climb the stairs.

On the third landing, the sound of a radio playing soft swing music came through a red-painted front door. He continued up the stairs, and as he was within four stairs of the fourth landing, he heard a door open and then slam shut.

Before he could make up his mind whether to turn around and bolt down the stairs, footsteps sounded on the landing, and a man appeared at the head of the stairs.

He was short, fat and going bald and he carried a snap-brim hat which he slapped against his thigh as he paused to stare at Ken.

In spite of his baldness, he couldn't have been much older than Ken. There was something repulsively soft about his appearance. He reminded Ken of a stale cream bun. He had great black, protruding eyes, the whites of which were bloodshot. A thin, ugly mouth, a small hooked nose, and sharply pointed ears that were set tightly against the sides of his head made him one of the most extraordinary looking men Ken had ever seen.

His suit was creased and baggy, and his orange and blue patterned tie was grease-stained.

Under his left arm he carried a fawn-coloured Pekinese dog whose long, silky coat told of hours of careful grooming. The dog was as immaculate as its master was shabby.

The fat man stepped back.

"Come up, sir," he said in a soft effeminate voice. "I never cross on the stairs. You weren't by any chance coming to see me?"

The black bloodshot eyes went over Ken, and Ken had an uncomfortable feeling the fat man was memorizing every little detail about him.

"No. I'm going further up," Ken said, hurrying up the stairs.

"We should have an elevator," the fat man complained. "These awful stairs are bad for my heart. Leo hates them too." He touched the dog's head with a fat, grubby forefinger. "Such a beautiful creature, don't you think?" He moved the dog forward a little as if inviting Ken's inspection. "Do you admire dogs, sir?"

Ken edged around the fat man.

"Yeah, I guess I do. He's certainly a fine animal," he said uncomfortably.

"He has won many prizes," the fat man went on. "Only this month he got a gold cup."

The dog stared at Ken. Its eyes were like those of its master: dark, protruding and bloodshot.

Ken went on up the stairs. When he reached the top landing he paused. As he had walked up the remaining stairs, he had been listening for sounds of the fat man going down, but he had heard nothing.

He stepped softly to the banister rail and looked over.

On the landing below, the fat man stood motionless, looking up. Their eyes met and the fat man smiled. It was a curious sly, knowing smile, and it startled Ken. The Pekinese also looked up. Its flat, black-muzzled face was stolid with indifference.

Ken moved hurriedly back, and turned to face the green-painted front door on the far side of the landing. He was aware that his heart was pounding and his nerves were jumpy. The encounter with the fat man had shaken him.

If he hadn't been sure the fat man was still standing on the lower landing, Ken would have about faced and got out of the house as quickly as he could. But the idea of having to pass the fat man again was more than his shaken nerves could stand.

Wishing now he hadn't been such a reckless fool as to come to this house, Ken gingerly pushed the bell button.

II

The front door opened almost immediately.

The girl who held the door open was dark, vivacious and pretty. At a guess she was twenty-three or four. Her hair, dressed to her shoulders, was as black as a raven's wing. She had wide-set, blue eyes, a big, generous, scarlet-painted mouth and a friendly smile that did much to restore Ken's shaken nerves.

She wore a pale blue summer frock, and the shape he saw under the frock set his heart thumping.

"Hello," she said, standing aside. "Come on in."

He was aware of her quick, searching scrutiny. What she saw seemed to please her, for she gave him another flashing smile as he walked awkwardly into a big, airy sitting-room.

Before the empty fireplace stood a massive leather couch. Three lounging chairs, a radiogram, a television set, a big walnut liquor cabinet, and a dining table that stood in the bay window completed the furnishing.

Bowls of flowers stood on the table, the top of the radiogram and on the mantelpiece.

The girl closed the front door and moved over to the liquor cabinet. She rolled her hips deliberately as she walked, and glanced over her shoulder to see his reaction.

Ken was reacting. He thought she had a sensational figure.

"Make yourself at home," she said. "Sit down and relax. I'm absolutely harmless, and you don't have to be shy or frightened of me."

"I'm not frightened of you," Ken said, warming to her. "It's just I'm not used to this sort of thing."

She laughed.

"I should hope not. A nice boy like you shouldn't need anyone like me." She quickly mixed two highballs as she talked. "What's the idea, Buster?" she went on. "Your girl let you down?"

Ken felt himself go hot.

"Not exactly."

She carried the drinks over to the couch and sat beside him.

"Sorry; that slipped out. I didn't mean to stick my nose where it isn't wanted," she said. "It's just you're not the type I usually meet." She gave him one of the tall glasses. "I'm in luck tonight. Here's to fun, Buster."

Ken was glad of the highball. He hadn't expected anything like this. The set-up wasn't sordid at all. The room was better than his own sitting-room. The girl was like one of the girls at his bank, only a lot prettier. He would never have guessed she was what she was.

"Are you in a rush to get away?" she asked, crossing one slim leg over the other and carefully adjusting her skirt to cover her knee.

"Why no. That is . . ."

"That's fine. There's nothing I hate more than the guy who tears in here, and tears out again. Most of them do. I guess their wives are waiting for them. Do you want to stay here?"

Ken hesitated. He would have liked nothing better, but he remembered his determination not to get himself involved in anything he would regret later.

"I guess not," he said awkwardly. "The fact is – I really only want – I thought we could do a show or something like that."

The girl looked quickly at him, then smiled.

"Of course, if that's what you really want. But look, Buster, it's going to cost you the same one way or the other. So you can please yourself."

"Let's go out," Ken said, feeling himself grow hot. He took out his billfold. "Shall we settle the financial arrangements now?"

"Twenty bucks: does that sound like hell?" she said, smiling at him.

"That's all right," Ken said, and gave her two tens.

"It's okay with me if you want to change your mind," she said, getting up. "Let's see how we go, shall we?"

She crossed the room went into another room and returned immediately.

"Well, now," she said, sitting on the arm of his chair. "What shall we do?"

He found her presence disturbing. Already his determination to behave was wilting.

"I thought we might go to a nightclub," he said. "I'll have to be careful not to be seen."

"Don't worry about that. We'll go to the Blue Rose. I bet none of your pals ever go to a joint like that. You'll have fun, and the drinks aren't too poisonous. I must change. Do you want to come in?"

Ken looked blank.

"That's all right. I'll sit here."

"You're a funny guy. I have to keep most of them out with a shot-gun. Don't be too shy, will you?"

"That's okay," Ken muttered, not looking at her.

She gave him a puzzled stare, shook her head, and went into the bedroom, leaving the door wide open.

Ken sat still while he wrestled with his conscience. It would have been easier and so much less complicated if she had run true to type. If she had been a hard little floosie, his coming here wouldn't have taken on this disconcerting personal atmosphere.

"For goodness' sake, Buster," the girl said, coming to the bedroom door, "stop looking like the wrath of God. What's the matter?"

She came over to where he was sitting took the highball out of his hand and put it on the table. She dropped on her knees in front of him.

"We have plenty of time," she said. "We can go out later." She slid her arms around his neck. "Kiss me, Buster."

Throwing caution to the winds, he caught her to him, his mouth coming down on hers.

III

It was ten-thirty when they left the apartment. They met no one on the stairs, and they picked up a passing taxi outside the house.

"The Blue Rose," the girl said to the driver. "122nd Street."

In the dark seclusion of the taxi she sat close to Ken, holding his hand.

"I like you, Buster," she said. "You don't know what a change you are to the usual guys I get snarled up with."

Ken smiled at her, not saying anything. He felt relaxed and happy. This night was off the record: hours that didn't count in his routine of life. In this way, he had got the better of his conscience. He knew he had been extraordinarily lucky to find a girl like Fay to share this stolen night out. By tomorrow the

21

whole episode would be behind him: a memory he would have for the rest of his days. It would never happen again, he assured himself. He wouldn't want it to happen again. But now it was happening, he would be a fool not to enjoy every second of it.

He looked at Fay as they passed a battery of neon lights advertising a cereal food. The blue, green and red lights lit up the interior of the cab.

She looked extraordinarily attractive, he thought, in the electric blue, full-skirted frock, cut low to show to advantage her creamy white shoulders. Around her throat she wore a necklace of dark blue beads that emphasized the blueness of her eyes.

He had forgotten he had paid her twenty dollars for this night out. It was odd, but he felt as if he had gone back five years and was spending the kind of night he had so often spent before he met Ann.

"Do you like dancing, Buster?" she asked suddenly.

"Sure; do you?"

"I love it. I used to earn a living as a dancer, then things went wrong. I lost my partner, and I couldn't find another, so I gave it up. We used to give exhibitions at the Blue Rose. It's not a bad little club. I think you'll like it."

"What happened to your partner?" Ken asked, merely to carry on the conversation.

He saw her face tighten.

"Oh, he went away. He wasn't the type to stick at anything for long."

Ken felt instinctively that this was a sore point with her, and he changed the subject.

"Who's the fat man who lives in the apartment below yours? The one with the Pekinese?"

She turned her head sharply to look at him.

"Did you see him, then?"

"I met him on the stairs."

Fay made a little grimace.

"He's a horrible little louse. No one knows what he does for a living. His name's Raphael Sweeting, believe it or not. He's always stopping me on the stairs. He uses that lap dog of his as an excuse to talk."

The cab slowed down and pulled up outside a tall, dark building.

They got out of the cab, and Ken paid off the driver.

"Is this it?" he said, staring up at the building.

"It's down this alley," Fay said, slipping her arm through his. "You needn't be scared you'll meet anyone you know. The members are strictly limited, and they don't come from your part of the world."

Ken followed her down the narrow alley. At the end of it was a heavy oak door with a judas window. Over the door, fashioned cleverly from neon tubes was a big blue rose. Its blue light reflected faintly on the gleaming brass of the door's fitments.

Fay touched a bell-push by the side of the door.

They stood, side by side, waiting.

Away in the far distance came a rumble of thunder.

"Hear that?" Ken said.

"I've been expecting a storm all the evening. Let's hope it cools the air."

The judas window slid back and a white thin face with hard expressionless eyes appeared for a brief moment, then the door opened.

"Evening, Miss Carson."

The man who had opened the door was short and thickset with a mop of blond wavy hair. He eyed Ken over, and gave him a brief nod.

"Hello, Joe," Fay said, smiling. "Busy tonight?"

"So, so," Joe returned. "Your table's free."

She nodded and led Ken across the bare lobby, down a passage to another heavy door. As she opened the door, the sound of a dance band reached them.

They walked down red-carpeted stairs where a hat check girl took Ken's hat. They went on into a big ornate bar.

There were a number of people in the bar, and Ken looked at them uneasily.

He saw at once he had nothing to worry about. Fay was right. These people certainly didn't come from his part of the world. The women were hard, showy and noisy. The men looked tough and sporting. Several of the women and a number of the men were in evening dress. None of them took any notice of Ken. Three or four of the men saluted Fay and then looked away.

The barman came over, wiping the shiny counter with a cloth.

"Evening, Miss Carson."

"Two martinis, Jack."

She climbed up on to a stool, while Ken stood at her side.

23

The barman served two martinis, and then moved away to serve a tall negro who had just come in.

Ken looked at the negro curiously.

He was a massive man, standing about six foot four, with shoulders that looked as wide as a barn door. His head was closely shaved, and he had a crinkled scar that began just under his right eye and went down in small puckers to his mouth.

He wore a lavender-coloured velveteen jacket, black trousers, a white nylon shirt and a mauve bow tie. A big diamond glittered in the centre of his shirt and flashed every time he moved.

"Hello, Sam," Fay said, lifting her hand and wriggling her fingers at the negro.

He gave a slow, expansive smile, revealing a mouthful of big, gold-capped teeth.

"Enjoy yourself, honey," he said in a deep, rich voice.

His black eyes dwelt on Ken for a brief moment, and then he gave him a little nod. He carried his drink across the room and sat down beside a thin mulatto girl in a low-cut green evening dress who was smoking a cigarette in a foot-long holder. She caught Fay's eye and waved.

"That's Sam Darcy," Fay told Ken. "He owns this joint. He gave me my first break. He's a swell guy. That's Claudette, his wife."

"What a size he is!" Ken said, impressed.

"He used to be one of Joe Louis's sparring partners. He built up this club from nothing. I wish you could have seen it when I first danced here. It was nothing but a damp cellar with a few tables and a pianist. In five years it's grown to this." She finished her martini and slid off the stool. "Let's eat. I'm starving."

Ken paid for the drinks and followed her across the bar, and into the restaurant.

Several couples were dancing, and most of the tables were occupied.

The Captain of waiters, a dark, hawk-eyed Italian, bustled forward, greeted Fay effusively and conducted them to a table against the wall.

It was while they were finishing an excellent mushroom and prawn omelette that Ken noticed a strikingly beautiful girl come to the door of the restaurant.

She immediately attracted his attention, and he wasn't the only man in the room to stare at her.

24

She was tall and willowy. Her blonde curls were piled high up on the top of her beautifully shaped head. She wore a sea-green evening gown, cut low enough to show an expanse of creamy white skin that made Ken's eyes pop. Her enormous eyes were emerald green and her eyelashes curled upwards and seemed to be touching her eyelids.

It wasn't so much her face that Ken stared at. Her figure would have stampeded an octogenarian. It stampeded Ken.

"Phew! Who's that?" he asked turning to Fay.

"Sensational, isn't she?" Fay returned, and he was startled to see how hard her face had become. "You're looking at the biggest bitch in town."

"You sound prejudiced," Ken said, and laughed. He looked again at the blonde. She glanced at him without interest, looked beyond him at Fay and then turned and went out of the restaurant. "Who is she, anyway?"

"Her name's Gilda Dorman," Fay said. "She and I used to share an apartment together once. She sings now. I guess if I had her shape, her morals and a voice like hers I'd be a success too."

The angry bitterness in her voice embarrassed Ken. He pushed back his chair.

"Let's dance," he said.

Fay made an effort and forced a smile.

"Sorry: I was just sounding off. I hate that bitch like poison. She broke up my dancing act." She got up. "Come on then; let's dance."

IV

Ken's wrist-watch showed twenty minutes past midnight as Fay and he walked into the bar.

"One quickie and then home," Fay said.

Ken ordered two highballs.

"I've had a wonderful evening," he said. "I've really enjoyed myself."

She gave him a saucy little look from under her eyelashes.

"You're not going to leave me now, are you?"

Ken didn't even hesitate. The damage was done. He had no intention of going back to the lonely, empty bungalow.

"You said I could change my mind. I've changed it," he said.

She leaned against him.

25

"Tell me, Buster, is this the very first time you have gone off the rails?"

He looked as startled as he felt.

"What do you mean?"

"I bet you are married, and I bet your wife's away. That's right isn't it?"

"Am I so damned obvious?" Ken asked, annoyed she could read him so easily.

She patted his arm.

"Let's go home. I shouldn't have said that. But you interest me, Buster. I've had such a nice evening with you. You're such a refreshing change. I just wanted to make certain you belong to someone. If you don't, I'll try and capture you for myself."

Ken reddened.

"I belong to someone all right," he said.

Fay lifted her shoulders, smiling.

"All the nice ones do." She slid her arm through his. "Let's go."

Sam Darcy was in the lobby as Ken collected his hat.

"Going early, honey?" he said softly to Fay.

"It's late enough for me, Sam. See you tomorrow."

"That's right."

Joe the doorman opened the door and stood aside.

"Good night, Miss Carson."

"So long, Joe."

They stepped into the still, hot night.

"It's like an oven isn't it?" Fay said, linking her arm through Ken's.

They walked down the alley to the main street and paused to look for a taxi.

"One will be along in a moment," Fay said, opened her bag and took out a pack of cigarettes. She offered one to Ken, and they both lit up.

Ken glanced across the road as he noticed a man come out of an opposite alley. He had a brief glimpse of him before the man stopped abruptly, moved quickly out of the rays of a street light into the shadows: a tall, thin, blond man not wearing a hat, young and from what Ken saw of him, good-looking.

Ken thought nothing of this at the time, but later he was to remember this man.

A taxi came around the corner and Fay waved.

They sat side by side in the darkness of the cab. Fay leaned against him, holding his hand, her head against his shoulder.

It was an extraordinary thing, he found himself thinking, but I feel I've known this girl for years.

He was completely at ease in her company now, and he knew he would have to make a very strong effort to resist the temptation of seeing her again.

"How long have you been on this racket?" he asked.

"About a year." She glanced up at him. "And Buster, darling, please don't start trying to reform me. It's such an old, old gag, and I get so tired of guys telling me I should be a good girl."

"I guess you would get tired of a line like that. It's not my business, but I should have thought you could have made a success of anything you took up. You dance so well. Isn't there anything in that for you now?"

"Maybe, but I just don't want to go back to dancing. Without the right partner it's no fun. What do you do for a living, Buster?"

He saw the danger of telling her that. There were only three banks in the city. It wouldn't be hard to find him again. He had read enough accounts of professional men getting themselves blackmailed to take the chance of telling her what he did.

"I work in an office," he said cautiously.

She looked at him and laughed, patting his hand.

"Don't look so scared. I've told you before: I'm perfectly harmless." She moved away so she could face him. "You took an awful risk tonight, Buster. Do you realize that?"

He laughed awkwardly.

"Oh, I don't know . . ."

"But you did. You are happily married and you have a position to keep up. Suddenly out of the blue, you call up a girl you don't know anything about and have never seen and make a blind date with her. You might have picked one of the floosies who live in my block. Any of those harpies would have battened on to you and you would have had a hell of a struggle to shake them off."

"It wasn't as bad as that. You were recommended to me by a friend."

"He wasn't much of a friend, Buster," she said seriously. "My old man had a saying that applies to you. Whenever I wanted to do something risky, he would tell me to watch my step. 'Be careful,' he would say, 'you might be catching a tiger by its tail.' I've never forgotten that saying. Don't you forget it either, Buster. You're going to forget all about me after tonight. If you get the wayward feeling again, don't call me up. I won't see you." She took his hand and squeezed it. "I wouldn't like you to get into trouble because of me."

Ken was touched.

"You're a funny girl: too good for this racket."

She shook her head.

"I wish I was. It just happens, Buster, there's something about you that's made me soft tonight." She laughed. "We'll be letting our hair down in a moment and sobbing over each other. Well, here we are."

Ken paid off the taxi, and together they walked up the steps and opened the front door.

They began the long climb to the top floor.

It was probably because she had underlined the risk he was running; something he knew for himself, but something he had dismissed because it had suited him to dismiss it, that, as he climbed the stairs, he was suddenly apprehensive. He should have dropped her at her apartment block and taken the taxi back to his own home, he told himself. He had had a swell evening. There was no point in continuing this escapade any further.

A tiger by the tail, she had said. Suppose now the tiger suddenly awoke?

But in spite of his uneasiness, he continued to climb the stairs after her, until they reached the fourth landing.

Facing them as they mounted the last few stairs, stood the fawn Pekinese. Its bulging bloodshot eyes surveyed them stonily, and it gave a sudden shrill yap that made Ken's heart skip a beat.

As if waiting for the signal, the fourth-floor front door opened quickly, and Raphael Sweeting appeared.

He wore a threadbare silk dressing-gown over a pair of black lounging pyjamas. Pasted to his moist thick underlip was an unlighted cigarette.

"Leo!" he said severely, "I'm really ashamed of you." He gave Ken that sly, knowing smile Ken had seen before. "The poor little fellow imagines he is a watch dog," he went on. "So ambitious for such a mite, don't you think?"

He bent and gathered the dog up in his arms.

Neither Fay nor Ken said anything. They kept on, both of them knowing that Sweeting was staring after them, and his

28

intense curiosity seemed to burn into their backs with the force of a blow-lamp.

Ken found he was sweating. There was something alarming and menacing about this fat, sordid little man. He couldn't explain the feeling, but it was there.

"Dirty little spy," Fay said as she unlocked her front door. "Always hanging about just when he's not wanted. Still, he's harmless enough."

Ken doubted this, but he didn't say anything. It was a relief to get inside Fay's apartment and shut the front door.

He tossed his hat on a chair and moved over to the fireplace, feeling suddenly awkward.

Fay went up to him, slid her arms around his neck and offered him her lips.

For a moment he hesitated then he kissed her. She closed her eyes, leaning against him, but now he suddenly wished she wouldn't.

She moved away from him, smiling.

"I'll be with you in two seconds, Buster," she said. "Help yourself to a drink and fix me one too."

She went into the bedroom and shut the door after her.

Ken lit a cigarette and moved over to the liquor cabinet. He was sure now that he shouldn't have come up to her apartment. He didn't know why, but the evening had gone dead on him. He was suddenly ashamed of himself. He thought of Ann. It was an inexcusable and disgraceful act of disloyalty. If Ann ever discovered what he had done, he could never look her in the face again.

He poured out a stiff drink and swallowed half of it.

The least he could do now, he told himself, moving slowly about the room, glass in hand, was to go home.

He looked at the clock on the mantelpiece. It showed a quarter to one.

Yes, he would go home, he decided, and feeling a little virtuous at making a sacrifice that most men, he felt, wouldn't have been able to resist, he sat down and waited.

A sudden rumble of thunder not far off startled him.

It was quite a walk from Fay's apartment to the parking lot. He wished she would hurry. He didn't want to get wet.

A flash of lightning penetrated the white curtains that were drawn across the window. Then thunder crashed violently overhead.

He got up, pushed aside the curtain and peered down into the street.

In the light of the street lamps he could see the sidewalk was already spotted with rain. Forked lightning lit up the rooftops and again thunder crashed violently.

"Fay!" he called, moving away from the window. "Are you coming?"

There was no answer from the bedroom, and thinking she might have gone into the bathroom, he returned to the window.

It was raining now, and the sidewalk glistened in the lamp light. Rain made patterns on the window, obscuring his view.

Well, he couldn't walk through this, he told himself. He would have to wait until it cleared a little, and his determination not to spend the night with Fay began to weaken.

The damage was already done, he thought, crushing out his cigarette. No point really in getting soaked. She expected him to stay the night. She would most certainly be offended if he didn't. Besides, it might be safer to stay here than return home so late. Mrs. Fielding, his next-door neighbour, was certain to hear his car and wonder what he had been up to. She was certain to tell Ann on her return that he hadn't come home until the small hours.

He finished his whisky and went over to the cabinet to make himself another.

She's taking her time, he thought, looking towards the bedroom door.

"Hurry up, Fay," he called. "What are you doing?"

The silence that greeted him puzzled him. What was she up to? he wondered. She had been in there for over ten minutes.

He stood listening. He heard nothing but the steady tick-tick-tick of the clock on the mantelpiece and the rain beating against the window.

Then suddenly the lights in the room went out, plunging him into hot, inky darkness.

For a moment he was badly startled, then he realized a fuse must have blown. He groped for the table and set his glass down.

"Fay!" he called, raising his voice. "Where's the fuse box? I'll fix it."

He thought he heard a door creak as if it were stealthily opening.

"Have you got a flashlight?" he asked.

The silence that greeted him sent a sudden chill crawling up his spine.

"Fay! Did you hear me?"

Still no sound but he was sure that someone was in the room. He groped in his pocket for his cigarette lighter. A board creaked near him.

He suddenly felt frightened, and he stepped back hurriedly, cannoning into the table. He heard his glass of whisky crash to the floor.

"Fay! What are you playing at?" he demanded hoarsely.

He distinctly heard a footfall, then a chair moved. The hair on the nape of his neck bristled.

He got out his lighter, but his hand was shaking so badly the lighter slipped out of his grasp and dropped on the floor.

As he bent to grope for it, he heard the sound of a lock click back, then a door creaked.

He looked towards the front door, trying to see through the darkness that enveloped him. He could see nothing.

Then the front door slammed shut, making him start violently, and he distinctly heard the sound of footsteps running down the stairs.

"Fay!"

He was thoroughly alarmed now.

His groping fingers found the lighter and he snapped down the lever. The flame made a tiny light but enough for him to see the room was empty.

Was it Fay who had just left the apartment or an intruder?

"Fay?"

The uncanny, frightening silence that greeted him stampeded him into a panic.

Shielding the flame of his lighter with his hand, he moved slowly across the room to the bedroom door.

"Are you there, Fay?"

He held the lighter high above his head. The flame was slowly diminishing. In another moment or so it would go out.

He moved forward, peering into the dark room. He looked towards the bed. What he saw there made him catch his breath.

Fay lay across the bed, her arms above her head. A narrow ribbon of blood ran between her breasts, crossing her arched ribs and making a puddle on the floor.

He stood paralysed, staring at her, unable to move.

The flickering flame of the lighter suddenly went out.

31

CHAPTER III

I

A VIVID streak of forked lightning lit up the room with an intense blue-white light, and the crash of thunder that followed rattled the windows.

In the brief moment of light, Ken saw a flashlight on the bedside table and he snatched it up and turned it on.

The hard circle of light fell directly on Fay as she lay outstretched on the bed.

Ken bent over her. Her half-open eyes stared blankly and fixedly at him. Blood, coming from a small blue-black puncture above her left breast, was now reduced to a trickle. Her lips moved, then a muscular spasm passed over her and she arched her back, her hands closing into tight, knuckle-white fists.

"For God's sake, Fay!" Ken gasped.

Into her blank eyes came an expression of terror, then as suddenly the terror went away, her eyes rolled back and her muscles relaxed. A quiet, gasping sigh came through her clenched teeth, and she seemed to grow smaller, suddenly doll-like, not human.

Shaking from head to foot, Ken stared stupidly at her. He had trouble in holding the flashlight steady.

He put a shaking hand over her left breast, getting blood from her on his fingers. He could feel no heart beat.

"Fay!"

His voice was a hoarse croak.

He stepped back, wanting to vomit, feeling a rush of saliva come into his mouth. He shut his eyes and fought back the sickness. After a moment he gained control of himself and, unsteadily, moved further away from the bed. As he did so, his foot touched something hard and he looked down, turning the beam of his flashlight on the object.

Lying on the carpet was a blue-handled ice-pick, its short, sharp blade red with blood.

He stared at it, scarcely breathing.

This was murder!

The discovery was almost too much for him. He felt his knees give, and he sat down hurriedly.

Thunder continued to rumble overhead, and the rain increased its violence. He heard a car coming swiftly up the road, its engine noisy and harsh. He held his breath while he listened. The car went on, passing the house, and he began to breathe again.

Murder!

He got to his feet.

I'm wasting time, he thought. I must call the police.

He turned the beam of the flashlight on Fay again. He had to convince himself that she was dead. He bent over her and touched the artery in her neck. He could feel nothing, and he had again to fight down the nauseating sickness.

As he stepped back, his foot slipped into something that made him shudder. He had stepped into a puddle of blood that had formed on the blue and white carpet.

He wiped his shoe on the carpet, and then walked unsteadily into the sitting-room.

The hot, inky darkness, pierced only by the beam of the flashlight, suffocated him. He made his way across the room to the liquor cabinet, poured himself out a stiff whisky and gulped it down. The spirit steadied his shaken nerves.

He swung the beam of light around, trying to locate the telephone. He saw the telephone on a small table by the settee. He made a move towards it, then stopped.

Suppose the police refused to accept his story? Suppose they accused him of killing Fay?

He turned cold at the thought.

Even if they did accept his story, and if they caught the killer, he would be chief witness in a murder trial. How was he going to explain being in the apartment when the murder happened? The truth would come out. Ann would know. The bank would know. All his friends would know.

His mouth turned dry.

He would be front-page news. Everyone would know that, while Ann was away, he had gone to a call-girl's place.

Get out of this, he told himself. You can't do anything for her. She's dead. You've got to think of yourself. Get out quick!

He crossed the room to the front door; then he stopped short.

Had he left any clue in this dark apartment that would lead the police to him? He mustn't rush away like this in a blind panic. There were sure to be some clues he had left.

He stood there in the darkness, fighting his panic, trying to think.

His finger-prints were on the glasses he had used. He was taking away Fay's flashlight: that might be traced to him. His prints were also on the whisky bottle.

He took out his handkerchief and wiped his sweating face.

Only the killer and himself knew Fay was dead. He had time. He mustn't panic. Before he left, he must check over this room and the bedroom to make absolutely certain he hadn't left anything to bring the police after him.

Before he could do that he must have light to see what he was doing.

He began a systematic search for the fuse-box, and finally found it in the kitchen. On the top of the fuse-box was a packet of fuse wire. He replaced the fuse, turned down the mains switch. The lights went up in the kitchen.

Using his handkerchief he wiped the fuse-box carefully, then returned to the sitting-room.

His heart was thumping as he looked around the room. His hat lay on the chair where he had dropped it. He had forgotten his hat. Suppose he had given way to panic and had gone, leaving it there? It had his name in it!

To make certain he didn't forget it, he put it on.

He then collected the broken pieces of the smashed tumbler, put them in a newspaper and crushed the pieces into fine particles with his heel. He carried them in the newspaper into the kitchen and dropped them into the trash basket.

He found a swab in the kitchen sink and returned to the sitting-room. He wiped the glass he had just used and also the whisky bottle.

In the ash-tray were four stubs of cigarettes he had smoked. He collected these and put them in his pocket, then wiped the ash-tray.

He tried to remember if he had touched anything else in the room. There was the telephone. He crossed the room and carefully wiped the receiver.

There didn't seem anything else in the room that needed his attention.

He was scared to go back into the bedroom, but he knew he had to. He braced himself, slowly crossed the room and turned on the bedroom lights. Keeping his eyes averted from Fay's dead and naked body, he put the flashlight, after carefully wiping it, on the bedside table where he had found it. Then he paused to look around the room.

He had touched nothing in the room except the flashlight. He was sure of that. He looked down at the blue-handled ice-pick, lying on the carpet. Where had it come from? Had the killer brought it with him? He didn't think that likely. If he had brought it with him, he would have taken it away with him. And how had the killer got into the apartment? Certainly not by climbing up to a window. He must have had a key or picked the lock of the front door.

But what did that matter? Ken thought. Time was getting on. Satisfied now he had left no finger-prints nor any clue to bring the police after him, he decided to go out.

But before going he had to get rid of the blood on his hands and check his clothes over.

He went into the bathroom. Careful to cover the taps with his handkerchief before turning them on, he washed the dried blood off his hands. He dried them on a towel, and then went to stand before the long mirror to take careful stock of his clothes.

His heart gave a lurch as he saw a small red stain on the inside of his left sleeve. There was also a red stain on the cuff of his left trousers leg.

He stared at the stains, feeling panic grip him. If anyone saw him now!

He ran more water into the toilet basin, took a sponge from the sponge rack and dabbed feverishly at the stains. The colour changed to a dirty brown, but the stains remained.

That would have to do, he thought, as he rinsed out the sponge, grimacing as the water in the basin turned a bright pink. He let out the water and replaced the sponge.

Turning off the light, he walked hurriedly through the bedroom into the sitting-room.

It was time to go.

He looked around once more.

The storm was passing. The thunder was now a distant rumble, but the rain continued to splash against the windows.

He had done all he could to safeguard himself. The time was twenty minutes to two. With any luck he wouldn't meet anyone at this time on the stairs. He crossed to the front door, turned off the light, and reached for the door handle. If he met someone . . . He had to make an effort to turn back the catch on the lock. Then he heard a sudden sound outside that turned him into a frozen, panic-stricken statue.

Against the front door, he heard a soft scratching sound.

He held his breath while he listened, his heart hammering.

To his straining ears came the sound of soft snuffling. There was a dog outside, and he immediately remembered the fawn Pekinese, and then he remembered Raphael Sweeting.

He had forgotten Sweeting.

Sweeting had seen him return to the apartment with Fay. Ken remembered how the fat little man had stared at him, as if memorizing every detail about him. When the police discovered Fay's body, Sweeting was certain to come forward with Ken's description.

Ken shut his eyes as he fought down his growing panic.

Pull yourself together, he told himself. There must be thousands of men who look like you. Even if he did tell the police what I look like, how could the police find me?

He leaned against the door, listening to the dog as it continued to snuffle, its nose hard against the bottom of the door.

Then Ken heard the stairs creak.

"Leo!"

Sweeting's soft effeminate voice made Ken's heart skip a beat.

"Leo! Come here!"

The dog continued to snuffle against the door.

Ken waited. His heart thudded so violently he was scared Sweeting would hear it.

"If you won't come down, then I must come up," Sweeting said. "It's most unkind of you, Leo."

More stairs creaked, and Ken stepped back hurriedly, holding his breath.

"Come along, Leo. What are you sniffing at?" Sweeting asked.

There was a long agonized silence, then Ken heard soft footfalls just outside the door. Then there was silence again, and Ken had a horrible feeling that Sweeting was listening outside, his ear against the door panel.

The dog had stopped snuffling. Ken could hear now only the thud of his heart and the sound of rain against the window.

Then he heard a sound that sent a chill up his spine. The door handle creaked and began to turn. He remembered he had unlocked the door. Even as the door began to move inwards, he rammed his foot against the bottom of it and jammed it shut. He put his hand on the door and leaned his weight against it while he fumbled desperately to find the catch on the lock.

There was only slight pressure on the door, and after a moment it went away.

"Come along, Leo," Sweeting said, slightly raising his voice. "We must go down. You will be waking Miss Carson."

Ken leaned against the door, feeling sweat run down his face. He listened to the soft creaking of the stairs as Sweeting descended, then, just as his nerves were relaxing, the telephone bell just above his head began to ring.

II

The thunder had died away now, and apart from the shrill, nagging sound of the telephone bell the house seemed wrapped in silence.

Everyone in the house must hear the bell, Ken thought frantically. Who could it be calling at this hour?

He waited, his nerves crawling, as the bell continued to ring. It must stop soon, he thought. It can't go on and on . . .

But it did go on, insistent and strident, until Ken could bear the sound no longer.

He turned on the light, blundered over to the telephone and lifted the receiver.

"Fay? This is Sam."

Ken recognized the deep rich voice of Sam Darcy, the big negro he had met at the Blue Rose.

"Listen, honey," Darcy went on urgently. "Johnny's been seen in town. He's looking for you. I got a tip-off he's been to the Paradise Club asking for you."

Ken held the receiver tightly against his ear, his mind bewildered.

Johnny? Who was he? Was it Johnny who had killed Fay?

"Fay?" Darcy's voice sharpened. "Do you hear me?"

With a shaking hand, Ken replaced the receiver.

He was sure Darcy would call back. He must stop the telephone bell ringing again.

He snatched up a newspaper lying in one of the chairs, tore off half a sheet and folded it into a small wedge. This he inserted between the telephone bell and the clapper.

He had scarcely done this when the clapper began to agitate, making a soft buzzing noise.

He took one last look around the apartment, turned off the

37

light, unlocked the front door and opened it a few inches. He peered out on to the landing. It was deserted. He remembered to wipe the door handle with his handkerchief, and then he closed the door after him.

He stood on the landing, listening. The house was silent. Tiptoeing across the landing, he cautiously looked over the banister rail to the landing below. That, too, was deserted, but he saw that Sweeting's front door stood ajar.

Ken stared at the door, his heart thumping.

That half-open door could mean only one thing. Sweeting was still on the prowl. He was probably sitting in his hall, out of sight, while he watched the landing.

There was no other way of leaving this house except by going down the stairs.

Ken hesitated. Should he wait Sweeting out or should he go down?

He wanted to wait, but he knew the risk of waiting. He could hear the soft continuous buzz of the telephone bell. Darcy might decide to come over and find out why Fay didn't answer his persistent calling.

Ken had to get as far away from this apartment house as he could before Fay's body was found.

It might be possible, if he were very quiet, to creep down the stairs and pass the half-open door without Sweeting seeing or hearing him.

It was his only hope.

He started down the stairs, leaning against the wall, keeping away from the banister rail, which he feared might creak if he touched it.

He went down slowly, step by step, not making a sound. As he reached the last step to the landing, he stopped to listen.

He was just out of sight of the half-open door. If Sweeting were sitting in the hall he would see him as Ken crossed the landing. But if Sweeting had dozed off, Ken might be able to reach the next flight of stairs without being seen.

He braced himself, and, just as he moved forward, the fawn Pekinese dog came through the half-open door and stood looking up at him.

Ken remained motionless, more frightened than he had ever been before in his life.

He and the dog stared fixedly at each other for a long, agonizing moment. Then before he could make up his mind what to do,

38

the front door opened wide and Sweeting came out on to the landing.

"Come along, Leo," he said gently. "Time little dogs were in bed."

He looked slyly at Ken and smiled.

"You have no idea, sir," he said, "what trouble I have to get this little fellow to go to bed."

Ken didn't say anything. He couldn't. His mouth was as dry as dust.

Sweeting picked up the Pekinese. His black eyes scrutinized Ken.

"I believe it has stopped raining," he went on, gently stroking the Pekinese's head. "Such a heavy storm." He looked at the cheap, nickel-plated watch he wore on his fat, hairy wrist. "I had no idea it was so late. It's nearly two."

Ken made a tremendous effort to control his panic. He moved across the landing to the head of the next flight of stairs.

"I must apologize. I talk too much," Sweeting went on, moving after Ken. "You will excuse me. It is a lonely man's failing. If it wasn't for Leo I should be quite alone."

Ken kept on, fighting down the increasing urge to rush madly down the stairs and out of the house.

"You wouldn't care to come in and have a drink with me?" Sweeting asked, catching hold of Ken's sleeve. "It would be a kindness. It's not often I have the opportunity to be a host."

"No, thank you," Ken managed to get out, pulled his arm free and went on down the stairs.

"You have a stain on your coat, sir," Sweeting called, leaning over the banister rail. "That brown stain. Do you see it? I have something that will take it out if you would care to have it."

Without looking back, Ken increased his pace. He reached the third-floor landing. The temptation to run was now too much for him, and he went down the next flight of stairs three at a time.

He bolted across the landing, down the next flight of stairs, across the first-floor landing to the dimly lit hall. He jerked open the front door and cannoned into a girl as she was about to enter the hall.

Ken was so startled, he jumped back.

"No need to knock me over, darling," the girl said, adjusting her pert little hat. She reached out and flicked down a light switch, flooding the hall with hard light.

She was a plump blonde with granite-hard eyes. Her black dress accentuated her curves.

"Hello," she said, giving him a bright, professional smile. "What's your hurry?"

"Sorry, I didn't see you," Ken said breathlessly. He took a step forward, but she blocked the doorway.

"Well, you do now." She eyed him over with professional interest. "Want a little fun, baby?" She pointed to a door to the left of the street door. "Just here. Come in and have a drink."

"Sorry; I'm in a hurry."

"Come on, baby, don't be shy." She sidled up to him.

"Get out of my way!" Ken said desperately. He put his hand on her arm and pushed her aside.

"Hey! Don't put your hands on me, you cheap bum!" the girl cried, and as Ken ran into the street, she started to yell abuse after him.

III

Rain was still falling as Ken hurried along the glistening sidewalk. The air was cooler, and overhead the black storm clouds were breaking up. From time to time the moon appeared and disappeared as the clouds moved across the sky, driven by the brisk wind.

Ken was thinking: Those two will know me again. They will give the police my description. Every newspaper will carry the description.

But why should anyone connect me with Fay? I had no motive for killing her. It's the motive that gives the police a lead. Without a motive, they can get nowhere. She was a prostitute. The murder of a prostitute is always the most difficult case to solve. But supposing Sweeting or the girl happens to come to the bank? He turned cold at the thought. Would they recognize me? Would they know me without a hat? They wouldn't expect to see me in a bank. But I must watch out. If I see them come in, I can always leave my till and get out of sight.

I must watch out.

He realized the horror of his future. He would always have to be on his guard; always on the look-out for these two. Not for a week or a month, but for as long as he remained at the bank.

The realization of his position brought him to a sudden halt. He stood on the edge of the kerb, staring blankly down the wet

40

street, his mind crawling with alarm.

For as long as he remained in the bank and for as long as he remained in town! The sight of any fat man with a Pekinese or any hard-eyed blonde would now send him scurrying for cover. He wouldn't be able to relax for a moment. It would be an impossible situation. The only way out would be to get a transfer to another branch in another city. He would have to sell his home. It might not be possible to get a transfer. He might even have to throw up banking and start hunting for some other job.

And what would Ann think? He had never been able to keep anything from her in the past. How could he hope to keep this from her? She always seemed to know when things were going wrong for him. There was that time when he had a forty dollar shortage in his takings. He hadn't told her. He had drawn the money from his own account to make up the shortage, but she had soon found out about it.

What a mad, crazy fool I've been! he thought. Why did I do it? Why the hell didn't I leave that girl and go home!

Across the road he caught sight of a moving figure, and he stepped hurriedly back into the shadows. His mouth turned dry when he saw the flat cap and the gleaming buttons of a cop.

Somehow he forced himself into a walk. His heart was thudding as he passed the cop who looked across the road at him, and it seemed to Ken the cop was suspicious. It was as much as he could do not to break into a run.

He kept on, not looking back, expecting to hear the cop shout after him. Nothing happened, and when he had walked twenty yards or so, he looked over his shoulder.

The cop was walking on, swinging his night stick, and Ken drew in a sharp breath of relief.

That meeting underlined again the horror of his future. Every time he saw a cop now he would be scared.

Would it be better to end it right now? Should he go to the police and tell them what had happened?

Pull yourself together, you spineless fool! he told himself angrily. You've got to think of Ann. If you keep your nerve you'll be all right. No one will suspect you. Get clear of here, get home and you'll be safe.

He stiffened his shoulders and increased his pace. In a minute or so he reached the parking lot.

Then a thought struck him that again stopped him dead in his tracks and filled him with sick panic.

Had the car attendants kept a book in which they entered the registration number of every car parked in the lot.

He was sunk if the attendant had taken his number. The police would be certain to question the attendant. They would give him Ken's description, and he must remember him. All he had to do then would be to turn up his book and give the police Ken's number. They would be at his house in half an hour.

Shaken by this thought, Ken stepped into a dark alley while he tried to think what to do. From where he stood he could see the entrance to the parking lot. He had a clear view of the little hut by the gates. A light burned inside the hut, and he could just make out the bent figure of the attendant as he sat by the window, reading a newspaper.

Ken had to know if there was a registration book in the hut. He daren't drive away without making certain the attendant hadn't his number. If the book existed he would have to destroy it.

He leaned against the wall of the alley and watched the hut. Perhaps someone would come for his car and the attendant would leave the hut, giving Ken a chance to slip in and see if the book was there. But it was now quarter-past two. The chances of anyone collecting his car at this hour was remote. Time was running out. He couldn't afford to wait.

He braced himself and, leaving the alley, he crossed the road and walked into the parking lot.

The door of the hut stood open, and he walked in.

The old attendant glanced up, eyed him over and gave him a surprised nod.

"You're late, mister."

"Yes," Ken said, and his eyes searched the hut.

There was a table near the window. Among the collection of old newspapers, a saucepan and a gas-ring, some dirty china mugs and a still dirtier hand towel, on the table was a dog-eared notebook, opened about half-way.

Ken moved closer.

"Some storm," he went on. "I've been waiting for it to clear."

His eyes took in the open page of the notebook. It contained a neatly written list of car numbers: third from the bottom was his own number.

"Still raining," the attendant said, busy lighting a foul-smelling pipe. "Well, I guess we can do with it. Got a garden, mister?"

"Sure," Ken said, trying to control the shake in his voice. "This must be the first rain we've had in ten days."

"That's right," the attendant said. "Do you grow roses, mister?"

"That's all I do grow: roses and weeds," Ken returned, moving so his back was now to the table.

"That's about my limit too," the old man said, and got stiffly to his feet and went to the door to look up at the rain-swollen clouds.

Ken picked up the book and held it behind him.

"Haven't you anyone to relieve you?" he asked, joining the old man at the door.

"I go off around eight o'clock. When you get to my age, mister, you don't need much sleep."

"Maybe you're right. Well, so long. I need all the sleep I can get."

Ken stepped out into the darkness, feeling the rain against his sweating face.

"I'll just mark you off in my book," the attendant said. "What's your number?"

Ken's heart stopped, then raced.

"My number?" he repeated blankly.

The old man had gone to the table and was pushing the newspapers to one side.

"Now where did I put it?" he muttered. "I had it a moment ago."

Ken shoved the notebook in his hip pocket. He looked across at a Packard, standing near the gates.

"My number's TXL 3345," he said, reading off the Packard's number plate.

"I had that darned book a moment ago. Did you see it, mister?"

"No. I've got to be moving." Ken offered the old man a half-dollar. "So long."

"Thanks, mister. What was that number again?"

Ken repeated the number and watched the old man scribble it down on the edge of a newspaper.

"I'm always losing things."

"So long," Ken said, and walked quickly across the lot to his car.

He got in the car, started the engine and, using only his parking lights, he sent the car shooting towards the gates.

The old man came out of the hut and waved to him.

Ken snapped off the parking lights, trod hard on the gas pedal and drove fast through the gates.

He didn't turn on his lights until he reached the main road. Then, driving at a steady pace, he headed for home.

CHAPTER IV

I

THE strident clamour of the alarm clock brought Ken out of a heavy sleep. He smothered the alarm, opened his eyes and looked around the bright familiar bedroom. Then into his sleep-heavy mind the events of the previous evening formed a stark picture, and immediately he was awake, a cold, sick feeling of fear laying hold of him.

He looked at the clock. It was just after seven.

Throwing his bedclothes aside, he swung his feet to the floor, slid them into his waiting slippers and walked into the bathroom.

His head ached, and when he looked at himself in the shaving mirror he saw his face was pale and gaunt and his eyes bloodshot and dark-ringed.

After he had shaved and taken a cold shower, he looked a little better, but his headache persisted.

He went into the bedroom to dress, and, as he fixed his tie, he wondered how long it would be before Fay's body was discovered. If she lived alone it might be days. The longer she remained undiscovered, the better it would be for him. People's memories became uncertain after a few days. The parking lot attendant would be unlikely to give the police a convincing description of him unless the police questioned him fairly soon. The plump blonde might also be a scatterbrain, but Ken had no delusions about Sweeting. His memory, Ken was sure, was dangerously reliable.

Goddam it! he said aloud, what a hell of a mess I've got myself into! What an utter fool I've been! Well, I've got to behave now as if nothing had happened. I've got to keep my nerve. I'm safe as long as Sweeting or that blonde doesn't run into me and I'll have to take good care to see them first.

44

He went into the kitchen and put on the kettle. While he was waiting for the water to boil, he wondered how he was going to get rid of his blood-stained suit.

He had read enough detective stories to know the danger of keeping the suit. Police chemists had methods of discovering blood-stains no matter how carefully they were washed out.

He was worried sick about the suit. He had only recently bought it, and Ann would know at once if it was missing. But he had to get rid of it: several people had seen him wearing it last night. If the police found it here, he would be sunk. It was easier said than done to get rid of it, but he had to think of a way, and think of it quickly.

He made the coffee, poured out a cup and carried the cup to the bedroom. Setting the cup down, he went over to the suit he had thrown over the back of a chair when he had stripped it off last night, and examined it carefully in the hard morning sunlight. The two stains showed up alarmingly against the light-grey material.

Then he remembered his shoes. He had stepped into a puddle of blood at Fay's apartment. They would also be stained. He picked them up and examined them. The side of the left shoe was stained. He would have to get rid of the shoes too.

He sat on the edge of the bed and drank the coffee. He wondered if he would ever be free of this empty sick feeling of fear and tension he now had. Finishing the coffee, he lit a cigarette, noticing how unsteady his hand was. For some moments he sat still, concentrating on ways and means of getting rid of the suit.

Fortunately he had bought the suit from one of the big stores. It had been ready-made, and he had paid cash for it. The same applied to the shoes. In both transactions it was extremely unlikely that the salesman who had served him would remember him.

He recollected the department where he had brought the suit with its rows of suits hanging in orderly lines, and that recollection gave him an idea.

He would take the blood-stained suit in a parcel to the stores this morning. He would buy a suit exactly like it. While the assistant was wrapping up his purchase, he would take the blood-stained suit out of the parcel and include it among the suits on the hangers. It might be weeks before the suit was discovered, and then it would be impossible for it to be traced to him.

His shoes were almost new too. He had bought them at the same store. He could work the same dodge with them. He would then have replaced the suit and shoes so Ann wouldn't know he had got rid of the original suit and shoes.

He made a parcel of the suit and another parcel of the shoes and put them in the hall. As he was turning back to the bedroom he saw the newspaper delivery boy coming up the path. As soon as the newspaper came through the letter-box, he grabbed it and took it into the sitting-room. He went through the paper from cover to cover, his heart thumping and his hands clammy.

He didn't expect to find any mention of Fay's murder, and he wasn't disappointed. If there was anything to report, the evening newspapers would have it.

It was almost time now for him to leave for the bank. He put on his hat, picked up the two parcels, locked the front door, and left the key under the mat for Carrie to find.

As he walked down the path to the gate, a car drew up outside the bungalow with a squeal of brakes.

Ken felt his heart turn a somersault, and for one ghastly moment he had to fight against a mad impulse to turn around and bolt back indoors. But he kept hold of himself with an effort, and stared at the car, his heart thudding.

Parker, red-faced and cheerful, waved to him from the car.

"Hello, sport," he said. "Thought I'd pick you up. One good turn deserves another. Come on – hop in."

Ken opened the gate and crossed the sidewalk to the car, aware that his knees felt weak and the muscles in his legs were fluttering. He opened the car door and got in.

"Thanks," he muttered. "I didn't know you were driving up this morning."

"I didn't know myself until I got home," Parker said gloomily. He took out his cigarette-case and offered it to Ken. "My ma-in-law's coming to spend a few days with us. Why the old cow can't take a taxi instead of expecting me to meet her beats me. It's not as if she's hard up, although the way she acts you'd think she was on relief. I told Maisie not to invite her, but she never does what I want."

Ken took the cigarette and accepted a light from Parker.

"Hello," Parker said, lifting his eyebrows, "so the lawn didn't get cut after all."

Ken had forgotten about the lawn.

"No; it was too hot," he said hurriedly.

46

Parker engaged gear and pulled away from the kerb.

"I thought you'd have better sense than to waste your time cutting a lawn." He gave Ken a dig in the ribs with his elbow. "How did you get on, you dirty dog?"

"I got on very well," Ken said, trying to sound casual. "I spent the evening weeding and went to bed early."

Parker gave a hoot of laughter.

"Tell that to your grandma," he said with a leer. "Have you seen your face this morning? Boy! Do you look washed out! Did you visit my little friend?"

"What little friend?" Ken asked, staring fixedly through the windshield at the line of traffic ahead.

"Come on, Holland, don't be cagey with me. You know you can trust me to keep my mouth shut. How did you like her?"

"I don't know what you're talking about," Ken said curtly.

"Well damn it! I gave you her telephone number. You called her, didn't you?"

"I've told you already; I stayed at home last night and weeded the rose bed."

Parker lifted his eyebrows.

"Well, okay, if that's your story, I guess you're stuck with it, but you don't kid me. But since I gave you the introduction you might at least admit she's a damn fine girl."

"I wish you'd shut up!" Ken snapped. "I stayed home last night. Can't you get that bit of information into your thick skull and stop all this nonsense?"

"I was only pulling your leg," Parker said, a little startled by the anger in Ken's voice. "I was doing you a good turn. If you're such a mug not to take advantage of my introduction, that's your funeral. Fay's sensational. When Hemingway put me on to her, he saved my life. I admit I took a chance, but I'm damned glad now."

"I wish you would get off this subject," Ken said. "Can't you talk about something else?"

"What else is there to talk about?" Parker said, and sniggered. "Well, okay, if that's the way you feel: tell me, what have you got in those two parcels?"

Ken had been expecting Parker to ask that question, and he was ready for it.

"Just some things Ann asked me to take to the cleaners."

"I don't know why it is but wives always find some errands for us guys to run. Maisie has given me a shopping list as long as my arm. I guess I'll have to get one of the girls in the office to handle it for me." Parker drove a couple of blocks without speaking: his plump red face thoughtful. "You know, I think I'll drive over to Fay's place in my lunch hour. It doesn't look as if I'll see much of her while my ma-in-law's with us. She's a regular old ferret, and if I stayed out late, she'd start putting a flea in Maisie's ear."

Ken felt a chill crawl up his spine.

"This afternoon? Is she likely to see you so early?"

"That's not early," Parker returned and laughed. "I once called on her at eight o'clock in the morning."

The thought of Parker going to that top-floor apartment and walking into the police turned Ken cold.

"You'll telephone her first?"

"Oh, sure. She might have someone there. But lunch-time is usually a good time to catch her in."

Ken began to breathe again.

"I should have thought it was damned risky to go to a place like that in daylight."

"Nothing to worry about at all. There's a parking lot not far from the house, and the street is screened by trees," Parker said airily. "You should try it one day, if you haven't tried it already, you sly dog."

"Keep your mind on your driving," Ken said, his voice sharp. "You nearly hit that truck."

II

Soon after half-past ten, when the first rush of business was over, Parker closed his till, and giving Ken a wink, said he was going to call Fay.

"Shan't be five minutes. Keep an eye on things for me."

Ken watched him cross the hall of the bank to a pay booth installed for the customers' convenience.

Ken's heart beat violently as he watched Parker shut himself in the booth. He waited while minutes dragged by, then the booth door opened and Parker came out.

Parker had lost his cocky, leering expression. He looked white and flustered, and he hurried across the hall as if anxious to gain sanctuary behind the grill protecting his till.

Ken pretended he hadn't noticed Parker's agitation. He was entering a pile of cheques into a ledger, and having difficulty, as

48

his hand was unsteady. He said as casually as he could: "Did you get fixed up?"

"My God!" Parker gasped, wiping his face with his handkerchief. "The cops are in her place."

Ken stiffened and dropped his pen.

"The cops?"

"Yes. Must be a raid. Suppose I had gone around there without calling her first?"

"How do you know it was the police?" Ken asked, groping on the floor for his pen.

"The guy who answered the phone said he was Lieutenant Adams of the City Police. He wanted to know who I was."

"You didn't tell him?"

"Of course not! I hung up on him while he was talking. Phew! What the hell does it mean? I've never known the police raid a call-girl's place before. They might have arrived when I was there."

"Lucky you called first."

"I'll say." Parker continued to mop his face. "You don't think they'll trace my call, do you?"

"Why should they?" Ken asked, and he suddenly saw the danger he was in. The police were likely to trace the call. If they came here with a description of him from Sweeting, they would catch him red-handed with the blood-stained suit still in his possession!

"Maybe she's been robbed or assaulted," Parker said nervously. "Maybe that's why they are there. Maybe someone's murdered her."

Ken felt a trickle of cold sweat run down the side of his face. He didn't trust his voice to say anything.

"These girls run a hell of a risk," Parker went on. "They don't know who they are taking on. She could have been murdered."

Before he could develop his theme a depositor came in, and then another followed. For some minutes both Ken and Parker were kept busy.

Ken was thinking of the blood-stained suit in his locker downstairs.

Damn Parker! If the police traced that call and came down here . . . ! He looked anxiously at his wrist-watch. He had another hour before he went to lunch. The police might be on their way over now. But before he could make up his mind what to do, a steady flow of customers began, and for the next half-hour he was too rushed to think of himself. Then there was a pause again.

Parker said sharply, "There's a guy just come in who looks like a cop."

Ken's heart stopped, then raced.

"Where?"

He looked around the big hall. Standing, half-concealed by one of the pillars, was a tall, heavily built man in a brown suit and a brown slouch hat.

He did look like a cop. His big fleshy face was brick-red and his small, green eyes had a still, intent quality about them that alarmed Ken.

"He must be a cop," Parker said, lowering his voice.

Ken didn't say anything. He watched the big man cross the hall to the pay booth.

"Do you think anyone saw me use the telephone?" Parker muttered.

"I don't know. It's out of sight of the door."

"If he asks me I'll tell him I called my wife, but I couldn't get an answer."

"He may not ask you."

"I hope to hell he doesn't."

They watched the big man come out of the pay booth and go over to speak to the messenger at the door.

The messenger looked startled as Ken saw the big man show him something he carried in his hand. They talked for some minutes, then the big man turned and stared directly at Ken.

Ken felt himself turn hot, then cold. He forced himself to continue to write in his ledger.

"He's coming over," Parker said softly.

The big man came up to the counter and his hard eyes went from Parker to Ken and back to Parker again.

"City Police. Sergeant Donovan," he said, his voice a harsh growl. "I'm making enquiries about a guy who used that pay booth about a half-hour ago. Did either of you see him?"

Ken looked at the hard, brick-red face. Donovan wore a close-clipped ginger moustache. A row of freckles ran across the bridge of his thick, short nose.

"No, I didn't see anyone," Ken said.

"I used the telephone a little while ago, sergeant," Parker said smoothly. "I was calling my wife. You don't mean me, do you?"

Donovan stared at Parker.

"Not if you called your wife. Did you see anyone else use the booth?"

"Well, there was a girl and an elderly man," Parker lied glibly. "But that would be about an hour ago, I guess. We've been busy, and I didn't notice anyone recently."

"Not too busy to call your wife," Donovan said, his hard little eyes boring into Parker.

"Never too busy to call my wife," Parker returned, and gave the sergeant a bright, false smile.

Donovan took a crumpled cigarette from his pocket, stuck it on his thin, brutal lower lip and set fire to it with a brass lighter.

"Did you see anyone use the phone?" he asked Ken.

"I've just told you: I didn't."

The green eyes forced Ken to look away.

"You might have changed your mind."

"I didn't see anyone."

Donovan made a grimace of disgust.

"No one ever sees nothing in this town. No one knows nothing, either."

He gave the two men a long, hard stare, then walked across the hall to the messenger.

"Phew!" Parker said. "Nice guy. I wouldn't like to be third-degree'd by him, would you?"

"I guess not," Ken said, his knees weak.

"I handled him rather well, don't you think?"

"Isn't it a little early to talk like that?" Ken returned.

They both watched Donovan as he talked to the messenger, then, nodding curtly, Donovan left the bank.

"It's a bad business," Parker said soberly. "They wouldn't have sent that sergeant here so fast unless there was something serious. My God! What an escape I've had!"

III

The City hall clock was striking the half-hour after one as Ken left Gaza's, the big store on the corner of Central and 4th Streets. Under his arm he carried two brown-paper parcels.

He walked rapidly along Central Street towards the bank. His plan to get rid of the blood-stained suit and shoes had worked. The suit now hung alongside the other hundreds of suits on display in Gaza's outfitting department. He hoped the blood-stained shoes were safely lost among the masses of shoes on the display counter of Gaza's shoe department.

There had been one nerve-shattering moment. The assistant who had sold him the light-grey suit, a replica of the one he had furtively included among the other suits, had asked him if he hadn't forgotten the parcel he had brought in with him.

Ken had managed to keep his head, and had said he hadn't been carrying a parcel. The assistant had looked puzzled, but having asked Ken if he was sure, he lost interest. But it had been an unpleasant moment.

Well, at least he had got rid of the suit and the shoes, and he felt safer.

On the other hand, through Parker's telephone call, the police had visited the bank, and this hard-faced sergeant had had a good look at him.

Would the sergeant link him with the description the police were bound to get once they began asking questions?

There was nothing in the mid-day papers about Fay, and when Ken got back to his till to relieve Parker, he shook his head at Parker's eager question.

"Nothing at all?" Parker asked. "Are you sure?"

Ken handed the paper over.

"Nothing: look for yourself."

"Maybe it isn't as bad as I thought," Parker said, glancing at the headlines. "She could have pinched something. These girls are always getting into trouble. Well I'm going to give her a wide berth from now on."

The afternoon dragged by. Ken kept watching the front entrance of the bank, half expecting to see the big sergeant come in again. The sick tension that had hold of him made him feel ill and tired.

When eventually the bank doors closed and he began to cash up, Parker said, "If that cop asks you questions about me, Holland, you'll keep your mouth shut, won't you?"

"Of course," Ken returned, wondering how Parker would react if he knew the truth. "You have nothing to worry about."

"I wish that were true," Parker said uneasily. "If they find out it was me who telephoned, the blasted news hounds will get after me. Can you imagine how old Schwartz would like it if he knew I'd been going to see this girl? That old blue-nose would kick me out like a shot. And there's my wife: I'd never live it down."

"Relax," Ken said, wishing he could relax himself. "I won't say a thing."

"This has taught me a lesson," Parker said. "Never again. From now on I'm going to keep clear of trouble." He locked his till. "Well, I've got to get off. Time to meet ma-in-law. Sorry I can't drive you home."

"That's okay," Ken said. "I've just got these cheques to enter up and I'm through. So long."

He took his time finishing his work to make certain Parker had gone, then he went down to the staff room, put on his hat, collected his two parcels from his locker and went up the steps to the rear exit.

He travelled home by bus, paused at the corner of his road to buy an evening paper and walked towards the bungalow; holding his parcels under one arm, he scanned the headlines of the paper.

There it was in the stop press.

He stopped, his heart hammering, to read the heavy print:

ICE-PICK SLAYING IN LOVE NEST
EX-DANCER MURDERED BY UNKNOWN ASSAILANT

He couldn't bring himself to read further, and folding the newspaper, he continued up the road, sweat on his face.

As he reached his gate, Mrs. Fielding, his next-door neighbour, bobbed up from behind the hedge to beam at him.

Mrs. Fielding was always bobbing up from behind the hedge.

Ann had tried to convince Ken that Mrs. Fielding meant well and that she was lonely, but Ken thought she was an old busy-body always on the look-out for a gossip or to stick her nose where it wasn't wanted.

"Just back from town, Mr. Holland?" she asked, her bright little eyes staring curiously at the two parcels he carried under his arm.

"That's right," Ken said, opening the gate.

"I hope you haven't been extravagent now your wife's away," she went on, wagging her finger at him. "I know how my dear husband used to behave as soon as I went away."

I wonder if you do, you silly old fool, Ken thought. I bet he kicked the can around as soon as he got rid of you.

"And you're keeping such late hours." She smiled archly at him. "Didn't I hear you come last night after two?"

Ken's heart gave a lurch.

"After two?" he said. "Oh, no. Couldn't have been me. I was in bed by eleven."

Her bright smile suddenly became fixed. Into her eyes came

an inquisitive, searching look that made Ken's eyes give ground.

"Oh. I looked out of the window, Mr. Holland. I am quite sure it was you."

"You were mistaken," Ken said shortly, caught with the lie and having to make the best of it. "You'll excuse me. I have to write to Ann."

"Yes." Still the bright eyes stared fixedly at him. "Well, be sure to give her my love."

"I will," Ken said, and forcing a smile, he hurried up the path, opened the front door and entered the hall.

He stood for a moment in the quiet hall, listening to the thud of his heart.

If the police took it in their heads to question her, she could give him away. He might have known she wouldn't have been asleep when he drove back last night. She would have to get of bed to spy.

She had seen the two parcels. If she remembered and if the police questioned her, how was he going to explain them away?

He now had a trapped feeling, and he went into the lounge, opened the liquor cabinet and poured himself out a stiff drink. He went over to the couch and sat down. After a long pull from his glass, he read the short paragraph in the stop press.

Early this morning, Fay Carson, one-time dance hostess at the Blue Rose nightclub, was discovered by her maid, stabbed to death and lying naked across her bed. The murder weapon is believed to be an ice-pick taken from the murdered woman's ice-box.

Sergeant Jack Donovan of the Homicide Department, in charge of the investigation, stated that he had already several important clues, and that an early arrest could be expected. He is anxious to interview a tall, well-built man, wearing a pearl-grey suit and a grey slouch hat who returned with Miss Carson to her apartment last night.

Ken dropped the paper and shut his eyes.

For a long, horrible moment he felt suffocated by the wave of panic that urged him to get in his car and get as far away as he could before they came after him.

A tall, well-built man in a pearl-grey suit and a grey slouch hat.

What a damn fool he had been to buy a suit exactly like the one he had left in the store. He had bought it because Ann would have missed it, but now he realized he would never dare wear it.

54

He ran his and over his sweating face.

Should he make a bolt for it?

Where would you go, you fool? he thought. And how far do you imagine you'd get? Your one and only chance is to sit tight and keep your nerve. It's your only hope. You've got to sit tight for Ann's sake as well as your own.

He got to his feet, finished his drink and set the glass down on the table. Then he unpacked the two parcels and carried the shoes and suit into his bedroom. He put them in his wardrobe.

He returned to his sitting-room and poured himself out another drink.

He thanked his stars Ann wasn't here, and that he could face this business on his own, but in six more days she would be back. He didn't kid himself this business would be over by then or, if it were, he would be in jail.

He set down his glass to light a cigarette. A movement outside made him look up towards the window.

A car had pulled up outside the bungalow. The car door opened and a massive figure of a man got out.

Ken stood transfixed, his breath coming through his clenched teeth in a little hiss.

Another burly man climbed out of the car, and together the two men moved across the sidewalk towards the gate.

The man who opened the gate wore a brown suit and a brown hat.

Ken recognized him.

It was Sergeant Donovan.

PART TWO

CHAPTER I

I

AT five minutes past nine a.m., seven hours after Ken Holland had furtively left 25 Lessington Avenue, a police car pulled up outside the tall, brown-stone building and parked behind two other police cars that had been there for the past fifteen minutes.

A patrolman stiffened to attention as Lieutenant Harry Adams of the Homicide Department got out of the car and came slowly up the steps.

"Top floor, Lieutenant," he said saluting. "Sergeant Donovan's up there."

"Where else would he be – in the basement?" Adams said softly, and without looking at the patrolman he walked into the hall.

He paused to read the names on the mail boxes, then he gave a snorting grunt.

"A cat house," he said under his breath. "The first murder in two years, and it's got to be in a cat house."

Adams was short, thin and dapper. The wings of his thick chalk-white hair looked dazzling against the black of his hat. His face was long and pinched, with deep hollows in his cheeks. His nose was sharp-pointed and long. When he was in a rage, which was often, his slate-grey eyes lit up as if an electric bulb inside his head had been switched on. His face never gave away what he was thinking. He was known to be a hard, ruthless, bitter man who was as heartily hated by his men as he was by the criminals who were unfortunate enough to cross his path.

But he was a first-rate police officer. His brain was four times as sharp as Donovan's and Donovan knew it. The big man lived in perpetual fear of Adams, knowing that if he gave Adams the slightest excuse, Adams had enough influence to have Donovan thrown back on a beat.

Walking slowly, Adams commenced the long climb to the top floor.

The house was silent. He met no one. It was as if the occupant of each apartment as he passed knew he was in the house and was crouching behind the shut door, breathless and frightened.

Jackson, a red-faced cop, was standing on the top-floor landing as Adams came slowly up. He saluted and waited. He knew Adams well enough not to speak to him unless he was spoken to.

Adams walked into the big, airy sitting-room where Fletcher, the finger-print expert, was already at work.

Donovan was prowling around the room, his set, heavy face dark with concentration.

Adams walked across the room and into the bedroom as if he knew instinctively that was where the body was. He went over to the bed and stared down at Fay's body. For several minutes he looked at her; then, still keeping his eyes on her, he took out a cigarette, lit it and blew a cloud of smoke down his thin nostrils.

Donovan stood in the doorway, tense and silent, watching him.

"Doc coming?" Adams asked, without turning.

"On his way now, Lieutenant," Donovan said.

Adams leaned forward and put his hand on Fay's arm.

"Been dead about six hours at a guess."

"That ice-pick, Lieutenant . . ."

Adams looked at the ice-pick lying on the floor and then turned to stare at Donovan.

"What about it?"

The big man flushed.

"I guess it's the murder weapon," he said, wishing he hadn't spoken.

Adams raised his thin, white eyebrows.

"That's smart of you. I was thinking it was something she took to bed with her to pare her nails. So you think it's the murder weapon?" His eyes lit up. "What else could it be, you fool? Keep your goddamn mouth shut!"

He turned away and began to move about the room while Donovan watched him, his eyes dark with hate.

"What have you found out about her?" Adams snapped.

"She's only been on the game for a year," Donovan told him. "She used to dance at the Blue Rose. She had no record, and she didn't work the streets."

Adams turned.

"Come in and shut the door."

Donovan did as he was told. He knew from past experience, and by Adams' quiet stillness, that something unpleasant was

58

coming, and inwardly he braced himself.

"The press haven't got on to this yet, have they?" Adams asked mildly. He sat on the edge of the bed, moving Fay's foot to give himself more room. The body so close to him might not have been there for all the feeling he showed.

"No, Lieutenant."

Donovan had a horror of the press. In the past he had had a lot of adverse criticism in the two local papers. They were always calling for better police action, and had singled him out for their more caustic remarks.

"They'll have to be told, but not until this afternoon. Give it to them in time for a stop press," Adams went on. "You'll have all day to-day and most of the night to get something for the morning's papers. This is the first killing we have had recently. They'll go to town it. The *Herald's* been picking on the Administration now for months. This will give them a club to beat us with unless we crack it fast." He reached out a thin, dry hand and patted Fay's knee. "She didn't amount to a damn while she was alive, but dead, Donovan, she becomes a very important person. You don't know what's going on behind the scenes at this moment, and you don't need to know, but this killing could be dynamite: a lot of people in the Administration could lose their jobs. It only wanted this to happen to set off the spark. Lindsay Burt has the backing of the press; the voters love him. He's been after the big boys for years, and in case you don't know, the Commissioner is a big boy, and Burt hates his guts. Burt's got a lot of ammunition. This killing could be his gun. Here in Lessington Avenue, less than a hundred yards from City Hall, is an apartment house full of tarts. Won't that make juicy reading after the Commissioner has stated again and again that this town is as clean as a whistle?" He stubbed out his cigarette into the ash bowl on the bedside table and fixed his eyes on Donovan's face. "I'm telling you all this so you don't kid yourself this case doesn't mean much. It does. It'll be headline news for as long as the case is unsolved, and you, Donovan, are going to solve. You can have all the help you want. You can have my advice for what it's worth, but the work, the credit or the dis-credit, is yours. Do you understand?"

"Yes, Lieutenant."

So here it comes, Donovan thought; the little punk has been after me ever since he took over his job. He knows this is a hell of a case to crack – any guy in town could have knocked her off –

and he's going to use it to get rid of me. That's my luck. A dame gets knocked off, and I find myself in the middle of a political jam.

"It won't be easy," Adams went on. "The guy who killed her might be a nut." He paused while he crossed one thin leg over the other, lacing his fingers across his knee. "Do you ever say your prayers, Donovan?"

The big man flushed, stared at Adams, then seeing he was serious, he muttered, "I guess so."

"Then take my tip and pray as you've never prayed before that this guy isn't a nut. If he is he may have enjoyed the experience of sticking this doll, and he may do it again. He may get into another cat house and give the press another club to hit us with. This isn't the only cat house in town. So get after him, Donovan, just in case he is a nut and is planning to do it again."

A tap sounded on the door and Donovan opened it.

Jackson said, "Doc's here, sergeant."

Adams joined Donovan at the door.

"Come on in, doc," he said, and waved to the bed. "She's all yours, and you're welcome."

Doc Summerfeld moved across to the bed. He was a big, fat, red-faced man, bald and placid looking.

"Hmm, a nice clean job, anyway."

Adams wasn't interested in Summerfeld's remarks. He went into the sitting-room where the police photographer was setting up his camera.

"Take your orders from Sergeant Donovan," Adams said to him and Fletcher. "He's handling the investigation."

Donovan saw the two exchange startled glances.

They know, he thought bitterly. The first killing in two years, but I get it. They're not fools. If this had been an easy one I wouldn't have got it. Well, okay. Maybe for the first time in my life I'll get a break. I'd like to see the little punk's face if I did crack it.

"What's your first move, sergeant?" Adams asked.

"I want to know who she was with last night," Donovan said slowly, carefully picking his words. "She didn't work the streets, so the guys either knew her or were recommended to her; that puts them in a different class to the ordinary masher. From what the cleaner woman tells me, this girl went for the middle-aged, upper income lecher. Maybe she tried blackmail and got knocked off to keep her mouth shut."

He saw both Fletcher and Holtby the photographer, were gaping at him.

Gape, you punks, he thought. You didn't imagine I had any ideas, did you?

"While doc's working on her, I'll go talk to the occupants of the other apartments. They may have seen the guy," he went on.

"You have a lot of faith, sergeant," Adams said. "That's all a tart lives for – to give information to the cops."

Holtby sniggered.

"One of their own people's been killed," Donovan said quietly. "May give them an incentive to talk."

Adams lifted his eyebrows. He stared at Donovan, his eyes suddenly thoughtful.

"Quite a psychologist, sergeant," he said.

Donovan turned to Fletcher who hurriedly wiped a grin off his face.

"There's an ice-pick in the bedroom. Check it for prints. Snap it up! I want a little more action and a lot less standing around from you."

Fletcher stiffened.

"Yes, sergeant."

Donovan walked out of the apartment.

Adams stared after him, then he went back into the bedroom to talk to Summerfeld.

II

Raphael Sweeting heard the urgent ring on his frontdoor bell, and he hastily wiped his sweating face on the sleeve of his dressing-gown.

He had seen the police cars arrive, and he knew, sooner or later, the front-door bell would ring.

What had happened? he asked himself. Something in the apartment above. He could hear the heavy footfalls overhead. His mind flinched away from murder, but he was sure she had been murdered. Just when he was settling down; just when he had been certain he had succeeded in dropping out of sight.

The bell rang persistently, and he looked hastily around the dusty, shabbily furnished room. All evidence of his evening activities had been hastily hidden. It had been a business to clear the room, but the arrival of the police cars had at least warned him a police visit was pending.

The big cupboard against the wall had been crammed with the mass of papers, envelopes, directories and the telephone books he used in his work, and the key had been turned. They wouldn't dare open the cupboard unless they had a search warrant. Even if they did open it, they couldn't pin anything on him, but it would tell them he was still up to his old tricks.

Leo, the Pekinese, crouched in the armchair, staring across the room at the front door, The dog breathed heavily, and looked with frightened eyes at its master as if it knew an enemy was on the far side of the door.

Sweeting touched the dog's head gently, but the dog sensed his fear and wasn't reassured.

Sweeting crossed the room, turned the key, braced himself and opened the door.

He stared up at the big man who towered above him, and it was a relief to see it wasn't Lieutenant Adams. This man he had never seen before.

"Did you want something?" he asked, trying to smile, but succeeding only in making a fixed grimace.

"I'm a police officer," Donovan said. He was asking himself where he had seen this fat little man before. His slow-thinking mind groped into the past, but failed to pin-point the irritatingly familiar features. "Who are you?"

"Sweeting is the name." The little man held the door against him, obstructing Donovan's view into the room. "Is something wrong?"

"A woman's been murdered in the apartment above," Donovan told him. "Did you see anyone going into her apartment last night?"

Sweeting shook his head.

"I'm afraid I didn't. I went to bed early; besides, I keep to myself. I don't pay attention to what goes on in this house."

Donovan had a frustrated feeling that he wasn't being told the truth.

"Did you hear anything?"

"I'm a heavy sleeper," Sweeting said. He realized that this big, hard-faced man wasn't dangerous. He hadn't been recognized. Sweeting had seen Adams arrive, and he had feared Adams would visit him. He knew the Lieutenant would have recognized him. "I'm sorry I can't be of assistance to you. I didn't even know the young woman. I've seen her once or twice, of course. We pass on the stairs. Murdered, you say? How dreadful!"

Donovan glared at him.

"You saw nobody and you heard nothing?"

"That's right. If there's nothing else, perhaps you will excuse me? You got me out of bed." Sweeting began to close the door very slowly, smiling at Donovan.

Donovan couldn't think of anything else to ask him. He realized he had lost the initiative, as he so often did, but there was nothing he could do about it. He nodded curtly and stepped back.

With a bland little smile, Sweeting closed the door and Donovan heard the key turn.

He pushed his hat to the back of his head, rubbed his jaw and crossed the landing to the head of the stairs.

Where had he seen that fat punk before? he asked himself. Had he a record or had he seen him on the street some time? He was sure Adams would know. Adams never forgot a face. With an angry shrug he went on down the stairs to the next-floor apartment.

Half an hour later he arrived in the hall; half an hour wasted. No one knew anything.

A tiny spark of panic was glowing inside him. To have to return to the top apartment and tell Adams, with Fletcher and Holtby listening. that he had discovered nothing, was not to be thought of. Savagely he rammed his thumb into the bell-push of the yellow-painted front door.

May Christie opened the front door. She, too, had seen the police cars arrive, and had known she was going to receive a visit from the police. She had fortified herself with a slug of gin, and Donovan could smell it on her breath.

"I'm a police officer," he said. "I want to talk to you."

He moved forward riding her back into the sitting-room.

"You can't come in here," she protested. "What will people think?"

"Shut up and sit down!" Donovan snarled.

Because she was itching with curiosity to know why the police had come to the house, and not because she was intimidated by Donovan, she obeyed him, reaching for a cigarette and lifting her plucked eyebrows at him.

"What's biting you?" she demanded.

"You know Fay Carson?"

May's face brightened.

"Is she in trouble?" she asked hopefully.

"She's been murdered."

He watched the quick change of expression and noted with satisfaction the fear that jumped into her eyes.

"Murdered? Who did it?"

"She was struck with an ice-pick. We don't know who did it yet. Was she working last night?"

"I wouldn't know. I was out."

Donovan drew in a slow exasperated breath.

"So you didn't hear or see anything, like the rest of them?"

"I can't help it, can I?" May said. "Murdered! Gee! I never liked her, but I wouldn't wish that on anyone." She got up and crossed the room to where the gin bottle stood on the window seat. "Excuse me, but my nerves are shot this morning." She poured a big drink. "Want one?"

"No. So you didn't see her last night?"

May shook her head, gulped down the gin, thumped herself on her chest and coughed.

"That's better. No, I didn't see her."

Donovan lit a cigarette.

"This killer may come back," he said, leaning forward to stare at May. "He may visit you. If you know anything, you'd better spill it."

"But I don't know anything."

"Didn't you see anyone? This would be between one and two o'clock."

May stared up at the ceiling. The fumes of the gin made her feel dizzy.

"I got back around two," she said. "I did meet a guy in the hall, but he could have come from any of the apartments."

Donovan edged forward in his chair.

"Never mind where he came from. What was he like?"

"He seemed in a hurry. He nearly knocked me over. He was tall, dark and good-looking. I thought he might like to have a drink." She gave Donovan a little leer. "You know how it is . . ."

"Never mind that," Donovan said curtly. "How was he dressed?"

"He had on a light-grey suit and a grey hat."

"Would you know him again?"

"I think so, but he didn't look like a killer."

"They never do. How old would he be?"

"About thirty."

Donovan grimaced. He remembered the cleaner woman had told him Fay specialized in old guys.

"Can't you tell me anything else about him?"

"Well, I asked him to have a drink, and he said he was in a hurry. He pushed me aside and ran into the street."

"Did he look upset?"

"I didn't notice. He just seemed to be in a hell of a hurry."

"Did he have a car outside?"

May shook her head.

"No one ever parks outside. If they have a car they leave it at the parking lot down the street."

Donovan got to his feet.

"Okay. Keep your eyes open, and if you see this guy again, call headquarters. Understand?"

It was just after ten o'clock when Donovan walked into Fay's sitting-room again.

Doc Summerfield had gone. Adams sat in an armchair, a cigarette between his thin lips, his eyes closed.

Fletcher and Holtby were working in the bedroom.

'Well, what have you got?" Adams asked, opening his eyes.

Donovan was having to make an effort to suppress his excitement.

"A description of a guy who could have done it," he said. "He was seen leaving the building around two o'clock and he was in a hurry."

"Most guys would be in a hurry to leave this joint," Adams said.

"I've checked back. None of the girls had a guy with them last night answering this one's description. That must mean he came to see Carson. Doc say when she died?"

"Around half-past one."

"Then he could have done it."

"Doesn't follow. He might have come up here, found her dead, and got out in a hurry."

A soft buzzing noise made both men look up. The sound came from the telephone bell. Donovan went over to the bell and stared at it.

"Look at this: someone's deadened the bell."

Adams picked up the receiver.

Donovan turned to watch him. He saw Adams frown, then he

said, "This is Lieutenant Adams, City Police, talking. Who are you?"

Donovan heard a click on the line and Adams hung up, shrugging.

"One of her mashers, I guess," Adams said. "He certainly got off the line in a hurry."

Donovan snatched up the receiver, called the operator and said urgently, "This is the police. Trace that call and snap it up."

Adams stared at him his eyes disapproving.

"What's the idea? You don't imagine the killer's going to call this number, do you?"

"I want to know who called," Donovan said obstinately.

The operator broke in. "The call came from the Eastern National Bank: from a pay booth."

"Thanks, sister," Donovan said, and hung up.

He went back to the telephone bell.

"Did she muffle the bell or did the killer?" he said.

Raising his voice, Adams called Fletcher.

"Did you check the telephone bell for prints?" he asked, as Fletcher came to the door.

"Yeah. It's clean."

"Didn't you see the bell was muffled?"

"Sure, but I didn't think anything of it."

"You wouldn't," Adams said in disgust. "No prints at all?"

Fletcher shook his head.

"Looks like the killer did it," Donovan said. "She would have left a print."

Adams waved Fletcher away.

"Better find out if anyone heard the bell ring during the evening."

"I'm going down to the bank," Donovan said. "I want to find out if anyone spotted that caller."

"What the hell for?"

"This girl didn't work the streets. She had regulars. Guys who recommended her. I want to talk to as many of them as I can find. One of them might be this guy in the grey suit."

Adams shrugged.

"Okay: you might do worse."

Donovan hurried out of the room. As he ran down the stairs, he was thinking at last he was getting a break. That's all he asked for. Given a little luck, he might crack this case, and then he would spit in Adams' right eye.

III

Police Commissioner Paul Howard sat behind his big mahogany desk, a cigar between his strong white teeth, his hard weather-beaten face worried.

Howard was fifty-one. He was an ambitious man, climbing laboriously up the political ladder, hoping soon to be made a judge and later a senator. He was well in with the political machine, willing to do as he was told, providing the rewards were adequate. He was in a good position to grant favours, and had acquired considerable wealth from the financial tips he had received for turning a blind eye to the corruption and racketeering running rife through the present Administration.

In an armchair by the window, Captain of Police Joe Motley sat with his legs outstretched, a cigar between his fingers, and his flabby, purple-bloomed face expressionless.

Motley was Howard's brother-in-law, the only reason why he remained Captain of Police.

When Howard first took over office, Motley realized his own job was in jeopardy. Motley had no interest in the police force. He was a racing man, but his position was a useful one and he had no intention of losing it. He was a judge of character, and it didn't take him long to discover Howard's weakness for young, attractive girls.

Gloria, Motley's kid sister, was young and more than attractive. Motley had had little difficulty in persuading her to show off her charms before Howard.

Within a month Howard had married her, realizing when it was too late that the Captain of Police he planned to get rid of was now his brother-in-law.

From that time on Motley was sacrosanct. Howard quickly found that if he put any kind of pressure on Motley, he was promptly shut out of his wife's room. So long as he let Motley alone, Gloria performed her wifely duties. Crazy about this vivacious, beautiful girl, he had now accepted the position and had taken the line of least resistance.

Adams sitting opposite the Commissioner, was aware of these facts. He knew Motley was useless, as a police captain, and he knew, if Motley went, he himself would be the automatic

67

choice to replace him. For months now he had been patiently waiting his opportunity to get rid of both Motley and Donovan. He had discovered, nowever, that it would need a major political explosion to blast Motley out of office, and even now, while he listened to Howard talking, his mind was trying to find a way to use Fay Carson's death as the spark to touch off the explosion.

"I want this cracked and cracked fast!" Howard was saying, in a soft furious voice. He looked across at Motley. "Get every man working on it! We've got to nab this killer! A house full of prostitutes! You told me there wasn't a call-house in town."

Motley smiled, showing tobacco-stained teeth.

"There are always call-houses," he said. "We shut them up and they open again."

"Why didn't you shut this one up?" Howard demanded.

Motley stared at him.

"You know why, don't you? It's one of O'Brien's houses."

Howard flushed, then went white. He looked quickly at Adams, who was staring down at his brightly polished shoes, his face blank. Howard was reassured: either Adams hadn't heard Motley's remark or O'Brien's name meant nothing to him.

But O'Brien's name meant plenty to Adams. He new O'Brien was the money behind the party. He knew he was the boss of the party machine. He felt a tingle run up his spine. This could be it. So O'Brien owned 25 Lessington Avenue. Here was the scandal he had been hunting for months. If he could trap Motley into giving O'Brien away, the explosion he had been waiting to touch off would take place.

Only a few of the higher-placed officers of the Administration knew O'Brien was behind the party. Adams wasn't supposed to know, but there wasn't much about the party he hadn't found out.

Howard felt a restricting band of rage tighten across his chest. This fat, loose-mouthed slob must be crazy to shoot his mouth off about O'Brien in front of Adams. He looked again at Adams. No, he didn't know about O'Brien. The remark had passed over his head. Adams was a good police officer, but that was all. He was only interested in his work: politics meant nothing to him.

Howard had no idea O'Brien owned 25 Lessington Avenue, and he was dismayed to hear it. If the press found out, the repercussions might very easily unseat the Administration.

It was essential that this killing should be cleared up as quickly as possible and the killer caught.

"How far have you got to now?" he asked Motley.

Motley waved an indifferent hand towards Adams.

"He's taking care of it. You know, Paul, you're making a hell of a fuss about the killing of this woman. Who cares, anyway?"

"You'll care when you see the press tomorrow morning," Howard said grimly. "Got any leads yet?" he went on to Adams.

"We have a description of a guy who could have done it," Adams said. "Donovan's working on it, now."

"Donovan? You should be working on it," Howard said violently. "Donovan . . . !" He stopped short, scowled down at the desk and then shrugged.

Motley watched him and concealed a grin.

Donovan was Motley's special pet. Howard and Motley had clashed over him before, and Adams knew it. He knew also that Gloria had been used to save Donovan from returning to a beat, and Howard wasn't likely to start trouble for Donovan again, unless he was forced to.

"Donovan's a good guy," Motley said, patting his heavy paunch. Although he was only thirty-eight, lack of exercise, heavy drinking and gross feeding had thickened his figure, making him look a lot older than he was. "We don't often get a murder case, and this could be Donovan's chance. I want him to re-establish himself. The press has been picking on him for months. It's time he had a chance to show what he can do."

"This isn't a one-man police force," Howard said, controlling his temper with difficulty. "I want every man working on it. We've got to nab this killer, Joe."

"Sure, sure," Motley said indifferently. He got slowly to his feet. "Well, I've got to run along. I'm going to the club tonight and I've got to get a haircut. Gloria said she'd be at the dance. You coming?"

"We have a murder on our hands, Joe."

Motley stared at him.

"So what? That doesn't mean you and I can't go to the dance does it? What the hell have we got Adams for? He'll take care of it."

"You go. I have things to do," Howard said curtly.

"Gloria won't like it. She's relying on you."

Howard started to say something, then stopped. To cover

his embarrassment, he stubbed out his cigar which was only half burned.

"It's up to you, of course," Motley went on.

"Well, I'll see how things work out. Maybe I'll look in later."

"Suit yourself," Motley said. "But there's no point in letting all the young punks fight over her. You know what it's like when she goes to a dance on her own. I have my own dish to look after."

Adams, watching and listening, saw Howard's face tighten, and he knew Motley had hit him where it hurt.

The fool! Adams thought contemptuously. What a sucker he is for a woman! He's scared stiff some young husky will make a pass when he's not looking. If I were a slave like he is to that little bitch I'd shoot myself!

When Motley had gone, Howard turned his attention to Adams. He realized Adams had heard a lot more than he cared for him to know, and he glared at Adams angrily.

But the Lieutenant looked as if he was either asleep or miles away somewhere with his thoughts and his complete lack of interest somewhat reassured Howard.

"What are you doing about this killing, Adams?"

Adams gave an elaborate start, blinked at the Commissioner and his face became alert.

"I'm following the usual procudure sir. You have my report on the desk. There are no clues. We have a description of a man whom we believe went to her apartment about the time she died. Donovan is working on that angle. The killing of a prostitute is always a tricky nut to crack. There seems to have been no motive. Nothing was taken."

"What are the chances of cracking this case in a hurry?" Howard asked, leaning forward across his desk and staring at Adams.

Adams shook his head.

"I wouldn't count on it, sir. The guy may be a nut. If he doesn't do it again, the chance aren't good. She may have tried to blackmail him and he killed her to shut her mouth. We have checked through her apartment: there was nothing in it to tell us she did collect material for blackmail, but she may have a deposit box somewhere."

"Do you think it was a nut?" Howard asked.

Adams shook his head.

"I guess not. A nut invariably strangles and then rips them. She was stabbed. Doc thinks she may have known the guy

70

because she was stabbed from the front. She must have seen him, and yet she didn't cry out. At least, no one heard anything."

Howard selected another cigar, bit off the end and spat angrily into his trash basket.

"We've got to get this killer fast. Donovan's okay on the routine stuff, but fast work isn't his strong point. I'm relying on you to crack this case, Adams. Hold your own investigation. Never mind what Motley and Donovan are doing. Get after this killer and nab him. There could be a shake-up here before long, and if you crack this one, you might do yourself a lot of good."

The two men looked at each other.

Adams' thin, pinched face was expressionless, but inside he was experiencing a surge of triumph.

"The Captain will know what I'm up to sir," he said. "He could block me off."

"I'll tell him you are working for me," Howard said. "You have orders from me to investigate and produce a report on the vice set-up in this town. I'll need the report, anyway. Get some-one to do the leg-work; you concentrate on this killing. I'll let you have duplicates of all reports sent in by Donovan. Now get moving: I want some action."

"You'll get it, sir," Adams said, and went out of the room.

For some moments Howard sat staring at his blotter, then he got up, went to the door and half opened it.

"I'm going over to City Hall," he told his secretary. "I'll be back in an hour."

He shut the door, put on his hat, crossed the room to the door leading to his private stairs, and hurried down to the street.

CHAPTER TWO

I

FOR the past three years, Séan O'Brien had been the secret political boss behind the present Administration. He had taken over at a time when the party was in very low water, and, by his enormous financial resources, had infused new life into it.

71

Ed Fabian, a fat, jovial, uninspired politician, had been the party's leader when O'Brien and his millions appeared on the scene. He had accepted O'Brien's offer of financial help without questioning where the money had come from or when would be the ultimate repayment.

The fact that O'Brien had insisted on complete anonymity should have aroused Fabian's suspicions, but Fabian had to have money to keep his party alive, and he couldn't afford to be curious.

Fabian now found himself a mere figurehead, but he was growing old, and had lost what fighting qualities he may have had. So long as he had the credit for running the party, he was content to take orders from O'Brien.

It would have severely jolted him if he had known that O'Brien had made his millions from large-scale, international drug trafficking. The drug traffic organization he had built up had eventually been smashed. He had always believed in being the unseen, unknown leader, and although the men who worked for him were now serving long sentences in French jails, he had managed to escape from France, taking his millions with him.

He had come to Flint City, California, to rest on his labours and enjoy his money. Pretty soon he became bored with an inactive life, and had decided to go into politics. He examined the political set-up in the town, picked on Fabian's party as the weakest reed, moved in and bought control.

In spite of his great care to remain anonymous during his drug-trafficking dealings, he hadn't been able to avoid contact with a few of the traffickers, and one of them, now serving a twenty years' sentence, had talked.

The police had from him only a vague description of O'Brien, but O'Brien knew they were still hunting for him. Publicity of any kind was dangerous. A chance photograph in the local press might be seen by an alert officer of the Division of Narcotic Enforcement, and O'Brien would find himself with a twenty-year rap hanging around his neck.

But after three years of security he wasn't unduly worried by his position. He had always avoided the limelight, always preferred to live quietly and not mix with people.

It amused him to control the activities of this prosperous town, and to know the voters had no idea he was the man who pulled the strings and to some extent directed their lives.

He had a big, luxurious bungalow with three acres of ornamental gardens, running down to the river. The grounds were screened by high walls, and it was impossible for the most curious passer-by to see behind the walls.

It took Police Commissioner Howard twenty minutes fast driving to reach the bungalow. As he drove up the long, winding drive, flanked on either side by large beds of gaily coloured dahlias, he could see a regiment of Chinese gardeners working to keep the vast and beautiful garden immaculate.

But the garden didn't interest Howard this morning. He knew it was unwise to call on O'Brien. Suspecting that there was something shady in the way O'Brien had made his money, Howard had been careful not to get his name too closely associated with O'Brien's, and if they had to meet, he made sure other members of the party were present. But he had to talk to O'Brien alone this morning, and he knew it was far more dangerous to say what he had to say over an open telephone line.

He pulled up outside the main entrance, got out of his car, hurried across the big sun porch, and rang the bell.

O'Brien's man, Sullivan, a hulking ex-prize fighter, wearing a white coat and well-pressed black trousers, opened the door. Sullivan's eyes showed surprise when he saw Howard.

"Mr. O'Brien in?" Howard asked.

"Sure," Sullivan said, stepping aside, "but he's busy right now."

As Howard entered the hall, he heard a woman singing somewhere in the bungalow, and he thought at first O'Brien had on the radio. The clear soprano voice had great quality. Even Howard, who didn't appreciate music, realized the voice was out of the ordinary.

"Tell him it's important."

"Better tell him yourself, boss," Sullivan said. "More than my life's worth to stop that hen screeching." He waved to the passage that led to the main lounge. "Go ahead and help yourself."

Howard walked quickly down the passage and paused at the open doorway, leading into the lounge.

O'Brien lolled in an armchair, his hands folded across his chest, his eyes closed.

At the grand piano by the open casement windows sat a tall willowy girl. She was strikingly beautiful; blonde, with big green eyes, a finely shaped nose, high cheek-bones and a large, sensuous mouth. She was wearing a white cashmere sweater and a pair of blue-and-white checkered jeans.

She was singing some soprano aria that was vaguely familiar to Howard. Her voice was as smooth as cream, and full of colour.

He stood motionless, watching her, feeling his pulse quicken. Up to now he had always imagined Gloria to be the most beautiful girl in town, but he had to admit this girl had her well beaten. Her figure, too, was sensational. Just like O'Brien to have found a beauty like this, he thought enviously.

The girl caught sight of him, standing in the doorway.

Her voice was moving up effortlessly, and she was about to hit a high note when their eyes met. She started, her voice trailed off, and her hands slipped off the keyboard.

O'Brien opened his eyes, frowning.

"What the hell . . . ?" he began, looking across at her, then swiftly he followed the direction of her staring eyes, and in his turn, he stared at Howard.

"I'm sorry to interrupt," Howard said, advancing into the room. "I wanted a word with you."

O'Brien got to his feet. He showed no surprise to see Howard, although Howard knew he must be surprised.

"You should have kept out of sight until she had finished," he said, coming across to shake hands. "Never mind. Music has never been your strong point, has it Commissioner? I want you to meet Miss Dorman, my future wife."

The girl got to her feet and came over. Her wide heavily made-up lips were parted in a smile but her eyes were wary. Howard had a puzzling idea that she was frightened of him.

"Your future wife?" he repeated, startled. "Well, I didn't know. My congratulations." He took her slim, cool hand as he smiled at O'Brien. "Well done! I was beginning to wonder if you were going to remain a bachelor all your life."

"I was in no hurry," O'Brien said, putting his arm around the girl's waist. "She's worth waiting for, isn't she? Gilda, this is Police Commissioner Howard. He is a very important person, and I want you two to be great friends."

Gilda said, "You know, Séan, all your friends are mine now."

O'Brien laughed.

"That sounds fine, but you don't kid me. I've seen the way you've looked at some of my so-called friends. Anyway, be nice to this guy. I like him." He looked at Howard. "Have a drink, Commissioner?"

"Well . . ." Howard glanced at Gilda and then at O'Brien. "There's a little business matter . . ."

"Now you're really going to make her love you," O'Brien said, shrugging. "Hear that honey? Business . . ."

"That's my cue to duck out," Gilda said, moving away from O'Brien's encircling arm. "Don't be too long, Séan."

She gave Howard a quick searching glance as she smiled at him. Then she left the room.

Howard followed her with his eyes, and again he felt his pulse quicken at the shape he could see under the sweater and jeans.

"Some kid, isn't she?" O'Brien said, who missed nothing. He knew Howard's weakness for beautiful young women. "And what a voice!" He went over to the liquor cabinet and began mixing two highballs. "Believe it or not I found her in a nightclub singing swing! As soon as I heard the quality of her voice I persuaded her to get down to serious work. She's on Mozart now. Francelli has heard her, and he's crazy about her. He says she'll be at the Met. in a couple of years."

Howard took the highball O'Brien offered him and sat down. He looked up at O'Brien.

Handsome devil, he thought. He can't be much older than forty, and he must be worth ten millions if he's worth a cent.

O'Brien was good-looking in a dark, showy way. His eyebrows that sloped upwards and his fine pencilled moustache gave him a satanic look.

"What's biting you, Commissioner?" he asked, sitting on the arm of a chair and swinging an expensively shod foot.

"Know anything about 25 Lessington Avenue?" Howard asked.

O'Brien's right eyebrow lifted.

"Why?"

"I hear you own the place."

"So what?"

"A call-girl was murdered there last night, and four other apartments in the house are occupied by call-girls."

O'Brien drank from his glass, set it down and lit a cigarette. His face was expressionless, but Howard knew him well enough to see his mind was working fast.

"You have nothing to worry about," O'Brien said finally.

"I'll take care of it. Who is the girl?"

"She called herself Fay Carson."

O'Brien's face remained expressionless but his eyes narrowed for a moment, and that was enough of a clue to tell Howard the information had shocked him.

"Press know yet?"

Howard shook his head.

"We'll have to give it to them in an hour or so. I thought I'd better have a word with you first. This could develop into something though."

"How did you know the house belongs to me?"

So he wasn't denying it. Howard's heart sunk. He had hoped Motley had been sounding off.

"Motley told me."

"That slob talks too much," O'Brien said. He rubbed his jaw and stared down at the carpet.

"Can the ownership of the house be traced to you?" Howard asked quietly.

"It might be. My attorney bought it, but if someone dug deep enough it could be traced to me. Let me think a moment."

Howard took a long pull at his glass. He felt in need of a stimulant. All along he had had an uneasy idea that O'Brien was shady. He had appeared from nowhere; no one had ever heard of him, and yet he had millions. Now he was calmly admitting to owning a call-house.

"Did you know what these women are?" Howard asked.

O'Brien frowned at him.

"Of course. They have to live somewhere, and besides they pay damn well." He got to his feet crossed over to the telephone and dialled a number. After a moment's delay, he said into the mouthpiece. "Tux there?" He waited, then went on, "Tux? Got a job for you, and snap this one up. Go to 25 Lessington Avenue right away and clear all the wrens out you find there. Get them all out. There are four of them. When you've cleared them out, get four people into their apartments. I don't care who they are so long as they look respectable: old spinsters would do fine. Some of the mob must have some respectable relations. I want the job done in two hours. Understand?" He dropped the receiver back on its cradle and came to sit down again. "Well, that takes care of that. When your news hawks arrive, they'll find the house so respectable they'll take their hats off and wipe their shoes."

76

Howard stared at him uneasily. This was too glib; too much of the rackateer.

"That's a relief off my mind. It didn't occur to me to do a thing like that," he said slowly.

O'Brien lifted his shoulders.

"I guess you have other things to think about. I specialize in keeping out of trouble." He reached for a cigar, tossed one into Howard's lap and lit one for himself. "Now tell me about this girl. Who killed her?"

"We don't know. The killer left no clues, but she must have known him. She was stabbed from in front with an ice-pick, and no one heard her cry out."

"Last night, you say? There was a hell of a thunderstorm raging wasn't there? Would they have heard her if she had cried out?"

Howard had forgotten the storm and bit his lip angrily.

"That's right. They might not have heard her."

"Who's handling the investigation?"

"Donovan, but I've told Adams to work on the side. Donovan has a description of a guy who could have done it."

O'Brien got up and moved over to the liquor cabinet. Howard wasn't sure, but he had a vague idea that O'Brien had become suddenly tense.

"What's the description?"

"It's not much: youngish, about thirty-three, tall, dark and good-looking. Wearing a light-grey suit and matching hat."

"Hmm, won't help you much, will it?" O'Brien said, bringing two more drinks to the table.

"It's better than nothing," Howard said, taking the drink. "A case like this is always tough to crack. There's usually no motive."

O'Brien sat down again.

"This could give Burt an excuse to start trouble. Have you talked to Fabian yet?"

"Not yet. There's nothing he can do, anyway. It's up to me. If I find the killer fast we should be all right. What worried me was hearing the house was a call-house."

O'Brien smiled.

"Well, I've taken care of that for you, so you can relax."

"Yes," Howard said uneasily. "Are there any more call-houses belonging to you in town?"

"There may be," O'Brien returned carelessly. "I own a lot of property. There may be."

"I have an idea Burt knows about you. It will be bad for us if he finds out about these call-houses of yours."

"Thanks for reminding me," O'Brien said, smiling. "I know the position as well as you do." He got to his feet. "Well, Commissioner, I don't want to hurry you away, but I have a whale of a lot of things to do this morning. Keep me in touch. I'd like to have a copy of all reports to do with the killing. I want them fast, too. Have someone bring them to me as soon as they are typed, will you?"

Howard hesitated.

"I don't think our reports should leave headquarters: that would be contrary to regulations. Suppose I keep you informed personally?"

O'Brien's eyes hardened although he continued to smile.

"I want the reports, Commissioner," he said quietly.

Howard made a little gesture with his hands.

"All right. I'll see you get them."

"Thank you. You had better have a word with Fabian. Warn him Burt is almost certain to try to start something. It can't be much if you find the killer fast. Play the girl down to the press. She can be a nightclub hostess."

"Yes."

Howard walked with O'Brien to the front door.

"Is Donovan such a good man to put on this case?" O'Brien asked as he opened the door.

"Adams is working on it too."

"Ah yes . . . Adams. He's a smart cop. So long, Commissioner, thanks for calling, and let me have those reports."

O'Brien stood in the doorway and watched Howard drive away, then he slowly closed the door and remained motionless, his face thoughtful.

Gilda, concealed behind the half-open door of O'Brien's study, felt a little chill of apprehension run through her at the hard, ugly set of O'Brien's mouth.

II

Detective Dave Duncan pasted a cigarette on his lower lip, scratched a match alight and lowered the cigarette end into his cupped hands.

78

He looked across the table at Sergeant Donovan who was finishing a ham sandwich, his heavy jaws moving slowly as he chewed, his face dark with thought.

Duncan had been a detective third for a long time. He had almost given up hope of promotion, but now he had been assigned to work with Donovan, he began to hope again. Not that Donovan rated high with him: but a murder case did give a guy a chance if he used his head.

"The old punk swears he kept a registration book." Duncan said. "He swears he entered all the cars parked in the lot last night, but the book's missing."

Donovan belched gently, pulled his coffee cup towards him and groped for a cigarette.

"It couldn't have got up and walked," he said. "It must be somewhere."

"This guy in the grey suit could have taken it," Duncan said. "He went into the hut and got talking with the old fella. He could have taken it, knowing his car number was in the book."

Donovan nodded.

"Yeah. If he did take it, it's destroyed by now. This guy in the grey suit looks like our man." He pulled his notebook out of his hip pocket and thumbed through the pages. "Let's see what we've got. At ten to nine last night, the guy leaves a green Lincoln, number not known, in the car park; tells the attendant if his friend is in he may stay the night. At half-past ten, he and the murdered woman pick up a taxi outside the house for the Blue Rose. The driver identifies him and Carson. Darcy and the doorman at the Blue Rose also identify him from our description. Darcy hasn't seen him before. He doesn't think he is an ordinary masher. Carson didn't take her clients to the Blue Rose. Our guy must be something special. Okay, Around twelve-thirty he and the girl take a taxi back to her apartment. The driver is sure it's our guy. According to Doc, the girl dies around one-thirty. Our guy is seen by this Christie dame leaving the house: he appears to be in a hurry. He then turns up at the parking lot. The attendant is sheltering from the rain in his hut. Our guy joins him and talks about the storm. Then he starts to go, but the attendant wants to mark off his car in his book, but he can't find it. He asks him for his number, and he gives him the number of a Packard that's been on the lot for a couple of days, and is still there now. Now why did he give the wrong car number unless he was in trouble?" Donovan closed his note book and ran his thumb nail across his ginger moustache. "That's not a bad day's work, Duncan. If we can find this guy, we've almost got enough on him to put him away."

"We have to find him first," Duncan said, finishing his coffee and standing up. "I have an idea, sarg; Darcy is holding out on us. I think he knows who this guy is."

Donovan shrugged.

"I don't know. He looked a little shifty, but maybe he has something to hide up himself," he said, getting off his stool. "You can't make a guy like Darcy talk unless he wants to. What I want to find out is if our guy was a regular customer of Carson's or just a chance caller. The fact she took him to the Blue Rose makes it look like he is a regular. What we've got to find out now is who her men friends are. She must have known a hell of a lot of guys, but there must have been several she knew better than others."

Duncan dropped his cigarette end on the floor and trod on it.

"How do we do that? Darcy said he didn't know who her friends were. Who else is there to ask?"

"I'm going to try that punk at the bank: the smooth, fat one who gave me that spiel about calling his wife. There was only one call from that pay booth around ten o'clock, and that was to Carson's apartment. This fat punk said a girl and an elderly man used the pay booth, and that he also used it. Well, he was lying; so we'll go along and talk to him."

"The bank's closed," Duncan said.

"Maybe the night watchman will know his address," Donovan said. "Come on; let's find out."

But the night watchman didn't know Parker's address. He didn't even know Parker.

"They are all gone by the time I take over," he explained. "Sorry, sergeant, you'll have to wait until tomorrow."

"Give me the manager's address," Donovan said shortly. "This is urgent."

"I haven't got it," the night watchman returned. "If I want one of the officials I have to get into touch with Mr. Holland: he's the head teller."

"Well, okay," Donovan said impatiently. "Let's have his address, and snap it up, will you? I'm in a hurry."

The night watchman wrote the address down on a scrap of paper, and the two detectives returned to their car.

"I'll get a newspaper," Donovan said, "hang on a second."

He bought two papers from the boy at the corner, and came back to the car.

"It's in the stop press," he said, and read the announcement. He felt no satisfaction to see his name in print. He knew if he didn't crack this one fast the press would turn on him.

During the afternoon he had returned to Fay Carson's apartment to meet the press. Anticipating the worst kind of trouble from the reporters, he had been relieved to find Captain Motley already there.

He was bewildered and astonished to find no sign of the cal-girls. The whole house had miraculously become respectable and, ferret as they could, the reporters found nothing to work on. They went from apartment to apartment. The elderly women who opened the door to them knew nothing and had heard nothing.

The reporters were highly suspicious because they had been called in so late, but Motley's smooth talk got over the awkward situation. Listening to him soft soap the press made Donovan thankful it wasn't he who had to handle them.

"Going to be a hell of a spread across the front page to-morrow morning," he said, getting into the car beside Duncan.

"Yeah," Duncan said, and sent the car shooting away from the kerb.

It didn't take them long to find the street.

"That's the place, over on your right," Donovan said.

They pulled up outside the neat, well-cared-for bungalow and got out.

"This guy can grow roses, can't he?" said Duncan, who was a keen gardener. "Look at that Mrs. Laxton."

"Who's she?" Donovan growled, staring around.

"Never mind, sarg," Duncan said, concealing a grin. "Pity he doesn't keep his lawn better. Reminds me I've got to cut mine."

"Keep your mind on your job!" Donovan snarled.

He rammed his thumb into the bell-push, kept it there for a couple of seconds, then stood away.

There was a long pause, then just as he was going to ring again, the front door opened.

He recognized the tall, good-looking guy who opened the door. He had been standing next to Parker at the bank.

Scared out of his wits, Donovan thought with sadistic satisfaction. Damn funny thing. I have only to ring a bell to frighten the life out of everyone in the house.

He shoved his heavy jaw forward aggressively.

"You Holland?" he growled.

Ken nodded dumbly.

Duncan was studying him, puzzled.

He looks as if he has robbed the bank and has the proceeds in the house, he thought. What the hell's the matter with him?"

"I want to talk to Parker. Where's he live?" Donovan demanded.

Ken opened and shut his mouth, but no sound came. He stared fixedly at Donovan.

"Where does he live?" Donovan repeated, raising his voice.

Ken made an effort, gulped, then said, "Why, he's just in the next road. 145 Marshall Avenue."

Duncan took out his notebook and jotted down the address.

"Did he tell you he was going to call his wife from the pay booth this morning?" Donovan demanded.

"He – he didn't say."

"But you saw him go to the pay booth?"

"Why – yes, I did,"

"What time was that?"

"I didn't notice."

Donovan glared at him, then he turned disgustedly to Duncan.

"Come on; we're wasting time."

He strode down the path, jerked open the gate and crossed to the car.

Duncan followed him. At the gate, he turned to look back. Ken was still standing motionless in the doorway, staring after them. Then, seeing Duncan looking at him, he stepped back and hurriedly shut the front door.

CHAPTER THREE

I

WHEN Commissioner Howard's car disappeared down the drive, Séan O'Brien walked slowly into the lounge and sat down. He waited, listening, and after a moment or so he heard footsteps. Gilda came into the room.

"Oh, he's gone, then," she said, but the assumed surprise in her voice didn't deceive O'Brien.

"Yes, he's gone," he said, and taking her hand, he pulled her down on to the arm of his chair. He put his arm around her waist and began to stroke her flank while he looked up at her.

Her great green cat's eyes were dark with anxiety.

"What did he want, Séan?" she asked. "Or shouldn't I ask?"

"This is the first time he has ever been here," O'Brien said, frowning. "He's an odd guy" He leaned his head against Gilda's arm. "He brought some bad news."

He felt her stiffen.

"Do you remember Fay Carson?" he went on, and looked up at her.

Her finely shaped nostrils contracted and her eyes hardened.

"Of course I do. What has she . . .?"

"Your brother and she were lovers, weren't they?"

He saw her flinch.

"But, Séan, that's ancient history now. Why bring it up?"

He abruptly got to his feet and moved away from her, his hands behind his back; a set, hard expression on his face.

"Maybe it's not so ancient. Now look, Gilda, before I say anything more about Johnny, I want you to understand our position. I don't have to tell you I'm crazy about you, and I'll do anything for you. Always remember that. You're the only woman I've ever loved. Oh, there have been plenty of the other type, but with you, it's different. You mean more to me than anything else in life. We are going to get married soon. As you know, I am in control of the administration of this City. It's important to me that I should remain in control. Politics is a dirty game, kid. Everyone is on the look-out to cut someone's throat. The quickest way to upset a political machine is to dig up a scandal that is big enough to hit the headlines. Then the voters take notice. Do you understand?"

She sat on the arm of the chair, her hands clenched tightly between her thighs; still, white-faced and frightened.

"Yes, Séan, but what has this to do with Johnny?"

He faced her.

"I told you Howard brought some bad news. Fay Carson was murdered last night."

Gilda shut her eyes. An uncontrolled shiver ran through her. For a long moment neither of them said anything, and only the busy ticking of the clock on the mantelpiece disturbed the silence. Then O'Brien said, "Did you know Johnny came back last night? One of my men saw him at the Paradise Club. Did you see him?"

She hesitated, not looking at him, then she nodded.

"I knew he was in town," she said, staring down at her clenched fists.

"Do you think he killed her?" O'Brien asked quietly.

She looked up, her eyes widening.

"Of course not! How could you say such a thing?"

Her vehemence was completely unconvincing. They looked at each other, then Gilda looked away.

"We must be frank with each other, kid," O'Brien said. "You know as well as I do why I asked you that. Before he went to the home, he threatened to kill her. He hasn't been out more than a few hours before she's murdered. You must face facts."

Gilda sat motionless. He could see she was holding on to herself in an effort to keep control, and he went over to her and put his arm around her.

"Now take it easy. This is something you don't have to face alone. You have me. There's not much I can't fix."

"He didn't do it," she said tonelessly. "He wouldn't do a horrible thing like that."

Knowing Johnny, O'Brien thought it was just the thing he would do.

"That's only your opinion," he said gently. "He's your brother and you're fond of him, but you've got to consider what other people will think. He's got a pretty bad reputation. He behaved badly . . ."

"I tell you he didn't do it!" she exclaimed, jumping up and facing him. "You talk as if you have proof . . ." She stopped, her hand going to her mouth. "That policeman doesn't think he did it, does he?"

O'Brien shook his head.

"He doesn't know a thing about Johnny."

She went over to the window, her back turned to him. He watched her, experiencing the sense of pleasure the sight of her tall, slim, beautifully proportioned body always gave him.

"Then why do you think Johnny did it?" she asked.

"Look, this will get us nowhere. He was in town last night and she was murdered. It's as simple as that."

"He didn't do it!" she said fiercely, without turning.

"Did you see him last night?"

"No. He telephoned."

"Why didn't you tell me?"

She turned then.

"I should have. I'm sorry, Séan, but he asked me not to. He wanted money. He said he was going to New York. I was leaving for the Casino when he called. I told him I'd meet him there and have the money for him. He didn't show up. He must have got the money from someone else."

"Did he get it from Fay?"

"No!" Her eyes flashed. "He didn't know where she lived, and he wouldn't take money from her. He never went near Fay last night."

"I hope you are right," O'Brien said soberly. "So you didn't see him?"

"I didn't."

He was far too shrewd not to see at once that she was lying. She had seen him, and she must be as convinced as he was that Johnny had murdered Fay.

This was serious. At all costs Johnny mustn't get into the hands of the police. He had to deal with this situation quickly and efficiently. Where was Johnny?"

"He's gone to New York then?" he said casually, watching her closely.

"Yes. I'm sure I shall hear from him soon," Gilda said, not looking at him.

"I see."

She was still lying to him. It suddenly occurred to him that she might be sheltering Johnny. He might be at her apartment at this moment.

"Well, so long as he is out of the way . . ." he said, and looked at his wrist-watch. "Damn it! I nearly forgot. I have to call a guy. Wait for me, will you? We've got to get this thing straightened out. I won't be a minute."

He went out of the room, into his study, and closed the door. He dialled a number, and, keeping his voice down, said, "Get me Tux."

After a short delay, a hard, rasping voice said, "Yes, boss?"

"You did a swell job on that apartment house. I have another job for you. Go around to 45 Maddox Court. It's Miss Dorman's apartment. Get in there and take a look around. Don't let anyone see you. I think Johnny Dorman's there. If he is, take him away and hole him up somewhere safe. It won't be easy, but you've handled tougher jobs than this one. Take Whitey along with you. The boy gets wild under pressure."

"I'll take care of him," Tux said.

"I want him somewhere where I can get at him in a hurry. I don't want anyone to see him, and be careful how you handle him. Don't hit him on the head: his roof's not all that strong."

"Leave it to me, boss," Tux said. "I'll call you back."

O'Brien replaced the receiver, lit a cigarette and returned to the lounge.

He thought from the look of Gilda's eyes that she had been crying, and he went to sit beside her on the couch.

"You mustn't let this upset you," he said gently. "Now, let's take a look at the set-up. You've got to be frank with me, Gilda. This could turn out to be unpleasant for both of us. We've got to think of ourselves. There are one or two things I want you to tell me about. Some time ago there was trouble between you and Fay and Johnny. At the time I felt it wasn't my business, but now it could be my business and I want to know what it was all about. You've got to remember that I have a lot of enemies. They know we're planning to get married. If they could put Johnny on a spot they'll do it to get at me. I must know the facts. I don't want them sprung on me. Someone might remember that Johnny threatened to kill Fay, and the police might be forced to dig into his past. I want to know what happened between you and Fay and Johnny. All I know is he suddenly went haywire and you put him in a home. I want the inside story, Gilda. I must have it."

"If Johnny is in trouble," she said quietly, "you don't have to marry me, Séan."

"I'm going to marry you," O'Brien said, looking fixedly at her. "That's about the one thing in life I am sure about. But I'm going to avoid trouble if I can. I must know what it was all about. Will you tell me?"

She lifted her shoulders wearily.

"Of course. It's all very sordid, but I have nothing to hide. I would have told you before if you had asked." She reached for a cigarette; accepted the light he offered, and went on, "Fay and I were once good friends. We shared an apartment. I did a little singing; she did a dancing act with her partner, Maurice Yarde. She was crazy about him. He wasn't the type of man any girl should be crazy about. He was selfish and utterly unscrupulous. One day she brought him to the apartment and introduced him to me. From that moment I never had a second's peace. He followed me everywhere. You can't imagine how crude he was. He forced himself on me. Fay wouldn't believe I wasn't encouraging him, and she quarrelled with me. Nothing I could say would convince her. She quarrelled with him, too. I left the apartment, but still he kept after me. Finally, I left town. He was so furious with Fay for interfering, he broke up the dance act and also left town. When I heard he had gone, I came back. Fay wouldn't have anything to do with me, and I wasn't sorry because she had gone completely off the rails. She wouldn't go on with her dancing, and she turned to men for money. One day she ran into Johnny, who was just out of the army. I don't have to tell you what a dreadful time he had had during the war. It left him unbalanced; he drank too much and got into violent rages. I was the only one who could handle him. Fay found out he was my brother, but he didn't find out what she was. She made up her mind to hook him to get even with me. She did hook him. I warned him about her, but he wouldn't listen. He became as crazy about her as she had been about Yarde. He wanted to marry her, but she held him off; neither refusing nor accepting him. Then one of his friends gave him her card, telling him if he wanted a girl, he could recommend her. I guess Johnny went off his head. He rushed around to her apartment, and if Sam Darcy hadn't arrived soon after, Johnny might have killed her. She was terribly beaten up. Sam got him under control and sent for me. I got Johnny into a home. Well, you know the rest of it, Séan. Johnny stayed in the home for nearly a year. The doctors have told me he has made a complete recovery. I was going there to bring him home, but he forestalled me. He got back last night."

O'Brien rubbed his chin thoughtfully.

"So Sam Darcy knows about Johnny and Fay?"

"He knows Johnny beat her up and threatened to kill her."

"Do you think Johnny went to him last night? Do you think Darcy knows he's in town?"

"I don't know."

"Well, all right," O'Brien said. "I now know the facts. We mustn't make too much of this. We mustn't jump to conclusions. Howard tells me they have a description of a man who was seen leaving Fay's apartment about the time she died. It's nothing like the description of Johnny."

"I tell you Johnny didn't do it!" she said sharply.

"I'm afraid it isn't very important what you and I think, Gilda," O'Brien said seriously. "The facts are he threatened to kill her before going into the home. As soon as he comes out, she's murdered. I only hope they catch this tall, dark guy in the grey suit. If they don't, someone may remember that Johnny could be a suspect, and because he's your brother, they may try to make something out of it."

"Surely the police will find this man," Gilda said anxiously.

"I hope so." He gave her a crooked little smile. "Let's get our minds off this for a moment. Lunch is ready."

She shook her head.

"I want to go home now, Séan. I have things to do."

"You are going to have lunch with me," he said firmly, and took her arm, walking with her down the passage to the dining-room.

An hour later, after she had driven away in her sports coupé, the telephone bell rang.

O'Brien picked up the receiver.

"Tux here," the hard, rasping voice said. "It's okay, boss. He was there, and I've got him."

O'Brien's face hardened.

"Where?"

"On the *Willow Point*."

"Fine. I'll be over in half an hour," O'Brien said. "Stick close to him, Tux."

He hung up.

II

Ken Holland closed the front door and walked with shaky legs back to the lounge. He rested his hands on the back of an easy chair and leaned his weight on them. His heart was still pounding. He still felt the suffocating fear that had gripped him at the sight of the two detectives as they had come up the path.

What an escape! he thought. Did they notice how scared I was? I've got to pull myself together. If they ever get on to me I'll give myself away if I behave like that again.

He suddenly thought of Parker.

He must be warned.

He hurried to the telephone, dialled and listened to the ringing tone.

Hurry up! he thought feverishly. They'll be around to you any moment. Hurry up!

There was a click on the line, and Mrs. Parker's chilly, pedantic voice asked who was calling.

"This is Kenway Holland. May I speak to Max?"

"Well, he's in the garden," Mrs. Parker said dubiously as if her husband was in China. "I'll see if I can get him. Hold on a moment."

Ken waited in an agony of suspense.

"Are you there?" Mrs. Parker asked after a long wait. "I'll get him to call you back. He's talking to two men at the moment. I can't imagine who they are, but I don't suppose he'll be long."

"Thank you," Ken said, and hung up.

He went over to the liquor cabinet, poured himself a shot of whisky and drank it. He lit a cigarette and sat down. There was nothing he could do now but wait.

What would happen to Parker? Would he be able to bluff Donovan? Would he admit knowing Fay Carson? Would he tell Donovan he had given Ken Fay's telephone number? Would Parker remember that Ken owned a light-grey suit?

Unable to sit still while his mind was crawling with alarm, Ken got up and went into the garden. He went down the path to the gate and stared up and down the street. He wanted to walk to the corner to see if the police car was still outside Parker's house, but he was scared the detectives might see him.

After a long moment of staring up and down the street, he returned to the bungalow.

Then from nowhere a sudden paralysing thought came into his mind.

What had he done with the registration book he had taken from the car attendant's hut?

He turned hot, then cold when he realized he had no idea what had become of the book. Until this moment he had completely forgotten about it.

He remembered slipping it into his hip pocket while he talked to the car attendant, but after that he had no recollection of what he had done with it.

It hadn't been in the suit. Before he had taken the suit back to Gaza's store, he had gone through the pockets most carefully.

Then where was it?

Had he dropped it in the street?

If it were found it would be recognized. The owner of every

car entered in the book would be investigated, and his car number was in the book!

He looked around wildly. If he had dropped it somewhere in the bungalow, Carrie might have found it and put it away as she put everything away.

He began a feverish and futile search.

It was growing dark by the time he satisfied himself the book wasn't in the bungalow. He was in a panic as he stood staring around the now disordered lounge.

Had the book slipped out of his pocket while he had been driving home?

What a fool he was!

Of course that was what must have happened. He should have looked in the car first.

He went to the front door, opened it and started down the path towards the garage when he saw Parker at the gate.

He stopped short, looking at Parker who came up the path in the gathering dusk, his head held low, a stoop to his shoulders.

"I want to talk to you," he said as he came up to Ken.

"Come in," Ken said, and led the way into the lounge. He turned on the light. "I'm sorry the place is in such a mess. I lost something, and I've been hunting for it."

Parker went over to an armchair and sank into it. His fat, usually red face looked flabby and pale, and his hands were unsteady as he rested them on the arms of the chair.

"If you've got a drink . . ." he said.

"Sure," Ken said, and fixed two highballs. "That detective fellow was here. He wanted your address. I tried to call you, but he got around to you too fast."

Parker stared at him in a disconcerting, searching way. Ken gave him the highball and then moved awkwardly to an armchair and sat down.

"What happened?" he asked after a long pause.

"They didn't get anything out of me," Parker said, his voice flat and cold. "I stuck to my story. I damn well had to. The sergeant said I was lying; he said I called Fay. I told him to prove it. He didn't rattle me, but he had a damn good try. When he saw he was getting nowhere, he said he didn't think I had killed her – that's nice, isn't it? He hoped I might know who her men friends were. I knew I didn't dare admit I knew her. I swore I hadn't called her. He said no other call had been made from the pay booth at the time I said I had called Maisie. I guessed by the way he talked no one but you had seen me use the booth, so I said I might have been mistaken about the time. I said it was possible I had called Maisie earlier than ten. So he said he would talk to Maisie." Parker took a long drink, wiped his face and stared down at his feet. "That was a pretty horrible ten minutes. I don't think I'll ever forget waiting in the garden with the other detective while the sergeant talked to Maisie. She was terrific. She must have guessed I had got myself into a mess. She lied her head off. She told the sergeant I had called her just after nine, and not after ten as I had said. The sergeant must have been a first-class fool. He actually told her I had called her at ten. She was so emphatic that he believed her. He even apologized to me."

Ken relaxed back in his chair.

"I can't say how glad I am . . ."

Again Parker gave him the odd, searching stare.

"When they had gone, I told Maisie the truth," he said slowly. "She's taken it pretty hard."

"You didn't tell her about the girl? That you and she . . .?"

"I had to. She knew I had lied to the sergeant. I couldn't look her in the face and lie to her. She asked me bluntly if I had been fooling around with Fay. I had to admit it."

Ken realized that if Ann had put the same question to him, he would have been unable to lie to her.

"I'm sorry . . ."

"Yes." Parker ran his hand over his face. "She's taken it pretty hard. Of course her mother heard all about it. She made things damned difficult. This could break up my home."

"I can't say how sorry I am."

"Well, I brought it on myself. It's damned funny, but I felt so safe with Fay. I thought I could get away with it. What a fool I've been!" He looked up suddenly and stared hard at Ken. "But that's enough about me. I'm not going to talk any more about my troubles. There's something else I want to say. The sergeant gave me a description of the man they want. They think he killed Fay. I've been thinking about what he said." He leaned forward and went on, "Are you quite sure, Holland, that you didn't go to Fay's apartment last night?"

Ken's heart skipped a beat, then raced. He felt himself change colour. He made a desperate attempt to meet Parker's eyes, but he couldn't do it. To hide his fear, he reached for a cigarette; lit it, then said, his voice hoarse and shaky, "I don't know what you're driving at, Max. I've told you before: I spent the evening here."

Parker continued to stare at him.

"I think you're lying," he said. "Did you go to her apartment?"

"I tell you I didn't!" Ken cried, starting to his feet.

"Good God!" Parker said, his face turning pale. "When he gave me the description it occurred to me it fitted you. I wondered if you had done it, but I couldn't believe you had. Now I know you did it!"

Ken felt so frightened he could scarcely breathe.

"They said they were looking for a tall, dark, good-looking man around thirty," Parker went on, his voice shrill. "He wore a grey suit and a grey hat. They said he owned a shabby green Lincoln." He got unsteadily to his feet. "Goddamn it! It must be you! You've got guilt written all over your face!"

The two men stared at each other, both shaking. Ken frightened; Parker horrified.

"I didn't do it!" Ken blurted out. "You've got to believe me, Max. I swear I didn't do it!"

"I don't want to hear anything about it!" Parker said violently. "I don't know what you've been up to, but whatever it is, you've got to keep me out of it. Do you understand? I know I gave you her telephone number, but for God's sake, don't tell the police that. You've already ruined my home. If it gets out I gave you her phone number, I'll lose my job as well. I'll be smeared over every newspaper in the country. You've got to keep me out of it!"

"I tell you I didn't do it!" Ken caught hold of Parker's arm. "You've got to believe me!"

Parker shook him off and backed away.

"It doesn't matter a damn if I believe you or not. That's for the police to decide. Sooner or later they'll catch up with you. They have your description. They'll find you before long, and when they do, you've got to keep quiet about me. Do you understand?"

"Oh, shut up about yourself!" Ken said, suddenly furious. "All you think about is yourself. What about me?"

"This is your mess, not mine!" Parker exclaimed.

"Is it? You are responsible. It was you who kept insinuating I should have a night out. All right, I was a damned fool to listen to your dirty suggestions, and a bigger fool to act on them. But if it hadn't been for you, I wouldn't . . ." Ken stopped, realizing what he was saying; then, seeing Parker's horrified expression, he couldn't contain himself any longer. "Yes, I admit it! I was with her last night! I was in her apartment, but I didn't kill her! She went into her bedroom and left me in the sitting-room . . ."

"Stop it!" Parker shouted, his face twitching. "You don't know what you are saying. I won't listen. You're trying to make me an accessory by telling me this. I won't listen! Keep me out of it! That's all I'm asking. This is your affair. It's nothing to do with me. All I ask you is not to tell them I gave you her telephone number!"

Ken stared at Parker's white, twitching face, and he suddenly gained courage from Parker's fear.

"Don't worry," he said. "I'll keep you out of it. But don't forget you are morally responsible. It was entirely due to you I went to her place. It is you who got me into this mess. Don't forget it. Now get out!"

Parker needed no encouragement. He hurried into the hall, opened the front door and went down the path at a shambling trot.

Moving to the window, Ken watched him go.

Well, at least he'll keep his mouth shut, he thought. He's even more frightened than I am.

But the pressure was on now. He thought with sinking heart of the shape of his future. There was Sweeting to watch out for. There was the blonde to be avoided, and now, every day, he would have to work side by side with Parker who knew he had been with Fay and who believed he had killed her. Sooner or later Ann would be back; then a new nightmare would begin for him.

He stared blindly out of the window, his fears pressing in on him. There seemed no way out, and his new-found courage deserted him.

He did something he hadn't done since he was a child. He went into his bedroom, and, kneeling down by the bed, he tried to pray.

III

Lieutenant Harry Adams walked down the dark alley that led to the entrance of the Blue Rose nightclub, his thin shoulders hunched against the rain.

He rang the bell and when the judas window slid back, he said, "I want Sam."

Joe, the doorman, stared at him, hesitated, then opened the door.

"I'll get him, Lieutenant," he said.

Adams lit a cigarette and looked around the ornate lobby. The hat-check girl started towards him, suddenly recognized who he was and stopped abruptly as if she had seen a snake in her path. She went quickly into the Ladies' room.

Adams was used to this kind of reception. It mildly amused him.

A red-head in a low-cut evening dress, wearing emerald green diamond-shaped frame glasses, came out of the Ladies' room, looked at him, began a professional smile which slipped off her heavily made-up lips as she caught Adams' frozen stare.

She moved hurriedly down the stairs to the restaurant, brushing past Sam Darcy as he came up.

"Evening, Lieutenant," Darcy said, his eyes wary. "We don't often see you here. Anything I can do, or are you here for a little relaxation?"

"I'm on duty, Sam," Adams said, looking the big negro over. He scarcely came up to the diamond in Darcy's shirtfront, but the negro's vastness didn't appear to impress him. "I want to talk to you. Let's go somewhere private."

"Okay," Darcy said reluctantly. "Come into my office."

He led the way down the passage and through a door into a big, luxuriously furnished room with a desk by the curtained windows.

Claudette, Darcy's wife, was counting a stack of money on the desk. Her great eyes opened wide when she saw Adams, and she looked anxiously at her husband.

"Run along, honey," Darcy said. "The Lieutenant and I have got business."

She gave Adams a scared look, hurriedly pushed the money into a drawer and went out, closing the door behind her.

Adams sat down.

"Drink, Lieutenant?"

"I'm on duty, Sam."

Darcy made himself a small whisky and soda and sat down behind his desk.

"Anything wrong?"

"Not unless you have a guilty conscience," Adams said, staring down at his small feet. "It's about Fay Carson."

Darcy had already guessed that was why Adams had called. He waited, not saying anything.

"Donovan been here yet?" Adams asked.

"Yes. He was here a couple of hours ago."

Adams nodded.

"If you see him again, don't tell him we've talked. I'm working on this independently. This could be a political jam, and it may need careful handling."

Darcy had already realized that as soon as he heard Fay had been murdered, but he didn't say so.

"That's okay, Lieutenant."

"I've always been pretty easy with you, Sam," Adams went on. "There have been times when I could have made things hot for you. There was that time the dame made an exhibition of herself. Most clubs would have been shut down after a scene like that. Then there was that shooting back in December. I guess you have had a little service from me. This might be a good time to show your appreciation."

"Anything I can do, Lieutenant, I'll do," Darcy said quietly.

Adams flicked ash on to the floor.

"I want to crack this one fast. I don't think Donovan will get very far." His cold blue eyes met Sam's. "He might get a break; stumble on something, but I doubt it. He needn't have any help from you."

"He hasn't got it up to now," Darcy said.

"Lindsay Burt could be the new political boss in a few months, certainly in a year," Adams went on. "This present set-up is on the skids. You, and to some extent me, have to look ahead. Burt could shut you down, Sam, once he got into office. This dive isn't as sweet-smelling as it could be. But if you were helpful, he might feel he owed you something. He might leave you alone."

"I understand, Lieutenant."

"Right." Adams stubbed out his cigarette, lit another and dropped the match into the ash bowl. "Did you see this Carson girl last night?"

"Yes."

"Who was she with?"

"A tall, dark, good-looking guy in a grey suit."

Adams nodded.

"That's the guy. Ever seen him before?"

"No."

"Did she say who he was?"

"No."

"Was he a friend or a client?"

"I don't know. They seemed to be getting along fine together. I've never known her to bring a client here before."

"So he could have been a friend?"

"I don't know, Lieutenant. She didn't introduce him to me, and I think she would have if he was a friend. I just don't know."

"Did he look like a guy who'd stab a girl with an ice-pick?"

Darcy shook his head.

"He certainly didn't. I liked the look of him."

"Maybe," Adams said, grimacing, "but it points to him. He was seen leaving her apartment about the time she died. But why should he kill her? What was she like, Sam? Would she try to blackmail a guy?"

"No." Darcy was emphatic. "She wasn't that kind of a girl at all, Lieutenant. Maybe she did go off the rails, but not to that extent. Blackmail is out."

Adams lifted his shoulders.

"Then why did he kill her? Think he was a nut?"

"He didn't look one. You can usually tell them. I was surprised to see him with Fay. He didn't look the type to be with her."

Adams brooded for a long moment.

"You've known Fay for some time, haven't you?"

"I've known her for about four years."

"Got any ideas who killed her if this guy didn't?"

Darcy shifted in his chair. He reached for his whisky, drank a little of it and sat back, nursing the glass in his enormous black hand.

"I wouldn't say this to anyone, Lieutenant, but since you've asked me, I have an idea," he said slowly. "It could be a wrong one."

"Never mind how wrong it is," Adams said. "What is it?"

"About a year ago, Fay and Johnny Dorman were always around together. He found out she was on the racket, and he beat her up. I caught him at it and stopped him. He might have killed her if I hadn't come along. He was in a pretty bad state. I had all I could do to handle him. I got his sister to come over. Fay was badly damaged. He had beaten her with a poker.

Johnny's sister got him into a home. He was there for about a year. He came out yesterday, cured. A guy I know saw him at the Paradise Club last night. He overheard Johnny asking Louie where he could find Fay. I thought maybe he was going to start trouble. I called her apartment, but couldn't get an answer." He looked hard at Adams. "It's my bet Johnny found her."

Adams sat motionless, staring down at his hands.

Johnny Dorman! He remembered him well: a fair, slim, good-looking boy who used to haunt the pool rooms on 66th Street.

"Did you tell Donovan this?"

Darcy shook his head.

"He didn't ask me for ideas."

Adams rubbed his jaw.

"Dorman: why, yes, that makes sense. Okay, I'll have him picked up. No harm in finding out where he was at the time of her death."

"You may not know it, Lieutenant," Darcy said quietly, "but Dorman's sister is going to marry Séan O'Brien."

Adams stubbed out his cigarette. His face remained expressionless.

"I didn't know." He stood up. "That could make the set-up tricky. Thanks for the information. Keep this close to your chest. I don't want anyone to know."

"No one will," Darcy said. "The guy who told me and Louie are the only two who know besides you and me, and I can take care of them."

Adams began to move slowly about the room.

"This is going to be damned tricky," he said. "If O'Brien finds out I want to talk to Johnny I could get blocked off. You don't know where Johnny is, do you?"

Darcy shook his head.

"Any ideas?"

"He might be holed up with his sister. She thought a lot of him in the old days."

Adams grimaced.

"That makes it worse. Yeah, he could be with her. Can you check for me, Sam? I'll have to keep out of sight on this. Will you see if you can find him for me?"

Darcy hesitated.

"It'll pay dividends," Adams went on, watching him. "I'm in

with Burt. I'll see you don't do it for nothing."

"Okay," Darcy said. "I'll pass the word around. I can't promise anything. But don't get the wrong idea, Lieutenant. He probably never went near Fay last night."

"Oh, sure. All I want is ten minutes with him. Find him fast, Sam. This is urgent."

Once more out in the drenching rain, Adams walked down the alley to his car. He got in and lit a cigarette. He sat staring emptily at the lighted dashboard, his brain busy.

So Dorman's sister was going to marry O'Brien. If Dorman had killed Fay, O'Brien could be in a hell of a spot.

Adams inhaled smoke deeply, and let it drift down his thin nostrils.

There were two ways of playing this hand, he thought. There was the long-term or the short-term policy. He could get in with O'Brien if he went to him, but it would be better to be patient and go to Burt. Before he could do either of them he had to prove Johnny Dorman did it.

He trod on the starter and the engine woke into life.

This could be big enough not only to unseat Motley, it's big enough to unseat O'Brien, he thought. This is the chance I've been waiting for, and brother! I've got to handle it right!

He engaged gear and drove fast to headquarters.

CHAPTER IV

_____

I

SÉAN O'BRIEN drove his big Cadillac along a lonely stretch of the river bank. The dirt road was pot-holed and dusty. No traffic came that way since the canning factory had closed down. The few remaining sheds and the broken-down jetty made a convenient place to leave a car and board the motorboat out to Tux's cruiser.

He drove his car into the rickety lean-to shed, cut the engine and got out of the car. He walked down to the jetty where the motorboat was waiting.

Willow Point, an ancient, rusty, eighty-foot cruiser, lay at anchor, half a mile from the mud flats. Ostensibly used by Tux to fish from when he happened to be in the mood for fishing, it also provided a convenient and safe hide-out for any of Tux's friends who were in trouble.

O'Brien climbed into the motorboat, nodded to the mulatto who sat in the stern and settled himself into the bucket seat.

The mulatto cast off, shoved the nose of the boat clear of the jetty, then started the engine and headed across the muddy estuary towards *Willow Point*.

Tux was leaning on the rail as the motorboat came alongside. He was thick-set, immensely powerful and swarthy. His washed-out blue eyes moved continuously and restlessly. His hard, brutal face was fleshy, and he badly needed a shave. He wore an open-necked black shirt, dirty white trousers and a yachting cap set jauntily over his right eye.

He was the only survivor of O'Brien's drug-trafficking days: a dangerous man with a knife or a gun. O'Brien found him invaluable. He paid him well, and he had never known Tux to fall down on any job, no matter how hard or dangerous.

Tux lifted a languid finger to his cap as O'Brien climbed on board.

"Where is he?" O'Brien asked.

"Below," Tux told him, and jerked his thumb to the companion ladder. Seated on an empty box, guarding the way down, was a big negro, naked to the waist, who grinned sheepishly at O'Brien, then got up and moved away from the door.

"What happened?" O'Brien asked.

"A little trouble," Tux returned indifferently. He had spent all his life dealing with trouble. "I had to tap him, but we got away without being seen. He tried to get rough as we were bringing him over, so Solly had to tap him again."

"Is he hurt?" O'Brien said sharply.

"Just a tap," Tux said, shrugging. He was an expert at tapping people. He knew just where and how hard to hit them. "Nothing to it. Want to talk to him, boss?"

"Yes."

Tux led the way below deck, along a passage to a cabin. He took a key from his pocket, unlocked the door and shoved it open. He walked in and O'Brien followed him.

Johnny Dorman lay on the bunk, one long leg hanging over the side. He opened his eyes as O'Brien came to stand at his side.

O'Brien looked at him, his face expressionless.

Johnny was uncannily like his sister, but without her strength of character. He had the same well-shaped nose and the green eyes, and his thick hair was the same shade as Gilda's.

A good-looking weakling, O'Brien thought. My luck she has to have a punk like this for a brother.

"Hello, Johnny," he said.

Johnny didn't move. He stared up at O'Brien, his green eyes watchful.

"What's the idea, Séan?" he asked. "Gilda's going to love this when I tell her."

O'Brien pulled up a straight-back chair and sat down. He waved to Tux, who went out, shutting the door behind him. Then he took out a gold cigarette-case and offered it to Johnny.

After a moment's hesitation, Johnny took a cigarette and accepted a light.

"We won't talk about Gilda just yet," O'Brien said. "We'll talk about you. How are you, Johnny?"

"Before that nigger knocked me around I was fine," Johnny said. "You don't imagine you're going to get away with this, do you?"

"I get away with most things," O'Brien returned. "I hear the doctors have given you a clean bill of health."

"So what? They would have given it to me before only they wanted to make as much out of me as they could," Johnny said with a sneer. "They're all alike. All they think about is what they can get out of me."

"I was under the impression your sister was paying the bills," O'Brien said quietly. "Nice of you to show so much interest."

Johnny laughed.

"That cat won't jump," he added. "Gilda's got all the money she wants at the moment; I haven't. If she had to go into a nut-house, I'd take care of her. Besides, she's going to marry you, isn't she? She'll have millions. It's not too much to expect her to pay my doctor's bills, is it?"

O'Brien had to make an effort to control his temper.

"You're a nasty little rat, aren't you, Johnny?" he said. "I'm damned glad you're not my brother."

"But I'm going to be your brother-in-law," Johnny jeered. "That is if Gilda will take you after what you've done to me. You must have been crazy to pull a stunt like this, but maybe I won't say anything about it. It'll cost you ten grand for me to keep my mouth shut. I don't suppose you'll find any trouble in raising ten grand, will you?"

"No trouble at all," O'Brien said mildly. "But you're not getting anything out of me. I'm surprised you haven't asked why you're here."

Into the deep green eyes came an uneasy expression.

"Well, okay: why am I here?"

"Obviously because the cure hasn't worked. You are still a mental case, Johnny."

Johnny's face went white and his eyes glittered.

"Yeah? You don't scare me. You know damn well you won't marry Gilda if you try to push me around. The doctors say I'm all right, and I am all right!"

"Then why did you kill Fay Carson?" O'Brien asked. "Not a very good recommendation for your sanity, is it?"

Johnny looked away.

"I don't know what you're talking about," he said uneasily.

"Oh, yes, you do. Last night you went to Fay Carson's apartment and stabbed her with an ice-pick."

"You're crazy! Last night I was with you, and you're stuck with it, Séan."

O'Brien shook his head.

"That won't work. I was at a party last night. Why did you kill her?"

"Who said I did?" Johnny asked.

"Why try and bluff with me?" O'Brien said curtly. "You threatened to kill her before you went into the home, the moment you come out she's murdered. Do you imagine you can get away with it?"

Johnny stared at him.

"I know I can get away with it!" he said.

"So you admit it, then?" O'Brien said.

"Okay, I admit it," Johnny returned. "I said I'd finish her and I like to keep a promise. She had enough warning. She went on with her dirty game and there wasn't any other logical thing to do with her."

O'Brien hadn't had any doubt that Johnny had killed Fay, but he hadn't expected him to be quite so brazen about it.

"And how long do you imagine it'll be before the police get on to you?"

Johnny laughed.

"Be your age! What's the use of having a political boss as a future brother-in-law if one can't knock off a dirty bitch when she needs killing? I've made it easy for you. There was a guy with her when I killed her. He can take the rap. It'll be easy for you to shift the rap on to him. You've got the Commissioner in your pocket, haven't you? He'll do what you tell him."

"You're taking a lot for granted," O'Brien said quietly. "Suppose I do nothing of the kind?"

"But you will," Johnny said easily. "You can't afford to let the cops catch me, Séan. I know just how besotted you are about Gilda. I'm not blaming you: she's a sexy piece, and any guy in his right senses would want to marry her. But if the police catch me, you won't dare marry her. I know just how much you've been avoiding the limelight ever since you took control of the Administration. You don't fool me, Séan. You have something to hide, and publicity is just the thing you don't want."

O'Brien studied him, his face expressionless. A cold, murderous rage had hold of him, but he didn't show it.

"I wonder if you did kill her," he said slowly.

Johnny laughed.

"You needn't believe me if you don't want to," he said indifferently. "It was easy. She had a rotten memory and was always locking herself out. The little fool used to keep a spare key under the mat. I went to her place, found the key and let myself in. I hid in the bedroom. She came back with this guy." His thin face hardened. "I had the ice-pick ready. She was so scared she didn't even scream. I wish you could have seen her face. She had taken off her clothes and was admiring herself in the mirror. I came up behind her. She saw me in the mirror and turned. I didn't think a human face could look so frightened. I stabbed her. There was nothing to it. She fell across the bed, looking up at me. The guy in the other room shouted out, asking her how long she was going to be. So I fused the lights and beat it. It was as easy as that, Séan."

"Did anyone see you leave the apartment?" O'Brien asked.

"Of course not. Do you imagine I'm a fool? I took care no one did see me."

"Gilda knows you're in town. Does anyone else?"

Johnny's eyes shifted.

"No."

"How did you know where Fay lived?"

Again Johnny's eyes shifted.

"I knew she often went to the Blue Rose. I took a chance and went down there. I saw her come out and I followed her."

O'Brien made an impatient gesture.

"Don't lie! You just said you were waiting for her when she came home. How could you have followed her if you were at the apartment before she arrived?"

Johnny grinned.

"You're quite a cop, aren't you, Séan? Well, if you must know, I asked Paradise Louie where she hung out."

"So he knows you were after her? You stupid fool! Do you think he'll keep his mouth shut?"

"That's up to you," Johnny returned carelessly. "You can handle Louie. You'd better see him and fix it."

O'Brien sat staring down at the floor, thinking.

"I wouldn't have touched her if I hadn't been sure of your protection," Johnny went on. He swung his legs off the bunk "I'm sick of this stinking cabin Let's go to your bank and collect ten grand, then I'll get off to New York "

O'Brien looked up

"You're kidding yourself, Johnny," he said, the edge of his rage showing in his voice He got up, went to the door, opened it and beckoned to Tux, who was waiting outside

"Come in here "

Tux moved silently into the cabin, closed the door and set his back to it

Johnny eyed him warily and moved back

"Now look here, Séan," he said, "I've taken as much as I'm going to from you Don't try any more funny stuff or you'll be sorry."

O'Brien ignored him.

"Johnny is to stay here," he said to Tux, "until I tell you to let him loose. You're responsible for him. If he tries to get away, I'll leave it to you to teach him not to try again. He's in your charge, Tux. If he doesn't behave, knock his goddamn head off!"

"Okay, boss," Tux said, and his brutal face brightened a little.

"You can't treat me that way!" Johnny exclaimed. "If you don't let me off this boat right now I'll ruin you!"

"You stupid punk!" O'Brien snarled. "You're staying here until I say so. Shut your trap or I'll have it shut for you!"

Johnny jumped across the cabin towards O'Brien, his fists swinging, but before he could come within striking distance, Tux had shuffled forward, blocked his rush and sent him reeling back.

"I'll make you pay for this!" Johnny snarled, glaring at O'Brien. "I'll see Gilda doesn't marry you, you big-head!"

O'Brien glanced at Tux, nodded, and opened the cabin door.

Tux shuffled forward, gave Johnny a light tap to turn him and then drove his fist into Johnny's face.

Johnny's head slammed against the wall and he slid down on his hands and knees.

O'Brien watched from the doorway.

"Soften him up a little," he said. "Don't do too much damage."

As he went out into the passage, Tux stepped back and kicked Johnny in the ribs, sending him over on his back.

O'Brien closed the door. He went up on deck to the motor-boat, showing his teeth in a fixed, mirthless grin.

II

Raphael Sweeting stood on the edge of the kerb, waiting for a break in the traffic before crossing to the far side. He carried his Pekinese under his arm, and the dog watched the traffic with the same impatience as its master.

The rain that had been falling had stopped, and the humid heat made Sweeting sweat. He watched the onrush of traffic as it flowed past him, and thought how pleasant it would be if he had enough money to buy a car.

At the moment Sweeting was worth exactly two dollars and sixty cents, and in spite of his inflexible optimism, he saw no possibilities of increasing his assets during the present week.

That morning, in spite of interruptions, the excitement of the police visit and the removal of Fay's body which he had watched with morbid interest from behind his window curtain, he had prepared and mailed his usual quota of fifty carefully written begging letters. He knew from experience it would take at least ten days before he had any returns, and he wasn't sure if the returns would amount to much when he did receive them.

For years now, Sweeting had relied on people's charity and gullibility for an income. It gave him tremendous satisfaction to be his own master. His beautifully written letters to anyone who happened to be in the news, especially those who had inherited money or who had had a spectacular success, explaining his distressed circumstances and asking them to send him a few dollars, thereby casting their bread upon the waters, brought him in enough to keep him in mild comfort. When the returns were bad, he resorted to blackmail or picking pockets, and in this sideline he had been unfortunate to come up against the police. He had already served, over a period of twenty years, eight years in jail, and he had no wish to go inside again.

As he stood on the edge of the kerb, he was thinking that he would have to pick a pocket if he was to pay his rent, due at the end of the week.

The events of the morning and the visit from Sergeant Donovan had badly shaken his nerve, and he tried to think of a less risky method to raise the money.

Then as he was about to step off the kerb, he saw a tall man come striding out of the side entrance of the Eastern National Bank.

Sweeting recognized him immediately. Here was the man who had brought Fay Carson home last night!

His mind in a flutter of excitement, Sweeting bolted across the road and set off after him.

Sweeting had long ago learned that it was fatal to his own interests to give information to the police. So when Donovan had asked him if he had seen anyone with Fay, he had kept his mouth shut.

If he had liked, Sweeting could have given Donovan a lot of useful information. He had seen Ken leave Fay's apartment, but some twenty minutes before Ken had left, Sweeting had heard someone bolt down the stairs from Fay's apartment.

He had rushed to his half-open door, but whoever it was who had come down the stairs had moved too fast for him, and he didn't catch a glimpse of the retreating person. He had at first assumed that it had been Ken leaving, but when he had heard Ken creep down the stairs later, and when he had gone to his door and had seen Ken, he realized that someone had been up in Fay's apartment besides Fay and Ken. When he had learned from Donovan that Fay had been murdered, he realized the person who had come down the stairs so quickly might easily have been the killer, and he was furious with himself for missing the chance of seeing who it was.

However, he wasn't going to lose by his mistake. This young fellow striding ahead of him must have also been in the apartment at the time of Fay's death. He must be worried sick that the police would assume he had killed Fay. Anyone with a guilty conscience was a potential source of income to Sweeting, and he happily stretched his short, fat legs to keep the young fellow in sight.

This was obviously his lucky day, Sweeting thought. The business would have to be handled carefully, but he had no doubt that he would be able to persuade this guy to part with a handsome sum in return for a promise of silence.

He had come from the side entrance of the Eastern National Bank, Sweeting thought, as he scurried along the sidewalk, clutching on to Leo; that must mean he worked at the bank. He wouldn't be a rich man, but he would have a good, steady income. Perhaps it would be better to ask for thirty dollars a month rather than put the bite on him for a large sum. But a guy in his position, Sweeting argued, was certain to have some savings. The best thing would be to ask for a lump sum; say a couple of hundred dollars, and then a regular payment of thirty dollars a month.

He followed Ken on to a bus, and, concealing himself behind a newspaper, he gave himself up to the excitement of the hunt.

Leo seemed to know what was taking place. He curled up on his master's ample lap and remained motionless, panting a little, his goggle eyes alert and interested.

After a twenty-minute ride, Ken got off the bus, brushing past Sweeting without noticing him.

Sweeting followed him, watched him buy a newspaper at the corner and pause to read the Stop Press while he struggled to hold two parcels under one arm.

Sweeting had already read the Stop Press announcement, and knew what it contained. He watched Ken's white, scared face with interest.

No wonder he looked scared, Sweeting thought, stroking Leo's silky head with the tip of a grubby finger. This should be easy: nothing more simple when they have had a good fright. This could be the most profitable job he had ever pulled off.

He watched Ken walk up the path to a small bungalow and pause to speak to a fat old woman who bobbed up from behind the next-door hedge. Then when he had gone into the bungalow, Sweeting crossed the road to a bench seat under the trees from where he had a good view of the bungalow and sat down.

There was no hurry, he told himself, setting Leo on the seat at his side. He removed his hat and wiped his glistening forehead. The next move was to find out who the young fellow was, and more important still, if he was married and had children.

A wife and children were very useful levers in the game Sweeting played.

He crossed one fat leg over the other, and sighed contentedly. He would watch the bungalow for an hour or so. It was a pleasant evening now, and with any luck the wife, if there was a wife, might come out into the garden.

Sweeting had infinite patience. All his life he had been content to wait for things to come to him, never attempting to make an effort himself, and he sat in the evening sunshine, his mind cloudy, his fat, dirty fingers gently stroking Leo's silky coat while he waited.

Then, after perhaps a quarter of an hour, he saw a car swing around the corner and come down the road fast.

Immediately he stiffened to attention when he recognized the driver.

The police!

He hurriedly opened his newspaper and concealed himself behind it.

His dream of a steady income exploded as he watched Sergeant Donovan climb out of the car.

Of all the filthy luck! he thought bitterly. How could they have got on to this guy so fast? What a bit of luck that he had waited instead of tackling him at once. He would have been in plenty of trouble if Donovan had found him inside the bungalow.

He watched the two detectives walk up the path and ring on the bell. He saw the door open and the young fellow come out on the step. The three men stood talking for some minutes, then to Sweeting's surprise, the two detectives turned abruptly away and walked back to their car.

What did it mean? he asked himself, peering around the edge of his newspaper. Why hadn't they arrested him?

He watched the police car disappear around the corner, and, getting to his feet, he picked up Leo and walked hurriedly to the corner of the street to make sure the police car had left the district.

He saw the car slow down and pull up outside a house, and the two detectives get out. He watched them speak to a fat, heavily built man who was in the garden.

After some minutes Donovan went on to the house while the fat man and the other detective remained in the garden.

All this intrigued Sweeting. He leaned against a tree, watching, but being careful to keep out of sight.

Some time passed, the Donovan came out and beckoned to the fat man. They all went into the house and shut the door.

Sweeting continued to wait. An hour dragged by, then the front door opened and the two detectives came out, walked down the path to their car and drove away.

Completely baffled as to why they hadn't made an arrest, Sweeting returned to the bench seat opposite Ken's bungalow and sat down again.

Who was the fat guy? he wondered, and why had the cops called on him? Why hadn't they arrested the young fellow? Even from this distance you could see how scared he had been. Had he satisfied them he hadn't been in Fay's apartment? Were they likely to return?

Sweeting decided to wait a little longer.

It was beginning to grow dusk when he saw the fat guy coming down the street.

Sweeting eyed him with interest.

My word! he thought, he looks as if he's had a shock.

He watched him pause outside the bungalow's gate, open it and walk up the path. The young fellow came to the door and let the fat guy in.

Sweeting waited.

Perhaps half an hour went by, then suddenly the front door opened and the fat guy came down the path. He walked hurriedly and unsteadily, his face was white and twitching.

Sweeting could contain himself no longer. He got to his feet, picked Leo up and crossed the road. At the gate, he looked to right and left. He was a little nervous in case the cops should suddenly appear. If it hadn't been for the urgent need to raise the rent money, he would have postponed his visit until the following day, but he couldn't afford to delay.

He lifted the latch and walked softly up the path to the front door. Setting Leo down on the step, he reached forward and pressed the bell with a dirty thumb.

III

Raphael Sweeting wasn't the only man in Flint City who had a nose for a fast buck. Paradise Louie, or to give him his correct name, Louis Manchini, also had talents in that direction.

He had read the Stop Press announcement in the *Herald*, and had instantly realized that Johnny had killed Fay.

He remembered that Johnny had come to him last night to ask for Fay's address. If Fay hadn't recently repulsed Louie's attentions, and no woman turned Louie down without regretting it, he wouldn't have told Johnny where he could find her, but it seemed to him poetic justice to give this wild-eyed nut the information he wanted.

Louie had hoped Johnny would beat Fay up as he had beaten her up before going to the home. He certainly hadn't imagined Johnny would kill her, and the news came as a shock to him.

He dropped the newspaper on his dusty desk, pushed back his chair and groped for a cigarette.

Louie was thirty-seven, thin, swarthy, with greasy black hair, a black pencil-line moustache and jowls that turned blue towards evening.

He realized that if he informed the cops that Johnny had been enquiring for Fay, even the cops dumb as they were, would jump to the conclusion that Johnny had killed her. The information he had was therefore valuable, and it was up to him to find the highest bidder.

He thought it unlikely that Johnny would stay around in town, and besides, Johnny never had any money. But his sister had.

Louie smiled.

This could be turned into something if handled right. Gilda was some dish. She was earning good money making gramophone discs and singing in the smart nightclubs. She might be persuaded not only to part with a sack of dough but she might, with a little pressure, become Louie's girl friend.

Louie lived for women. He had a lot of success, but he was sharply aware that so far his women weren't class. Now Gilda was class. The set-up could definitely be turned into something outstanding.

He got up and walked over to the fly-blown mirror and surveyed his blue chin. A shave perhaps and a clean collar, he thought. She was appearing at the Casino tonight. He would drop in and have a little talk with her. He had no doubt he could persuade her to invite him back to her apartment. He had heard she was very fond of Johnny. He was confident she wouldn't be difficult. He might even pass up the money if he could come to a satisfactory arrangement with her. This would make a refreshing change after mixing with the tough floosies who haunted the Paradise Club. After all, he could always make money, whereas

109

to have a girl friend like Gilda was a once-in-a-lifetime experience.

A couple of hours later he entered the lush hall of the Casino. He followed the Captain of waiters along the gangway to a badly placed table behind a pillar. The Casino management wasn't wasting valuable space on a heel like Louie, but that didn't worry him. He had no wish to be seen. He offended the Captain of waiters by ordering a straight whisky and a plate of ham. Then he settled down to wait for Gilda's act.

She came on some twenty minutes later, dressed in a tight-fitting, strapless evening gown of gold lamé, and he watched her hungrily.

Some dish! he thought. Brother! What I would do for that dame is nobody's business.

Her singing left him cold. He preferred his own crooners who worked at his club: girls who screeched their lungs out and who got their songs through even to the drunks at the back of the restaurant. This smooth, velvety voice with its colour and range didn't appeal to him.

When she had taken her encores and had disappeared behind a curtain, Louie pushed back his chair and went around to the dressing-rooms.

The star on a door at the end of the corridor told him where she was, and he tapped with a long, glossy fingernail.

Gilda opened the door.

She had on a pale-green wrap that enhanced her colouring, and it was as much as he could do not to make a grab at her.

She looked him over; her great green eyes cold and steady.

"Yes?"

Louie remembered she had given him that look before. Before she had become an established singer she had once sung at his club and he had tried to preposition her without success. His leering little smile stiffened.

This wren would have to be taught a lesson, he told himself. He would take a lot of pleasure knocking the starch out of her when he got her where he wanted her.

"I saw Johnny last night," he said, leaning against the door-post. "Want to talk about it?"

That cracked her veneer, he noticed. She lost the high-hat look and the anxious expression that came into her eyes gave him confidence.

"What's there to talk about?" she asked sharply.

"Plenty, baby, plenty," he said, and moving forward, rode her back into the room. He closed the door and set his back against it. "Sit down and let's be pally."

"I don't want you in here. Get out!"

"You'll get to like it," he said, wandering across the room and sitting in the only armchair. "Most wrens find me an acquired taste. I grow on them."

She studied him, then moved over to the couch and sat down. "What is it?"

"Johnny came to see me last night. He wanted to know where he could find Fay. I told him. I wouldn't have if I had known he was going to kill her. I thought maybe I'd see you first before I told the cops."

Gilda sat motionless, her face white, her eyes glittering.

"He didn't kill her!"

"The cops will think so," Louie said, and smiled. "They want to crack this one fast. They'll love Johnny for the job."

She stared at him for a long moment.

"How much?" she said, clenching her fists.

Louie looked surprised.

"You're quick, baby," he said admiringly. "Some wrens would have . . ."

"How much?"

"Well, I thought we might go back to your apartment to-night. There could be other nights. I have an idea we could have plenty of fun together."

"So you don't want money?" she said, and he was surprised to see she had suddenly relaxed.

"I have money," he said airily. "I haven't got you. If it doesn't work out the way I think it will, then we'll make it money, baby, but we'll try the other way first."

She reached for a cigarette, lit it and tossed the match into the ash-tray.

"I'd like to think about this, Louie."

"It's going to be tonight, baby, so think fast."

She stared down at her hands.

"And you won't say anything about Johnny?"

"Not a thing, baby. Play with me and I'll play with you."

"I'd like a little time. You don't expect me to . . ."

"You have until you leave the club, baby. No longer. It's up to you."

She suddenly shrugged.

"All right. It can't kill me, can it? It's a deal."

Louie beamed. Any other man would have been instantly suspicious, but Louie had an enormous opinion of his charms. He believed all women found him irresistible, and he accepted Gilda's apparent surrender as his due.

"You're being smart, baby," he said, got up and went over to her. "This could be the beginning of a long and beautiful friendship." He caught hold of her, pulled her upright and made an attempt to kiss her.

Gilda shoved him off with strength that startled him.

"You'll spoil my make-up!" she said sharply. "Keep away from me!"

"Take it easy, baby," he said, grinning at her. "None of those tricks tonight."

She gave him a long, steady stare.

"Meet me at the stage door in an hour," she said, crossed the room and opened the door. "I have to change."

"That's okay. I've grown up," Louie said. "I'll stick around and watch."

"You'll get out!" she said curtly. "You don't own me, Louie, and I don't have men in my room when I change."

"I don't own you – yet, baby," he said, "but I will."

He drifted through the doorway, turned and leered at her.

"If you're as good as you look, you're good," he said.

She shut the door in his face.

For some moments she stood motionless, breathing with difficulty, then she opened the door again and made sure he had gone.

She shut the door, turned the key and went quickly over to the telephone.

She knew Séan O'Brien was at his club. After a minute or so he came on the line.

"Séan, I'm in trouble," she said.

"Okay, kid," he said. "That's why you have me. What can I do?"

She drew in a deep breath of relief. It was so comforting to have someone as powerful as him behind her. She felt no matter what the emergency might be he would take it in his stride. His confidence in himself to cope with any situation scared her sometimes.

"Louis Manchini has just left. Johnny got Fay's address from him last night. Manchini is trying to blackmail me. I'm supposed to take him back to my apartment tonight or he'll tell the police about Johnny."

"What are you worrying about, honey?" O'Brien asked, his voice deceptively mild. "You're not in trouble; Manchini is. I'll take care of it. Just forget about him. You won't be bothered by him any more. Is he in the club?"

"He'll be at the stage door in an hour's time."

"Fine. Just relax. I'll be along as soon as you've finished your act. We'll leave by the front entrance. Just forget Manchini."

Because of his deadly calmness she was suddenly frightened.

"You won't have him hurt, Séan? He's dangerous. If he told the police . . ."

"That's okay," O'Brien said smoothly. "I know how to shut his mouth. Forget about him, kid. I'll be along," and he hung up.

At twenty-five minutes to eleven, Louie left the Casino and sauntered around to the stage door.

He was in a jubilant, excitable mood. By tomorrow morning he would have something to tell his pals, he thought, as he stood under the light immediately above the stage door.

Louie always boasted of his conquests, and for the first time in his life he felt he would really have something to boast about.

He looked at his wrist-watch. He was a minute or so early. Well, she had better not keep him waiting. A guy could be kind or rough with a dame; she better not give him any reasons to be rough.

Tux, looking short and squat in the shadowy darkness, walked down the alley, his hands in his coat pockets.

"Hi, Louie," he said. "What do you think you're doing here?"

Louie eyed him irritably. Where the hell did this punk spring from? he wondered.

"I'm waiting for a wren," he said airily. "Give me some room, Tux. You're in the way."

Tux smiled. It wasn't a nice smile, and Louie suddenly felt uneasy.

"You're not after Gilda Dorman, are you?" Tux asked.

"What the hell's that to do with you?" Louie demanded, backing away.

"Plenty, pally," Tux said, and his hand came out of his pocket. The squat-nosed automatic threatened Louie. "Come on. Didn't you know she belongs to O'Brien?"

Louie stiffened, his face went white and his mouth turned dry.

He stared at the gun as if hypnotized.

"Come on," Tux repeated. "You've been playing with dynamite."

"O'Brien?" Louie croaked. "Why didn't she tell me?"

"Why should she?" Tux said, and dug the gun into Louie's ribs. "Let's go, pally."

Louie walked to the end of the alley on unsteady legs. He knew enough about Tux not to try to run.

There was a car at the end of the alley. Whitey, a fat, jovial-looking ruffian, his chin unshaven and a lank lock of hair hanging over his ear from under his hat, sat at the wheel.

"Hi, Louie," he said, grinning through the open window. "Long time no see."

Louie got into the back seat of the car, feeling Tux's gun ramming against his kidneys. He began to shake.

"Where are we going, Tux?" he asked, in a faint, muffled voice.

"We're taking you home, pally," Tux said amiably.

"But this isn't the way," Louie wailed. "Now listen, Tux, I didn't know she was O'Brien's girl."

"We live and learn," Tux said. "What's all this about Johnny Dorman coming to see you last night?"

Louie stared at him, feeling sweat running down his face.

"That was just talk, Tux. I – I thought I'd scare the wren. There was nothing to it."

"The boss doesn't like his wrens scared," Tux said. "Okay, Whitey, this'll do."

Whitey trod on the brake and the car skidded to a stop.

Louie looked with horror at the plot of waste land stretching out before him. Beyond the plot was the river.

"Tux! Listen! I swear . . .!"

"Save it, pally," Tux said, as he got out of the car. "Come on." He threatened Louie with the gun. "Step out and snap it up."

Whitey had already got out of the car. He took a bicycle chain from his pocket and began lovingly to wrap it around his right hand.

Louie got out of the car. His legs shook so violently he nearly fell.

Tux put his gun away, took a bicycle chain from his hip pocket and, following Whitey's example, he, too, began to wrap the chain around his right hand.

"I wanted to kill you, pally," he said softly, "but the boss doesn't like killings. He asked me to soften you up a little just to make sure you don't bother the girl again, and just to make sure you don't yap to the cops. If you do, pally, I'll come after you next time with the heater, and you'll get it in the gut."

"Keep away from me!" Louie yelled, throwing up his hands to protect his head. "Keep away from me!"

The two men suddenly closed in on him.

CHAPTER V

I

KEN was in his bedroom when he heard the front-door bell ring. For a long moment he stood motionless, too scared to move. Had the police returned? Was that sergeant going to question him again? Had he given himself away? He looked at the clock on the bedside table. It was ten minutes past nine. Who could it be if it wasn't the police?

He went furtively to the window and looked out. There was no car at the gate. Then it couldn't be the police. He crossed the room, opened the door and stepped into the passage.

If he peered around the corner of the passage and across the hall he would be able to see through the glass panel of the front door who the caller was without being seen himself.

He began to edge forward when a movement just ahead of him brought him to an abrupt standstill.

Standing in the middle of the passage, looking up at him, was a fawn Pekinese dog.

The dog stared up at him, its bulging eyes frog-like and expressionless.

Ken turned cold. He stood rooted, paralysed with shock.

He heard a soft footfall in the hall, then around the corner Sweeting appeared. He looked at Ken slyly, then he bent and picked up the dog.

"I must apologize for Leo," he said. "He shouldn't have pushed in like that, but I believe he must have taken a liking to you."

Ken tried to say something, but the words wouldn't come.

"I wanted to talk to you, Mr. Holland," Sweeting went on. "You are Mr. Holland? There were some letters in the hall I glanced at: they were addressed to you, or have I made a mistake?"

Ken was in no state to attempt to bluff. His mind was paralysed with panic.

"What do you want?" he said hoarsely.

"Just a few minutes with you," Sweeting said, stroking Leo's head with his finger-tip. "Perhaps we could sit down? I have had a very tiring day. I won't keep you long. It's a business matter." He looked into the lounge. "That looks most comfortable. Shall we go in there?"

Without waiting, he walked into the lounge.

"How very nice!" he said, looking around. "How very pleasant! I envy you, Mr. Holland, having such a delightful home." His beady little eyes went to the silver-framed photograph of Ann. "Is that your wife? What a charming girl! How pretty! She isn't in, is she?"

Ken watched this fat, oily little man walking around his lounge as if he owned it. He was slowly recovering from the shock of finding him in his home. How had Sweeting found him? What was going to happen? Was he going to blackmail him?

"Oh, and I see you keep whisky in your house," Sweeting said, pausing beside the liquor cabinet. "How pleasant! You know, Mr. Holland, I have always wanted to own one of these cabinets. They are so useful, and they do establish a standard, don't they? I'm afraid I haven't been a great success in my life. Some people are a lot more fortunate than others. Would it be discourteous of me if I had a drink? With a whisky and a comfortable chair one can always discuss a business proposition more congenially, don't you think?"

He set Leo down on the couch, poured himself a big shot of whisky, carried the glass to an armchair and sat down. He took off his hat, which he placed on the floor at his side and drank some of the whisky.

"Most refreshing," he said, looking up at Ken. "Won't you sit down, Mr. Holland?"

Ken came slowly into the room and sat down.

"What do you want?" he asked.

"It's about last night. A young woman was murdered in the apartment above mine. I have some information that would be of interest to the police." Sweeting paused to smile knowingly.

"I'm not anxious to become a police informer, Mr. Holland. I realize it is my duty to tell them what I know, but they seldom show any appreciation. After all, one has to consider one's own interests first, I always think."

So it was to be blackmail. Ken reached for a cigarette and lit it with an unsteady hand.

"I had nothing to do with the murder," he said steadily.

Sweeting inclined his head.

"I am quite sure of that. If I thought you had I wouldn't be here. I am a cautious man. I wouldn't allow myself to become an accessory to murder. No, of course you had nothing to do with the murder, but you were in Miss Carson's apartment when it happened, weren't you?"

Ken didn't say anything.

"I'm sure you're too sensible to deny it, Mr. Holland," Sweeting went on after a pause. "I saw you leave. I noted the time." He shook his head sorrowfully. "You are in an awkward position. You must realize that it is almost impossible for you to convince the police that you didn't murder the girl. They are always so anxious to make an arrest."

Ken began to feel a rising anger against this fat hypocrite who was so obviously enjoying his power.

"All right, I admit all that," he said curtly. "Suppose we get to the point. What do you intend to do about it?"

Sweeting lifted his fat shoulders.

"That depends entirely on you, Mr. Holland."

"It's blackmail, is that it?"

Sweeting smiled.

"Some people might call it that," he said, shaking his head. "It's a nasty word. I would prefer to say that in return for keeping my information to myself you will give me a small pecuniary reward."

"What do you want?"

Sweeting couldn't conceal his satisfaction. The interview was going along splendidly: exactly how he had planned it to go.

"I am a poor man, Mr. Holland. In fact, to be frank with you, I am in urgent need of funds right now. I thought you might let me have two hundred dollars as a first payment and a small sum each month."

"How small?" Ken said, an edge to his voice.

"Well, perhaps thirty dollars, perhaps thirty-five."

Ken realized that if he agreed to pay Sweeting, there would be no end to it. He would be bled white. He had to take a stand. He had to think of Ann. He would probably need every dime he could lay hands on for his defence.

"I should only be buying time," he said quietly. "The police could find me without your help. You had better tell them what you know. You're getting nothing out of me."

Sweeting had had many years' experience of petty blackmailing. He was a little surprised that Ken should attempt to bluff, considering the dangerous position he was in, but he was quite prepared to accept Ken's attitude for the moment. So many of his past victims had tried to bluff, but they had always toed the line in the end.

"Let's be sensible about this, Mr. Holland. My evidence would send you to the chair. After all, I am the only witness who saw you leave the house at the time the police say she died. If I kept quiet . . ."

"You're mistaken," Ken said, getting to his feet. "Someone else saw me: the woman who lives on the ground floor. Your evidence is not so exclusive as you think."

Sweeting stared up at him, taken aback.

"Now wait a moment, Mr. Holland. We mustn't be too hasty about this. This woman doesn't know who you are: I do. It would be stupid of you to sacrifice your life for a few dollars. Besides, you must think of your wife. Think how hurt she will be to learn what you have done."

"We'll leave my wife out of this!" Ken said savagely. "I'm not paying you a dime. Get out!"

Sweeting lost his genial smile. His face became hard and spiteful.

"You mustn't talk like that to me, Mr. Holland. You are in no position to be discourteous. I shan't hesitate to go to the police if we can't come to terms. I tell you what I will do. I'll settle for two hundred dollars. I won't press you for any monthly payments. I can't be fairer than that, can I? Two hundred dollars in cash."

Ken's rising temper exploded. He stepped forward and knocked the glass of whisky out of Sweeting's hand. His grim, furious expression alarmed Sweeting, who had a horror of violence.

"Mr. Holland!" he gasped, cringing back into the chair. "That was quite unnecessary . . ."

Leo, as if sensing that his master had failed in his purpose, slunk off the couch and trotted, tail between his legs, to the door.

Ken grabbed hold of Sweeting's coat front and hauled him to his feet.

"You miserable little rat!" he said furiously. "You're not getting a dime out of me! I've had enough of this! I won't be shoved around any more by you or the police!"

"Mr. Holland!" Sweeting gasped, his eyes popping out of his head. "Don't let us have any violence. If you feel that way . . ."

Ken released him, stepped back and hit Sweeting in his right eye with all his weight behind the punch. He felt an enormous satisfaction as his knuckles thudded against Sweeting's face.

Sweeting gave a squeal of pain, tripped over the rug and fell on his back with a crash that shook the bungalow.

"Get out!" Ken shouted at him. "If I ever see you again, I'll beat the hell out of you!"

Sweeting crawled to his feet, still holding his eye. He made a frantic bolt across the room to the front door, pulled it open and clattered down the steps.

Leo was already streaking down the street, and his master went after him.

Breathing heavily, Ken stared through the window until he lost sight of Sweeting. He had no doubt that Sweeting would tell the police. In a few hours he would be arrested. The thought scared him, but he knew it was something he had now to face up to.

It didn't cross his mind to make a bolt for it. He had been cowardly enough already. He had made a complete fool of himself, and it was now time to face the music. The only possible solution was to give himself up, tell the truth and hope the police believed him. He hadn't much hope that they would, but anything was better than these past hours.

He had no time to lose. He must get to police headquarters before Sweeting gave him away.

He looked around the lounge and wondered if he would ever see it again. He looked at Ann's photograph and his heart contracted. What a shock it was going to be for her! What a crazy, irresponsible fool he had been!

He wondered if he should write to her, but there was no time. He had better get down to headquarters at once.

He went quickly into the hall, put on his hat, locked the front door after him and, seeing a taxi crawling past, he waved, ran down the path and jerked open the cab door.

"Police headquarters, and snap it up!" he said to the startled driver.

II

Detective Dave Duncan glanced at his wrist-watch and sighed. The time was just after nine o'clock. He had hoped to get home for supper, but the hope had long faded. He wondered gloomily what his wife was thinking. Whenever he was late she always accused him of fooling around with some woman. He could never convince her that police officers had to keep irregular hours. Maybe she would be more amenable when he told her he was working with Donovan on a murder case, but he doubted it.

He looked at the rough draft that lay on the desk before him. Sergeant Donovan had told him to prepare a report on the Carson murder for the Commissioner, and Duncan had just finished it. The report would take forty minutes or so to type. Then Donovan had to read it and he would be certain to make a lot of alterations. It would have to be re-typed. Duncan didn't see any hope of getting home before half-past twelve. There would be another tow waiting for him just when he wanted all the sleep he could get.

He lit a cigarette and settling down in the uncomfortable desk chair he began to read what he had written.

Half-way through the report he made a discovery that snapped him upright and sent a tingle of excitement up his spine. He hadn't time to consider this discovery before the door kicked open and Sergeant Donovan came in.

"Hey! I've got something!" Donovan said, slamming the door and coming to sit on the desk. "We've got our guy's grey suit. There are blood-stains on it! What do you know?"

Restraining his own excitement with difficulty, Duncan pushed the report aside; lit a cigarette before asking, "Where did you find it?"

Donovan grinned.

"I got a break. I was chewing the fat with the desk sergeant; by the merest fluke he mentioned that Gaza's stores had reported finding a grey suit with stains on it amongst their suits on display. O'Malley went down and took a statement from one of the assistants. While he was there another assistant from the shoe department found a pair of used shoes amongst the shoes on

120

display. One of them was stained. O'Malley made a routine check and found they were blood-stains: on the suit and on the shoes. The assistant remembers a guy who had a parcel with him when he came to buy a grey suit and he hadn't the parcel with him when he left. His description fits the guy we want for the Carson killing, and the blood-stains belong to Carson's group." He tossed a sheaf of papers on to the desk. "That's O'Malley's report with the statements. We've got to hook it up to our report. You'd better snap it up. The Commissioner expects to hear from me before he leaves tonight."

Duncan shoved the report aside.

"I've got something for you, sergeant. I'll take a five buck bet I know who the killer is."

Donovan's beefy face changed colour. He stared at Duncan, his hard little eyes narrowing.

"What the hell do you mean?"

"That guy Holland killed her!"

"Are you crazy?" Donovan exploded angrily. "Now look, if you can't talk sense, get down to that report. I want to get home some time tonight."

Duncan shrugged.

"Okay, if that's the way you feel about it. If I handle this myself, I'll get the credit."

Donovan's face turned purple.

"If you talk like that to me . . .!" he began furiously.

"I tell you he's the guy we want, and I can prove it!"

Donovan controlled himself. He got off the desk and went over to his own desk and sat behind it.

"Go ahead and prove it," he grated.

"Remember how scared Holland was when we called on him?"

Donovan snorted.

"That doesn't mean a damn. You know as well as I do when a cop calls unexpectedly whoever answers the door lays an egg. If you can't do better than that you'd better keep your trap shut!"

"This guy did more than lay an egg. I was watching him while you talked to him," Duncan said quietly. "He was really scared: like a man with a guilty conscience. That doesn't prove my case, but it did set me thinking. Doesn't he fit the description of the guy we want? He's tall, dark, good-looking and around thirty. That's the exact description of the guy we're after, isn't it? But this is the clincher. Do you remember his roses? Nothing but roses in the garden, and good ones? Remember them?"

Donovan drew in a slow, exasperated breath.

"What the hell have his roses got to do with it?"

Duncan picked up the report he had written.

"Listen to this. This is the car attendant's statement just as he made it. This is what he says: 'The guy said something about the first rain we've had in ten days. I said he was right. I asked him if he grew roses. That's about all I do grow, he tells me. Roses and weeds.' " Duncan looked across at Donovan, his eyes triumphant. "Sort of hangs together, doesn't it?"

Donovan sat still while his slow-working brain tried to cope with this unexpected situation.

"You don't call that proof, do you?" he said finally, glaring at Duncan.

Duncan refused to be intimidated. He knew if Donovan had made the discovery himself he would be crowing his head off.

"The guy is scared stiff; the description matches and he grows roses," he said quietly. "It's enough for me to dig further. I want to know what make of car he runs. If it's a green Lincoln I know I won't have to look further for the guy we want."

"If he runs a green Lincoln then he is our guy," Donovan said, shrugging, "but I'll bet he doesn't run one."

Duncan shoved back his chair and stood up.

"Shall we go and find out?"

"May as well," Donovan said grudgingly.

Twenty minutes later, Duncan pulled up some hundred yards from Ken's bungalow.

"Do we walk?" he asked. "No point in warning him we're on to him."

"Yeah."

Donovan got out of the car, and together the two detectives walked quickly down the street to the gate of Ken's bungalow. Donovan crossed the uncut lawn to the small garage.

By now it was dark. No lights showed in the bungalow.

They arrived at the garage. The double doors were locked. While he was trying to open the padlock, Duncan went around to peer through the side window, shining his flashlight on the car inside.

"Hey, sarg! It's a green Lincoln!" he called excitedly.

Donovan joined him and looked through the window.

"We've got him!" he exclaimed, and he felt a tingle of elation

122

run up his spine. "This will make that punk Adams bleed at the nose. We've cracked this one in eighteen hours!"

"I'd like to look at that car," Duncan said.

"What's stopping you?" Donovan went around to the padlocked doors again. "There's a tyre lever in our car; go and get it."

He leaned against the garage doors while he waited for Duncan to return. This would shake Adams, he thought. It would shake the Commissioner, too.

What a break! He wouldn't write a report. He would see the Commissioner personally and tell him. There was no need to mention Duncan's contribution. After all, Duncan had years ahead of him to get promotion. No need to tell the Commissioner who cracked the case. If he said nothing the Commissioner would assume he had thought up the angles.

Duncan returned with the tyre lever. They broke the padlock and opened the door. Donovan snapped down a light switch and lit up the garage.

While Duncan examined the back seat of the Lincoln, Donovan looked over the driving seat.

"Here we are," Duncan said suddenly. "This clinches it."

He handed Donovan a much-thumbed notebook. It was the car attendant's missing registration book.

"On the floor behind the driving seat. Must have slipped out of his hip pocket."

Donovan grinned.

"And it's got his car number in it, too! Yeah, this clinches it!"

"Let's go talk to him, sergeant."

Together the two detectives walked up the path. Donovan stuck his thumb against the bell-push and kept it there. They waited several minutes while the bell rang continuously, then Donovan stepped back with an exclamation of disgust.

"Looks like he's out," he said.

Duncan was already walking around the bungalow, peering through the windows. He came back after completing the circuit.

"No sign of him."

Donovan looked at his watch. It was now getting on for ten o'clock.

"We'd better stick around."

"Think he's lost his nerve and skipped?"

"He might have done. I'll send out a general call for him. Let's see if we can bust in."

It didn't take Duncan long to find a window that wasn't latched. He climbed through the window, went to the front door and let Donovan in.

"I'll take a look around while you're calling headquarters."

When Donovan had talked to the desk sergeant and had given his orders, he went into the hall to see what Duncan was doing.

Duncan came out of the bedroom, grinning. He carried a grey suit and a pair of shoes.

"Here you are, sarg. Just out of their wrapping, straight from Gaza's stores. This guy certainly knows how to work his way into the chair, doesn't he?"

Donovan grunted. He was getting a little fed-up with Duncan's persistent successes.

They went into the lounge and Duncan went over to the trash basket. He turned it upside down while Donovan watched him, scowling.

"It falls into my lap, doesn't it?" Duncan said suddenly. "Look at this."

He put two small pieces of card on the desk.

"We're home now," he said. "I knew I was right. Here's Carson's telephone number on the back of that guy Parker's card. I bet Parker recommended Holland to go and call on Carson. Sweet as honey, isn't it?"

III

Lieutenant Adams eased back his chair, yawned and decided to call it a day. There was nothing he could do now until he got a copy of Donovan's report and had found out how far he had progressed. He had also to wait for Darcy to get a line on Johnny Dorman. He couldn't expect much to happen until the following morning.

He was about to leave the office when the telephone bell rang. Frowning, he returned to his desk and picked up the receiver.

"Desk sergeant here, sir," a voice barked in his ear. "There's a guy just come in who wants to talk to the officer in charge of the Carson killing. Sergeant Donovan's out. Do you want to see him?"

"Yes: send him up," Adams said, hung his hat on the rack and sat down behind his desk.

After a three- or four-minute wait, a knock came on the door and a cop came in, followed by a tall, dark man whose pale face and haggard looks caught Adams' interest.

"What can I do for you?" he asked.

"I'm Kenway Holland," Ken said breathlessly. He waited until the cop had gone, then went on, "I'm the man you're looking for. I was with Fay Carson last night."

Adams stiffened, stared, then pushing back his chair he stood up. For a moment he was so surprised that he couldn't think how to handle this unexpected situation, but he quickly recovered.

He looked steadily at Ken. Yes, the description matched. This guy looked too scared and ill to be a faker.

"Did you tell the desk sergeant who you are?" he asked sharply.

"Why, no," Ken said, surprised. "He didn't ask me."

Adams was now in control of himself. What a break! he thought. If that fool Donovan had been in I wouldn't have known about this until it was too late. What the hell am I going to do with this guy? If Donovan gets hold of him before I get hold of Dorman, they'll pull me off the case, and this guy won't know what's hit him until he's sitting in the chair.

It didn't take him more than a second or two to make up his mind.

"Why didn't you come here before?" he asked sharply.

"I – I hoped to get away with it," Ken said, "but I've found it's not possible. I want you to know I didn't kill her. I want to tell you exactly what happened."

"Okay," Adams said, "but this isn't the place where we can talk. The telephone rings, people come in and out." He reached for his hat and put it on. "You come with me." He had a sudden alarming thought. "Did you bring your car with you?"

Bewildered, Ken stared at him.

"I came in a taxi."

Adams nodded. Another break! If he had parked his green Lincoln outside headquarters some smart Alec would have been sure to have had something to say about it.

"Come with me," Adams said, and set off down the passage.

Ken followed him to the street where Adams' car was parked.

"Get in," Adams said.

"But I don't understand," Ken said blankly.

"Why should you? Get in!"

Ken got into the car and Adams drove off, heading for his own apartment. He didn't say anything until he pulled up outside a house in Cranbourne Avenue.

"I live here," he said as he got out of the car. "You can talk your head off in my apartment without interruption."

Ken followed him into a ground-floor, comfortably furnished sitting-room.

"Make yourself at home," Adams said, tossing his hat on to a chair. "Have a drink?"

"I don't understand what all this is about," Ken said, facing him. "Why have you brought me here? I want to make a statement to the officer in charge of the murder. Who are you?"

Adams smiled as he fixed two highballs.

"I'm Lieutenant Adams of the Homicide Department. Take it easy. You don't know it yet, but the last thing you want to do is to make a statement to the officer in charge of the Carson killing. He's got a one-track mind. Now sit down and stop wasting time. I want your story. I want to know who you are, how you met Fay Carson and what happened last night. Don't rush it. I want as many details as you can remember. Now start talking."

Ken made his statement. He told Adams what had happened the previous evening, omitting no details, and as he came to the end of his story there was something about the little Lieutenant's expression that gave him hope.

"I know I have behaved badly," he concluded, "and I'm paying for it, but I didn't kill her. I should have come to you before this, but I funked it. I wasn't so much thinking of myself, I had to think of my wife. I wanted to keep it from her, but I don't see how I can now."

Adams stared at him for a long minute, then he pulled thoughtfully at his nose.

"If I were married, which fortunately I'm not," he said, "and if I had been mug enough to have gone to a callgirl, I would have acted as you did in the same circumstances."

"Does that mean you believe me?" Ken asked eagerly.

Adams shrugged.

"It doesn't matter a damn if I believe you or not. The final word is with the jury. Now, let's check on a few details. You had no idea there was someone else in the apartment beside you until the lights went out?"

"No idea at all."

"You didn't see this guy?"

"No. It was pitch dark. I heard him cross the room and bolt downstairs, but I hadn't a chance of seeing him."

"You didn't hear her cry out?"

"There was a thunderstorm on. I don't think I should have heard her if she had cried out."

"Hmm . . ." Adams crossed one leg over the other, then asked, "This fat guy with the Pekinese: is he bald with a hooked nose and pointed ears?"

Ken looked startled.

"Why, yes. That exactly describes him. Do you know him?"

"I know him," Adams said. "You don't have to worry about him. He won't give you any trouble. He's only been out of jail six months. You can forget about him."

"You mean he was bluffing?"

"Sure," Adams said, and took a cautious sip from his glass. "He saw you last night going up and coming down. He might have seen this other guy. Did you ask him?"

Ken shook his head.

"I didn't think of it."

"I'll ask him," Adams said grimly. "You've told me everything? There's nothing else you can remember?"

"I don't think so," Ken said, thought for a moment, then he remembered the tall, fair man who had ducked out of sight when he and Fay had come out of the Blue Rose. "There was a guy outside the Blue Rose I noticed. He seemed anxious not to be seen. He was tall and fair and good-looking. When he saw I had spotted him, he ducked back out of sight."

Adams frowned.

"Tall, fair and good-looking?" he asked, and he was thinking of Johnny Dorman. "Would you know him again?"

"I think so. The light wasn't too good, but I think I would."

"Nothing else?"

Ken shook his head.

There was a long silence, then Ken asked, "Do you believe my story, Lieutenant?"

"Sure, it hangs together and makes sense, but don't kid yourself that puts you in the clear. You're in a hell of a jam; a far worse jam than you imagine."

As Ken began to ask him what he meant, the telephone bell rang.

"Let me get this," Adams said, and picked up the receiver.

"Yeah? What is it?" he said into the mouthpiece. He lay back in the easy chair, listening to the excited voice that came over the line. "Okay, sergeant. I'll be right over. Yeah, if Donovan isn't there, someone's got to be. Okay, I'm coming," and he hung up. He looked at Ken and grimaced. "There's a general call out for you. They've found your suit and shoes at Gaza's store. My two bright assistants have also found your car and the card Parker gave you with Carson's telephone number on it. Right now every cop in town is looking for you."

Ken sat rigid.

"But they can't prove I killed her!" he exclaimed. "You believe me! You've just said so. You can call them off . . ."

Adams lit his cigarette, stretched out his short legs and shook his head.

"Know anything about politics, Mr. Holland?" he asked.

"What has politics to do with this?"

"Everything. You'd better get a picture of the set-up." He sank further into the chair. "The boss behind the present Administration is a guy named Séan O'Brien. He intends to marry Gilda Dorman, a nightclub crooner. O'Brien has money, power and ability. If he wants anything, he has it, and nothing stands in his way. He wants this woman. Her brother is Johnny Dorman who was Fay Carson's lover before he was put in a nut-house. He came out yesterday. He was the guy who killed Fay Carson. I can't prove it yet, but I'll bet my last buck he was the guy. O'Brien isn't likely to let him go to the chair for murder. He'll cover him up, and he can do it. He'll look around for a fall guy, and the fall guy is you."

Ken stared at him.

"You must be joking," he said blankly.

"It's no joke. You'll find that out fast enough. What O'Brien says goes in this town. Sergeant Donovan will turn in a report. The Commissioner will hand it over to O'Brien. They have a certain amount of evidence against you. Any other evidence in your favour will be suppressed. They have enough on you to put you into the chair right now."

Ken grappled with the feeling of rising panic.

"Then why are you telling me this? Why don't you go ahead and arrest me?" he said angrily. "You're a member of the police. Why bring me here?"

Adams crossed and uncrossed his legs.

"I happen to be in the opposition camp. I guess I must be

128

crazy to stick my neck out, but that's the way it is. If I could pull the rug from under O'Brien I would do it. I have an idea I might do it through you. If I can prove Dorman killed this Carson girl, I might force O'Brien to show his hand. Dorman's sister would put pressure on O'Brien, and he might make a false move. I want my men to be hunting you so I can hunt Dorman. That's why I've brought you here. It's essential they don't catch you before I catch him. I want to get Lindsay Burt interested in you. He'll take care of you if I can convince him you are being framed. But you've got to have patience. This could take a few days, even a few weeks. You're safe here, but don't go showing yourself on the streets. My men are efficient. They're looking for you, and they'll find you if you show yourself."

"But my wife will be coming home soon," Ken said anxiously. "I've my job to think of. You can't expect me . . ."

Adams raised his hand.

"Wait a minute. I've told you already: you're in a jam. Your wife and your job aren't important. It's your life you have to think of. If they catch you, you're through, and don't forget it!"

"But this is fantastic! Suppose you don't find Dorman? What happens to me?"

"We'll think about that when the time comes."

"What about my wife?"

"You should have thought about her before you played around with Fay Carson." Adams finished his drink and set down his glass. "Now, take it easy. You stay here. I'm going back to headquarters. I want to find out what they are doing."

"I forgot to tell you I saw Gilda Dorman at the Blue Rose that night," Ken said. "Did you know she and Fay Carson once shared an apartment together?"

Adams put on his hat.

"I didn't know, but I can't see it has anything to do with our problem. You take it easy. Leave this to me."

"I'd better see a lawyer," Ken said uneasily.

"Plenty of time to see a lawyer. Relax, can't you? You're safe here. Go to bed. The spare room is through that door. I've got to go," Adams said, and nodding, he left the apartment.

Ken got to his feet, went over to the window and watched the Lieutenant drive away. His mind was in a whirl. This was an incredible position to be in. He had a disturbing idea that Adams was only using him as a political pawn. If the gamble came off, all would be well, but if it didn't, then Adams might wash his hands of him.

He thought of Ann returning to the empty bungalow. He couldn't remain in this apartment indefinitely. The best thing he could do was to consult a first-class attorney and put himself into his hands.

He was still trying to make up his mind which attorney to go to when the telephone bell rang. He hesitated for a moment, then, thinking it might be Adams to tell him what was happening at headquarters, he lifted the receiver.

"That you, Lieutenant?" A deep, rich voice, which Ken instantly recognized as Sam Darcy's, whispered in his ear.

"The Lieutenant's out. I think he's at headquarters."

There was a pause, then Darcy said, "Can you take a message?"

"I guess so."

"Okay, tell him a guy who looked like Johnny Dorman was seen on Tux's cruiser, *Willow Point*. My man only caught a glimpse of him and he won't swear it was Johnny."

Ken felt a tingle of excitement run up his spine.

"I'll tell him."

"The cruiser's anchored in the estuary. He'll know."

"Okay," Ken said, and hung up.

For a long moment he stood thinking, then he put a call through to police headquarters.

"Give me Lieutenant Adams," he said to the desk sergeant.

"He's not here. Who's calling?"

"He's on his way down. Hasn't he arrived yet?"

"He's been in and he's gone out again. What is it?"

Ken replaced the receiver.

Suppose Dorman left the cruiser before he could tell Adams where he was? he thought. If he were to get out of this jam, he had to help himself. He would go to the waterfront and watch the cruiser until Adams came.

· He went to Adams' desk, wrote down Darcy's message, added that he was going to try to find the *Willow Point* and urged Adams to come as quickly as he could. He left the message on the table, grabbed his hat and left the apartment. He cautiously opened the front door.

Rain was falling, and the wet darkness gave him a feeling of security. He went down the steps and, turning left, he walked as quickly as he could towards the river.

CHAPTER VI

I

Séan O'Brien tapped on Gilda's dressing-room door, waited a moment, then turned the handle and entered.

Gilda was changing. She reached hurriedly for her wrap, then changed her mind when she saw O'Brien, and went to him quickly.

"Sorry," he said, smiling at her. "I should have waited a little longer."

"Is it all right, Séan?" she asked, her great green eyes dark with anxiety.

"Of course." He took her in his arms and kissed her. "You should lock the door, kid. Anyone could have walked in."

"I thought I had. What happened, Séan?" She moved back to the dressing-table while he watched her, thinking how beautiful she was.

"Manchini won't worry you again. I've had a scare thrown into him, and he scares fast."

She slipped into a simple white evening dress that made her look, to O'Brien's eyes, much more seductive than when she was wearing her nightclub finery.

"I don't know what I should do without you," she said, going to the dressing-table and sitting down.

He laughed.

"That's what I'm here for." He took a cigar from his case, sat sat down and slowly removed the band. "So Manchini saw Johnny last night?"

"That's what he said, but I don't believe him. He was trying to scare me into taking him back to my apartment."

"Then you don't think he gave Johnny Fay's address?"

She hesitated, then turned to face him.

"I know he didn't. Darling, forgive me, I didn't tell you the truth about Johnny. I did see him last night. He was at my apartment when I returned from the Casino. He's scared of you, Séan. He thinks you made me put him in the home. He made me promise not to tell you I had seen him. I've told him over and over again you had nothing to do with putting him in the home, but he doesn't believe me. He stayed the night with me. That's why I know he couldn't have killed Fay."

O'Brien nodded, and wondered why she continued to lie to him.

"You should have told me that before, kid. Never mind. Is he still at your place?"

"No. He's gone. I'm worried, Séan. He left no note. He's just vanished. You don't think the police have arrested him?"

O'Brien shook his head.

"Of course not. I should have heard. Relax, kid. He's probably decided to get out of town. Didn't you say he was going to New York?"

"He did say he might go, but he hadn't any money. That's what worries me. He can't have gone to New York . . ."

"How do you know he hasn't borrowed money from someone? He always was an opportunist. Don't worry about him. He can take care of himself. Come and have supper with me."

"Not tonight, Séan. I want to go home. He may have returned."

O'Brien lifted his shoulders good-humouredly.

"Okay. Do you want me to come back with you?"

"I'd rather go back alone."

"Anything you say, kid."

He got out of the chair and handed her her wrap.

"I'll see if I can find out anything. If I get news of him I'll call you."

"You're terribly good to me, Séan."

She raised her face and he kissed her.

"It's my job to be good to you."

When she had driven away in a taxi, O'Brien walked slowly over to the parking lot, got into his Cadillac and stared emptily into the darkness.

Johnny was a nuisance, he decided. He always would be a nuisance. Even if he were lucky enough to get out of this mess, there would be other messes. Sooner or later he would get into the kind of trouble O'Brien couldn't handle. It was a bleak outlook to be saddled with a brother-in-law like Johnny. Now he had Johnny where he wanted him, he would be a mug not to settle him once and for all.

He brooded for several minutes, playing with the idea of being rid of Johnny for good. The more he thought about it, the more of a temptation the idea became.

In the past, O'Brien had never hesitated to get rid of trouble-makers, but he had got out of the habit of wiping out his enemies. He should have let Tux knock off Paradise Louie instead of beating him up. The quiet, secluded life he had been living for the past three years had made him soft, he thought, grimacing. With a set-up like this before him he couldn't afford to be soft. He knew Lindsay Burt would try and make capital out of Fay's murder. Someone in his camp would be certain to remember Johnny had threatened Fay, and knowing Johnny was Gilda's brother and Gilda was going to marry O'Brien, pressure would be brought to bear on the Commissioner to find Johnny.

Besides, O'Brien had no illusions about Johnny. As soon as he became his brother-in-law, he would be after money. The safest way would be to make sure Johnny didn't become a bigger nuisance that he was now.

O'Brien lit his cigar, started the car engine and drove over to the Country Club.

On the first of every month there was a dance at the club, and everyone who was anyone went. O'Brien guessed Commissioner Howard and Police Captain Motley would be there. He wanted the latest news of the murder before finally deciding what he was to do with Johnny.

He could see the crowd of dancers through the big windows as he drove around the circular drive. The dance would go on until the small hours: there would be a lot of drinking and necking, and probably some horseplay by the young members.

O'Brien wasn't interested in this kind of shindig, but he usually put in an appearance. All the party members went, and it was an opportunity to have a private word without the press wondering what was being said.

He drove into the parking lot, that was packed solid with cars. He got out and glanced up at the dark, swollen clouds. It would rain before long, he thought, as he made his way along the narrow gangway between the cars.

He became aware of a man and woman ahead of him. The woman held a car door open. He thought he recognized her in the half light, and paused to look more intently.

"If you're going to behave like a goddamn dummy, I'm going back," the woman said in a shrill, angry voice. She sounded drunk to O'Brien.

"We've got to be sensible, Gloria," the man said anxiously.

"Your husband may be coming out. Can't we wait until he's gone?"

"I'm damned if I'm going to wait," the woman said, and got into the back seat of the car. "Are you coming?"

The man got in beside her and shut the car door. O'Brien saw the woman throw her arms around him and pull him to her, and he made a little grimace. Commissioner Howard's young wife and some punk, he thought. Well, the old fool shouldn't have married a girl half his age.

He went on towards the club house.

He found Commissioner Howard and Motley on the verandah.

Motley was saying impatiently, "For the love of Mike, let the girl alone. She's enjoying herself somewhere. If we're going, let's go."

"Leaving already?" O'Brien said, coming out of the darkness.

"Hello, there," Motley said, turning. "I have news for you. Donovan's cracked the Carson case!"

O'Brien lifted his eyebrows.

"That's quick work."

"Yeah. I've always said if Donovan was given a case worth a damn, he would show what he was made of. In the next hour or so he will make an arrest."

"Who did it, then?"

"Kenway Holland, a young bank clerk. It's an open and shut case. We have enough evidence to put him in the chair three times over."

"But you haven't arrested him yet?"

"My men are at his house now. He may have lost his nerve and skipped, but it's just a matter of time before we get him."

"That's damned good work," O'Brien said without any enthusiasm. He looked over at Howard. "You'll let me have the report and see the evidence?"

"You'll get the papers tomorrow morning," Howard said curtly. He looked worried, and having seen what his wife was up to, O'Brien wasn't surprised. "You'll excuse us. I want to get back to headquarters. Now we have got so far I don't want any slip-up."

"I keep telling you we can leave it to Donovan to handle," Motley said impatiently.

"I'm going back, even if you aren't," Howard snapped, and nodding to O'Brien he went down the steps and towards the parking lot.

"Your sister is amusing herself with a guy in a car," O'Brien said softly. "Watch the Commissioner doesn't spot her."

Motley swore under his breath.

"I'll break that little bitch's neck one of these days," he said. "Why the hell can't she wait until Howard has left?" He went off hurriedly after the Commissioner.

O'Brien stroked his jaw thoughtfully. Just like that numbskull Donovan to find the wrong man, he thought. What was the evidence they were talking about? They seemed pretty certain that they had enough on this guy to convict him.

He leaned against the verandah rail while he thought about Johnny. If this Holland guy was caught and convicted, it would let Johnny out, but sooner or later he would get into more trouble. Now he had him under lock and key it would be flying in the face of providence not to be rid of him.

He watched Howard and Motley drive out of the parking lot, then, his mind now made up, he went down the steps towards his car.

II

Before going to his office, Adams looked into the charge room.

"Anything new?" he asked the desk sergeant, who stiffened to attention at the sight of him.

"The Commissioner and the Captain are on their way over, sir," the sergeant said. "This guy Holland hasn't been picked up yet. We have a couple of men and Detective Duncan waiting for him at his house. Sergeant Donovan has just come in and is waiting for the Commissioner."

Adams grunted.

"I'll be in my office if the Commissioner wants me," he said. "Nothing else?"

"Nothing that'd interest you, sir. Paradise Louie is in trouble. He was picked up ten minutes ago on a vacant lot on West Street. Someone has given him the treatment. O'Sullivan, who found him, reports he isn't likely to live. He's had a beating, and whoever beat him hit him a little too hard."

Adams remembered what Darcy had told him. Paradise Louie had told Johnny where he cold find Fay Carson and now he had been beaten up. A coincidence?

"Where is he?" he asked sharply.

"Ward Six, County hospital," the sergeant told him.

"Tell the Commissioner if he wants me I'll be back in an hour," Adams said, and went quickly back to his car.

He got over to the County hospital in five minutes.

"Manchini?" the house surgeon said when Adams asked him if he could talk to Louie. "Not much hope for him. He has an abnormally thin skull. Someone hit him with a bicycle chain. I doubt if he'll last the night."

"Is he conscious?"

"No, but he might come round at any moment. One of your men is with him. You can go up if you want to. There's nothing more we can do for him."

Paradise Louie lay in bed, his bruised and broken face swathed in bandages. Detective Watson sat glumly at his side. He got up hurriedly when he saw Adams, nearly upsetting his chair.

"Is he conscious?" Adams asked.

"Yes, sir, but he's pretty bad."

Adams bent over the still body.

"Louie! Wake up!" he barked, and shook Louie's arm.

Louie opened his eyes and stared up at Adams.

"Leave me alone, can't you?" he snarled faintly. "Get the hell out of here!"

Adams sat on the edge of the bed.

"Who did it to you?" he said.

Watson automatically opened his notebook and waited expectantly.

"I'm not talking, copper," Louie said. "Leave me alone."

Adams took out a box of matches, struck one and held the flame to Louie's hand while Watson watched, goggle-eyed.

Louie snatched his hand away, his lips coming off his teeth.

"Next time I'll hold your wrist," Adams said quietly. "Who did it?"

The thin, ruthless face that hung over him scared Louie.

"Tux and Whitey," he mumbled. "Leave me alone, can't you?"

"Why did they do it?"

"I don't remember," Louie said, but went on hurriedly as Adams struck another match. "Okay, okay, I'll tell you."

He gave Adams a watered-down account of his attempt to blackmail Gilda. It took some minutes, but Watson got it down after Adams had made Louie go over it again.

"Did you give Johnny Fay Carson's address?" Adams demanded.

"I told him where he could find her."

"Where was that?"

"I told him she went to the Blue Rose most nights."

"You didn't give him her address?"

"I don't know it."

"What time did you tell him?"

"About eleven, I think it was."

"So Tux works for O'Brien?" Adams said, aware he had made an important discovery.

"Yeah. O'Brien has always been his boss."

Adams looked at Watson.

"Got it all?"

"Yes, sir."

"Louie, you're going to sign this."

He read Louie's statement over to him, held the book while Louie scrawled his signature on each page, then he got Watson also to sign each page.

"I'll take it," he said to Watson, and slipped the notebook into his pocket. "Come on, you don't have to waste any more time with this punk."

Outside in the passage, he went on, "Keep your mouth shut about this statement, Watson. There's a political angle to it that could be tricky. Understand?"

"Yes, sir," Watson said blankly. He didn't understand, but he had long ago learned it wasn't safe to ask Adams questions.

"Okay. Come with me. I have a job for you."

Bewildered, Watson followed Adams down the steps and across the sidewalk to his car.

III

It took Ken forty minutes to reach the waterfront. He was afraid to get on a bus or take a taxi. Adams had said every cop in town was looking for him by now, and he wasn't taking any chances of being recognized.

He kept to the back streets, walking close to the buildings and shops where the shadows were darkest.

From time to time he spotted ahead of him a patrolling cop, and he hastily turned down a side street to avoid passing him.

When eventually he arrived at the waterfront, the rain that had been falling began to ease off.

It was dim, damp and smelly by the water. On the street side was a row of cafés, popcorn stalls, shops selling fishing tackle and nets, a dingy hotel and an amusement arcade.

Ken stood on the edge of the wharf and looked across the broad stretch of oily water to the distant estuary. It was too dark to see if any boats were anchored out there, but Darcy had said that was where *Willor Point* was, and Ken had no reason not to believe him.

He would have to find a boat to take him out there. He had little money on him and he might need every nickel before he was through. He wouldn't be able to afford to rent a boat, he would have to borrow one.

But before he tried to find a boat, he had to know exactly where *Willow Point* was anchored.

He looked over at the lighted amusement arcade, hesitated, than walked slowly across the wet street and glanced in.

There were only a few youths playing the pin-table machines. A girl in a grubby white overall leaned against one of the machines while she cleaned her long painted finger-nails with a chip of wood. She was white-faced and tired; a kid of about eighteen, old in sin and experience if he could judge from her hard expression. She had a leather satchel for giving change hung over her shoulder.

He walked into the arcade and, going to a pin-table machine near where the girl was standing, he began to play, shooting the balls up the channel, watching the coloured lights spring up as each ball tapped the pins.

After he had shot off a complete row of balls, he paused to light a cigarette, and he was aware the girl was looking curiously at him.

He met her blue, dark-ringed eyes and he smiled.

"Some way to waste an hour, isn't it?" he said.

She lifted her shoulders indifferently.

"No one's asking you to do it."

He left the machine and came over to her.

"Would you know anything about the boats anchored in the estuary?" he asked. "I'm looking for *Willow Point*."

Surprise and suspicion jumped into her eyes.

"I'm not stopping you," she said, slid her hand through the opening in her overall and scratched herself under her arm.

"Would you know where it's anchored?"

"I might. Why?"

"I want to find it," he said patiently.

"Are you sure you do, handsome?" she asked, leaning her hips against the pin-table machine. "Do you know who owns *Willow Point*?"

He shook his head.

"Tux," she said, "and he's a guy you want to keep away from."

"I've got to find the boat," Ken said.

She studied him.

"Look, handsome, hadn't you better go home? You're likely to get into trouble if you start messing around with Tux."

"I'm in trouble already," Ken said.

"Well, I don't have to be," she said, and abruptly moved away to give change to a fat man who was tapping impatiently on the glass top of a pin-table machine.

Ken lit a cigarette and went back to his machine. He began to play again, watching the girl out of the corner of his eye.

She moved around the arcade aimlessly, and after about five minutes she came slowly back to where he was standing.

She leaned against the machine he was playing and began to clean her nails again with the chip of wood.

"Won't you help me?" Ken said, keeping his voice low. "Won't you tell me where *Willow Point* is?"

She gave a little shrug.

"Last time I saw it, it was anchored off North End."

"That doesn't tell me anything. I don't know the river. How far out?"

"Half a mile. North End is the light you can see from the wharf."

He looked up and smiled.

"Thanks."

She shook her head at him.

"You're heading for trouble, handsome. Tux is a mean guy."

He shot another ball up the channel before saying, "I want a boat, but I can't pay for it. I've got to to to *Willow Point*."

"What do you expect me to do?" she asked, not looking at him. "Steal one for you?"

"I'd do that myself if I knew where to find one."

"Does Tux know you're coming?"

Ken shook his head.

"How hot are you?" she asked. "Is it the cops?"

"Something like that."

"You'll find a boat under the jetty. The guy who owns it

leaves around dawn, so you'd better get back before then."

"Thanks," Ken said.

"Watch your step, handsome. Tux doesn't like unexpected visitors. He's tough."

"I'll watch out," Ken said, and walked out into the drizzling rain.

He found a dinghy berthed under the jetty. A rod, can of bait, an oilskin and oars lay in the bottom of the boat. He swung himself down into the boat, cast off and began to row towards the distant light that she had told him was North End.

It seemed to him he rowed for a long time before he saw some way ahead of him the shadowy outlines of a cruiser, silhouetted against the dark skyline.

Ken rested on the oars and watched it, wondering if it were the *Willow Point*. As he sat in the gently bobbing boat he heard the sound of a distant motorboat engine. He looked quickly across the waterfront, half a mile from him.

He saw a powerful motorboat leaving the jetty. It headed towards him. He wondered in alarm if it were a police boat. He began to row away from the course set by the motorboat, then shipping his oars, he crouched down in the boat so his head and shoulders weren't outlined against the skyline.

He watched the approaching motorboat anxiously.

It was coming fast, but he saw with relief it would pass him by some three or four hundred yards unless it altered course.

The boat roared past him, and its wash sent his boat bouncing violently. He heard the engine suddenly cut out. The motorboat vanished into the darkness of the cruiser's side.

Ken straightened up, grabbed the oars again and began to row. It took him over ten minutes to come within forty yards of the cruiser. He rested on his oars and let the boat drift while he examined the deck of the cruiser for any sign of life.

He spotted the motorboat tied up to the cruiser. He could see no one on deck, and he began to row again until he came up alongside the cruiser. He stared up at the deck rail while he listened.

He imagined he heard the faint sound of voices, and he wondered if he should take the risk of climbing on board. If anyone came up on deck his boat would be seen. He decided against the risk.

Rowing slowly and quietly, he passed under the stern of the cruiser and came up on the port side.

One of the port-holes showed a light, and as he let his boat drift silently up to the cruiser, he heard a voice coming from the port-hole say, "It's time we had a straight talk, Johnny. You are in no position to dictate terms. You either accept my conditions or you'll stay here until you change your mind."

Ken quietly paddled his boat up alongside the cruiser and shipped his oars, taking care to stop the boat from bumping against the cruiser's side. He caught hold of an iron bracket near the port-hole, steadied the boat while he stood up and took a quick look into the cabin.

The tall, fair, good-looking man he had seen outside the Blue Rose nightclub the previous evening was lounging on a bunk facing him. A tall, dark man in an expensively cut suit leaned against the wall, smoking a cigar.

Ken drew back quickly; then, keeping his boat steady, he listened to what was being said.

IV

Solly caught the rope O'Brien tossed to him, held the motor-boat steady while O'Brien scrambled aboard.

"Tux here?" O'Brien asked abruptly.

"Yes, boss," Solly said, startled that O'Brien had brought the motorboat over himself.

"Where is he?"

Tux came out of the shadows, buttoning up his shirt. He had been asleep, but had wakened when he heard the motorboat and had scrambled, cursing, into his clothes.

"I want you," O'Brien said curtly.

Tux led the way down the companion ladder, along the dimly lit passage to his cabin. He sat on his bunk, stifled a yawn and looked enquiringly at O'Brien.

"Did you fix Louie?" O'Brien asked.

"Sure," Tux said, looking a little uneasy. "Whitey hit him a shade too hard."

O'Brien stared at him, his eyes intent.

"What does that mean?"

"I don't reckon Louie is feeling too good right now," Tux said guardedly. "He's got a dome like an egg-shell."

"Does that mean he's dead?"

Tux lifted his shoulders.

"He could be. He spilt a lot of brain."

O'Brien rubbed his jaw.

"This set-up is getting out of hand," he said, took out a cigar and bit off the end. "It might be a good thing if Louie did croak."

Tux looked relieved.

"It'll surprise me if he doesn't."

"We don't want any death-bed confessions."

"He was too far gone to talk when we left him."

O'Brien lit his cigar, blew smoke to the ceiling while he eyed Tux thoughtfully. This was the beginning, he thought. Rough stuff again after four years. Well, it couldn't be helped. He had to keep control of the situation, and if guys were a nuisance they must expect trouble.

"I've decided to get rid of Johnny," he said, lowering his voice.

Tux was surprised, but he didn't show it.

"Anything you say, boss."

"I want him planted where he won't be found," O'Brien went on. "He must never be found."

"I can fix that," Tux said. "I have a barrel on board that'll fix him. I've plenty of cement, too. He won't be found."

O'Brien nodded.

"You mustn't slip up on this, Tux. I'll go along and talk to him now. I'll let you know when to do it."

"Tonight?" Tux asked, thinking longingly of his much-needed sleep.

"It'll be tonight. Better get that barrel and the cement ready."

"I'll tell Solly."

"Do it yourself," O'Brien said sharply. "Solly is to keep out of this. I'll take him back with me. I don't want him to know anything about it. Only you and I are to know about it, Tux."

Tux grimaced.

"That barrel's going to be goddamn heavy. I can't handle it alone. I'll have to have Solly."

O'Brien took his cigar from between his lips, stared at the glowing end, then said, "Please yourself, but if you have Solly, you'll have to take care of him. He'll have to go the same way."

Tux was fond of Solly. Besides, Solly was as strong as a bull and as quick as a rattlesnake.

"He'll keep his trap shut. You don't have to worry about him," he said.

O'Brien looked at him.

"If you don't want to handle it my way, Tux, just say so." The threat in his voice was unmistakable.

Tux eyed him, then shrugged.

"Okay, I'll manage on my own."

"You'd better make a job of it."

"I'll make a job of it."

O'Brien got up, opened the cabin door and went into the passage. He walked to Johnny's cabin, turned the key that was in the lock, pushed open the door and entered.

Johnny was dozing. He opened his eyes, blinked, then sat up.

"Hello, Johnny," O'Brien said quietly.

He looked at Johnny's bruised face with satisfaction. It was about time someone pushed this punk around, he thought as he closed the door and leaned against it.

Johnny eyed him warily.

"What do you want?"

"I've decided to make you a proposition," O'Brien said.

"Yeah?" Johnny swung his legs off the bunk. "Well, okay, but it's going to cost you plenty."

O'Brien shook his head.

"It's time we had a straight talk, Johnny. You are in no position to dictate terms. You either accept my conditions or you'll stay here until you change your mind."

"What are the conditions?" Johnny asked, touching his bruised face with his finger-tips.

"You'll leave here tonight, go to the airport and fly to New York. One of my agents will meet you at the airport and put you on a plane for Paris. Another of my agents will meet you in Paris and take you to an apartment there. You will remain in Paris until I give you permission to leave."

"And that will be after you've married Gilda, I suppose?" Johnny said with a sneer. "Do you imagine she'll marry you unless I'm there to give her away?"

"You will write and tell her you are leaving for Paris tonight, and you won't be back," O'Brien said quietly. "She knows you're in trouble, and she won't be surprised you are clearing out."

"Why are you so anxious to get rid of me?"

"Need you ask?" O'Brien returned. "You are a damned nuisance. I know what I'm in for taking you on as a brother-in-law. I can do without your company."

Johnny laughed.

"You're kidding yourself, Séan. If you want Gilda you'll have to put up with me. I'm not going, so get that idea out of your head. I'm sticking to you and Gilda and your dough."

O'Brien shrugged.

"Please yourself. You'll either go or stay on this boat until you rot. You have no other alternative, and if you think you can escape, try it and see how you get on!"

Johnny grimaced.

"I might go if there was some money in it. Is there?"

"I didn't expect to get rid of you without it costing me something," O'Brien said. "I'll give you ten grand in return for the letter to Gilda and your promise to remain in Paris until I tell you to return."

"Ten grand?" Johnny said incredulously. "You'll have to do better than that. Make it fifty, and it's a deal."

"Twenty-five, but no more."

"I'll close at thirty," Johnny said, watching O'Brien closely.

O'Brien appeared to hesitate, then he shrugged.

"Okay: thirty. My agent will give you half in New York and you'll get the other half in Paris."

"You wouldn't double-cross me, would you, Séan? If I don't get the money, I'll come back."

"By then the police may be looking for you. You seem to have forgotten you killed a woman last night."

"Why shouldn't I forget it? That's your headache. I want some money now. How about my air passage?"

"My agent will take care of that," O'Brien said glibly. He took out his billfold, counted three hundred dollars on to the table and waved his hand. "There you are: take it."

Johnny didn't need a second invitation. He slid off the bunk, collected the money and put it in his pocket.

"You must want her, Séan," he said, grinning. "Brother! You must want her to part with all that dough. I wouldn't give all that for her or any woman."

O'Brien had to make an effort to hide the fury that was raging inside him.

"There's notepaper in that drawer. Write to Gilda and tell her you're going to Paris and won't be coming back for some time," he said curtly.

"Oh, the hell with that!" Johnny said impatiently. "You tell her. Why should I bother to write?"

"Write to her or the deal's off!" O'Brien said, his rage sounding in his voice.

"What are you worrying about?" Johnny asked, suddenly

eyeing him suspiciously. "Scared she'll think you've knocked me on the head and dropped me into the river?"

"Don't be a fool!" O'Brien was secretly startled that Johnny should have got so near to the truth. "She's fond of you and she deserves to hear direct from you."

"Well, okay, I'll call her from the airport."

"I'm not having you hanging around the airport where a cop might spot you. You'll write now or the deal's off."

Johnny shrugged.

"Okay, okay. Shall I tell her how your thug knocked me around? I can't imagine she'll be soft and sweet to you if she knew how you've been treating me."

"Get on with it!" O'Brien snarled, and turned away, his face ugly with suppressed rage.

Johnny sat down and began to scrawl on a sheet of notepaper. He hummed under his breath, then he tossed the paper over to O'Brien. "There you are," he said. "Now let's get off this stinking boat."

O'Brien picked up the note, read it, nodded and pointed to an envelope.

"Address it to her."

Johnny obeyed and O'Brien put the note in the envelope, sealed it, and put it in his billfold.

He was elated. He could now deal with Johnny without making Gilda suspicious.

"You're not coming back with me," he said. "I'm not taking the risk of being seen with you. I'll take Solly and he can come back with the motorboat for you. And understand, do what I tell you or you'll be sorry."

"Suppose I go first for a change?" Johnny said. "I've been on this goddamn boat longer than you have."

"Shut your trap!" O'Brien snarled, his face suddenly murderous. "You stinking little rat! I've had about enough of you!"

The expression in his eyes startled Johnny.

"Take it easy, Séan," he said uneasily. "I was only kidding."

"Yeah? Well, I don't like kidders, and you'll damn well find out just how much I don't like them before long!"

O'Brien went out, locked the door after him and went up on deck. He was shaking with rage. Now he had the letter, the sooner Johnny was out of the way the better. He could tell Gilda in a little while that Johnny had been killed in a brawl in Paris. It would never occur to her that he had ordered Johnny's death.

Solly stood by the deck rail. As soon as he saw O'Brien he scrambled down into the motorboat.

Tux joined O'Brien.

"Go ahead and take him," O'Brien said, keeping his voice low. "You're sure you can handle this, Tux? I don't want any slip-up."

"That's okay," Tux said. "I'll roll the barrel overboard. There's plenty of water. It'll be okay."

"When Solly comes back, come over and call me. You'd better tell Solly you took Johnny ashore in the dinghy. I'll keep him with me for an hour. Will that give you enough time?"

"Sure," Tux said indifferently. "I'll fix him as soon as you're gone. There's nothing to it. The barrel's a big one. He'll fit in it easily. I have plenty of cement. An hour's fine."

"Don't use a gun, Tux. Someone may hear it from the water-front."

"I'll use a knife."

"Make a job of it," O'Brien said, crossed the deck and climbed down into the motorboat.

Solly cast off, started the engine and sent boat shooting away into the darkness.

CHAPTER VII

I

O'BRIEN'S and Tux's voices came clearly to Ken as he clung to the side of the cruiser, but it took several moments before he realized what was about to happen to Johnny.

They were going to murder Johnny and dump him in the river!

Ken turned cold.

With Johnny at the bottom of the river, how could he hope to convince anyone he hadn't murdered Fay? He had to rescue Johnny get him back to land and hand him over to Adams. That was his only chance of ever proving his innocence.

But the thought of tackling Tux single-handed turned his mouth dry and made his heart beat violently. Ken didn't pretend to be a man of action. He knew, too, he wasn't in any physical shape for a hand-to-hand grapple with Tux. But there was no alternative. He had to rescue Johnny if he was to save himself.

As he tied his boat to the iron bracket by Johnny's port-hole, he wondered if it would be safe to attract Johnny's attention and warn him what he planned to do, but Tux was still somewhere on deck and he decided against the risk of being heard.

His first move was to get on board. If he could sneak up on Tux and hit him over the head, the rescue would be simple.

He reached up and caught hold of the bottom rail, then cautiously pulled himself up until his eyes were level with the deck.

In the shadowy darkness he caught sight of Tux on the far side, outlined against the skyline. He was busy trying to pry off the head of a big cask that stood against the far deck rail, his back turned to Ken.

His heart hammering, Ken lifted one leg, hooked his foot around the rail support and pulled himself up. He shifted his grip, reached for the top rail and swung himself on deck.

He crouched down on hands and knees, his eyes fixed on Tux's broad back.

Tux was making enough noise while hammering a chisel into the head of the cask to cover the slight sounds Ken had made getting on deck.

Ken watched him. The thirty-foot gap that separated him from Tux was too wide to risk a rush. Besides, he hadn't a weapon and he had no intentions of tackling Tux with his fists.

He decided his only chance against Tux was to combine forces with Johnny. The two of them should be able to handle Tux. He began to creep towards the companion ladder.

Tux got the head off the cask, straightened and turned suddenly.

Ken flattened out and lay still, his heart doing a somersault while he watched Tux walk along the deck and disappear behind the bridge house. He came into sight again before Ken could move, carrying a sack of cement on his shoulder. He emptied the cement into the barrel, then he went back for another sack.

Ken darted across the deck, reached the companion ladder and scrambled down it as Tux reappeared.

He found himself in a narrow, dimly lit passage. One of the four doors on either side of the passage had a key in the lock. He could hear Tux moving about above him, and guessed he hadn't much time. He turned the key, pushed open the door and entered the small cabin.

Johnny was lolling on the bunk. He stared at Ken blankly, then sat up.

"Who are you?" he said sharply.

Ken closed the door and leaned against it. He was in such a state of nerves he had difficulty in controlling his breathing.

"I happened to be near this boat and heard them planning to murder you," he said, his voice shaking. "They're going to put you in a barrel and drop you in the river."

Johnny stiffened.

"Is this one of O'Brien's tricks?" he snarled. "You can't scare me, you fool! Get out!"

"We haven't a second to lose! Tux's getting the barrel ready now," Ken said. "The two of us can tackle him, but we've got to take him by surprise."

It suddenly dawned on Johnny that this tall, haggard, frightened man, facing him, wasn't trying to kid him. He remembered O'Brien's murderous expression when he had left the cabin. He remembered, too, how persistent O'Brien had been that he should write to Gilda. It would suit O'Brien to be rid of him for good.

He slid off the bunk, feeling cold sweat on his face.

"He's got a gun!" he said. "We haven't a chance against him."

"We've got to tackle him," Ken said sharply. "Come on. We can't handle him in here."

"Give me the key," Johnny said wildly. "I'll lock myself in. You go for the police."

"Don't be a fool! He'd break the door in and get to you. We've got to handle this ourselves!"

Ken's heart sank at the sight of Johnny's white, twitching face. He wasn't surprised when Johnny said, "Leave me out of it! I'm not going up there."

Any moment now Tux would be down. He had to find a weapon. A quick look around Johnny's cabin convinced him there was nothing he could use except a rather flimsy chair, so he stepped into the passage and opened the door opposite, groped for the light switch and turned it on.

The only likely weapon he could see was a half-empty bottle of whisky that stood on the table. He rammed in the cork and picked it up. As he moved back to the door, he heard Tux coming down the companion ladder.

There was no time to reach Johnny's cabin. He snapped up the light switch, and, his heart hammering, he leaned against the wall by the door and waited.

Tux came along the passage, humming under his breath. Ken caught sight of him through the half-open door. His fingers tightened on the neck of the bottle.

Johnny had also heard Tux coming and had hastily shut his door.

Tux paused outside Johnny's door, attempted to turn the key, but finding it unlocked, he abruptly stopped humming.

Ken watched him through the crack between the hinges end of the door and the door-post. He held his breath as Tux suddenly jerked out a snub-nosed automatic from inside his coat.

Tux turned the handle and kicked the door wide open. Over his shoulder, Ken could see Johnny backed up against the opposite wall, his face waxen.

"Hello, Johnny," Tux said softly. "Who unlocked the door?"

"How do I know?" Johnny said hoarsely, staring at the gun. "Maybe O'Brien forgot to lock it. What does it matter? I'm leaving, anyway."

"That's right," Tux said, and he slipped the gun back into his hip pocket. "You're going on a hell of a long journey."

Ken began to creep across the passage towards him.

The boss is sick of you, Johnny, and I don't blame him," Tux said. "I've got a barrel for you and a snug-fitting cement overcoat."

"You wouldn't do that to me!" Johnny gasped, his eyes bolting out of his head. "O'Brien wouldn't stand for it! Keep away from me!"

Ken jumped forward and aimed a violent blow at Tux's head with the bottle, but Tux was too quick for him. He heard Ken's movement behind him and the swish of the descending bottle and he ducked sideways.

The bottle crashed down on his right shoulder, making him stagger. Fragments of glass and whisky exploded over him.

Cursing, his arm momentarily numbed, Tux spun around.

More frightened that he had ever been before, Ken swung a wild, hard punch at Tux's head, but Tux slipped the punch and caught Ken under the heart with a jarring left jab that staggered him.

Johnny made a rush for the door, but Tux kicked out, catching Johnny above the knee, bringing him down.

Before Tux could get his eyes back on Ken, Ken had jumped in close and grabbed his arms. It was like catching hold of a gorilla. Tux threw him off with a heave of his massive shoulders. He jumped away and set his back against the cabin wall.

Johnny scrambled up and backed away while Ken stood by the door, staring at Tux.

"So you've found a pal," Tux said, his small eyes gleaming viciously. "Well, okay, the barrel's big enough to take you both." His hand whipped behind him and reappeared holding a short stabbing knife. "Who's first?"

Both Ken and Johnny recoiled at the sight of the knife and Tux grinned. He began to edge forward.

Ken snatched up the chair and thrust it at Tux. One of the legs narrowly missed Tux's face as he ducked under it, and he cursed; catching hold of the chair leg with his left hand, he tried to pull Ken on to the knife blade.

He was too strong for Ken, and to prevent himself being pulled forward, Ken had to let go of the chair.

Tux tossed the chair away and darted forward. Ken hit out blindly, and his fist crashed into Tux's face as the knife flashed.

Ken had no idea how he avoided the thrust. He felt the blade cut into his coat and he twisted sideways. He fell against Tux, grabbed hold of Tux's knife wrist with both hands and threw his whole weight on Tux's arm.

"Get him!" he shouted frantically to Johnny, who, instead of going to Ken's help, tried to reach the door. As he shoved past the struggling men, Tux grabbed him by the throat with his left hand and pinned him against the wall.

It was as much as Ken could do to control Tux's right arm. He hung on, his fingers squeezing Tux's fingers against the knife handle, trying to make him drop it.

Tux hooked his leg around Ken's, heaved and upset Ken, sending him sprawling on the floor. He tried to hang on to Tux's wrist, but the fall broke his hold.

Tux swung around on Johnny and again the knife flashed, but in falling, Ken had grabbed hold of Tux's trousers cuff and he jerked with all his strength, bringing Tux over backwards on top of him.

Johnny kicked violently at Tux's head. The toe of his shoe smashed against Tux's temple, and for a second or so Tux went limp, the knife falling from his hand.

Ken grabbed the knife and threw it across the room, shoved

Tux away from him and scrambled up on hands and knees.

Tux was up at the same time. Blood ran down his face from a cut on the temple where Johnny had kicked him. His face was convulsed with murderous rage.

Before Ken could get out of the way, Tux belted him in the face with a half-arm punch that sent Ken over on his back, but Johnny had snatched up the chair and crashed it down on Tux's head and shoulders.

Johnny suddenly seemed to have found some courage. His white, thin face was as murderous and as vicious as Tux's now. He hit Tux again, driving him to his knees as Ken rolled away and staggered to his feet.

Tux tried to shield his face with his arms as he came off the floor, but Johnny battered his arm down and again hit him on the top of his head with the chair.

The back of the chair snapped and Tux flattened out on his face.

Johnny jumped forward, grabbed a handful of Tux's thick hair and, lifting Tux's head, he slammed it down on the floor.

Tux gave a strangled grunt and went limp.

The two stood over him, panting.

"Let's get out of here!" Ken gasped. "Come on!"

Johnny gave Tux a hard, vicious kick in the side of his neck, then bending over him, he rolled him over and pulled out Tux's automatic from his hip pocket.

"Come on!" Ken said again.

Johnny followed him along the passage and up on to the deck.

II

The lighted clock on the dashboard showed twenty minutes past eleven as Adams pulled up outside 25 Lessington Avenue.

During the short drive from the hospital he had remained silent, hunched up behind the driving-wheel, while Watson sat beside him, hoping for some explanation which didn't come.

Adams got out of the car and Watson followed him.

They walked up the steps, opened the front door and, with Adams leading, they climbed the stairs to Raphael Sweeting's apartment.

As Adams paused outside the door, he said, "This guy's going to make a statement. Get it down!"

"Yes, sir," Watson said, wondering who the guy might be.

Adams rang the bell and waited.

There was a long delay, then the door opened cautiously and Sweeting, a damp sponge held to his right eye, looked first at Adams and then at Watson. He seemed to shrivel under Adams' hard stare, and he stepped back hurriedly.

Adams walked into the room, and Watson followed him.

"So this is where you've holed up," Adams said, glancing around the room. "How's business, Raphael?"

"Now look, Lieutenant," Sweeting said urgently, "I'm going straight. How can a guy settle to anything if you cops keep pestering him?"

"I wouldn't know," Adams said mildly. He wandered over to a chair and sat down. "Must be difficult for you. How's the blackmail business flourishing?"

"I don't know what you mean," Sweeting said indignantly. "I've given that up months ago."

"Have you? What's the matter with your eye? Someone paid a debt?"

"I had an accident," Sweeting said sullenly. "Can't you leave me alone, Lieutenant? I'm trying to earn an honest living."

"Finding it difficult?" Adams said, taking out his cigarette-case and lighting a cigarette. "It might be easier for you if I put you inside for ten years."

Sweeting stiffened.

"You've got nothing on me, and you know it."

"But I could easily fix something, Raphael. The easiest thing in the world. Don't forget that. I can put you away for ten years just when I want to, but I'll leave you alone if you play along with me. I want some information."

Sweeting sat down. This had been a hell of a day. His eye ached and he felt old and tired. He looked across the room to where Leo crouched, panting, and he sighed.

"What do you want to know, Lieutenant?"

"I want facts. You told Donovan you saw no one go up or come down and heard nothing. You were lying. Are you going to tell me?"

"I'm always ready to talk to you, Lieutenant," Sweeting said. "I didn't know the other other guy."

Adams looked over at Watson and tossed him his notebook.

"Take it down," he said curtly. "Talk away," he went on to Sweeting. "I know most of it so don't skip the details. Start where you met Holland on the stairs."

Sweeting flinched.

"Have you arrested him, Lieutenant?" he asked uneasily. "You can't believe a word that guy says. I'll bet he said I tried to blackmail him."

"He told me he punched you in the eye," Adams said unfeelingly. "Start talking!"

Sweeting talked.

Half an hour later, Adams lit his fourth cigarette, stretched, yawned and nodded his head.

"That seems to take care of that. You're sure you didn't see this other guy who left Carson's apartment before Holland did?"

"I didn't see him," Sweeting said miserably. He had parted with valuable information for nothing, and it grieved him.

"Okay. Got it all down?" Adams said to Watson.

"Yes, sir."

"Sign it, Raphael," Adams said. "Each page and you countersign it, Watson."

When both men had finished signing the statement, Adams took charge of the notebook again.

"You can go home," he said to Watson. "Keep your mouth shut about this."

When Watson had gone, Adams lit his fifth cigarette, settled himself more comfortably in his chair and stared at Sweeting thoughtfully.

"We're going to have a little talk, Raphael. Strictly off the record, and you're going to be helpful. I want to crack this case. It's important to me. There's not much you don't see and hear. You may have some ideas. If you play with me, I'll play with you, so keep on the right side of me."

"Yes, Lieutenant," Sweeting said, dabbing his eye. "But I don't know a thing."

"You might," Adams said, stretching out his short legs. "I had an idea Johnny Dorman knocked this girl off. How do you react to that one?"

Sweeting looked startled.

"Johnny? He wouldn't kill anyone!"

"Don't talk through the back of your neck! Of course he would. He's as vicious as they come. You knew him pretty well, didn't you?"

"I played billiards with him from time to time," Sweeting said. "Yes, I guess I knew him well, but I haven't seen or heard from him since he was put in that home. What makes you think he did it?"

"I don't think he did it now. I said I liked him for the job, but I've changed my mind. He threatened to kill her before he went into the home, and that made me think maybe he'd done it."

"He wouldn't kill her," Sweeting said. "He was through with her. I know. He told me. She meant nothing to him after he had beaten her up."

"Okay. Do you think Holland did it?"

Sweeting hesitated. He wanted to get Ken Holland into trouble if he could, but he decided Adams might not like him to side-track him because of his own private hate.

"I guess not. Why have you changed your mind about Johnny, Lieutenant?"

"I don't reckon he could have done it. Holland saw him outside the Blue Rose. He didn't know Carson's address. He couldn't have got there and hid in her bedroom before they returned, could he?"

Sweeting inclined his head.

"Maybe you're right."

"I think I am. Okay, if it wasn't Johnny and it wasn't Holland who was it?"

Sweeting blinked.

"Are you asking me?"

"I'm asking you, Raphael. You spend all your life sticking your snout into other people's affairs. Don't tell me you didn't stick it into Carson's affairs as well."

Sweeting hesitated.

"Well, I'd like to help you, Lieutenant, but I don't know."

"Have a guess," Adams said quietly.

Sweeting again hesitated.

"If I were you," he said slowly, "I'd talk to Maurice Yarde. He might have a few ideas."

"Who's he?"

"He used to be Fay's dancing partner before they quarrelled."

"What did they quarrel about?"

"She and Gilda Dorman used to share an apartment. Yarde fell for Gilda. He broke up the act and Gilda and he went to Los Angeles. She came back after six months alone. Yarde came back a couple of days ago. He came to see Fay. I happened to see him. They had a quarrel. I heard her cursing him. When he left I heard him tell her he would cut her throat."

Adams removed his hat and ran his fingers through his thick white hair.

"You're sure Gilda went away with Yarde?"

Sweeting nodded.

"Johnny told me. He hated the idea. Yarde's a bad man, Lieutenant: a bad man with women."

Adams scratched the side of his jaw. This set-up was getting complicated. He would have preferred to tie Johnny to the murder, but if he couldn't do that, Yarde would do nearly as well. In both cases Gilda was hooked up to it, and that meant O'Brien was hooked up in it too.

"Where do I find Yarde?" he asked.

"He usually hangs out at the Washington Hotel. He could be there, Lieutenant."

Adams got slowly and stiffly to his feet. This was turning out to be a hell of a night.

"Okay, Raphael. Keep your mouth shut and your legs crossed. Stick right here and don't try to leave town. I may need you for a witness. Play along with me and you won't get into trouble."

"Yes, Lieutenant," Sweeting said, and for the first time since Adams had been in the apartment, he began to breathe freely.

As Adams moved to the door, Sweeting went on, "Excuse me, Lieutenant, but you wouldn't happen to have a spare buck on you? I have my rent to meet tomorrow and I find myself a little short."

Adams opened the door and went slowly down the stairs as if he hadn't heard his head bent, his brow furrowed in thought.

Sweeting leaned over the banister rail but resisted the temptation of spitting on the Lieutenant's hat. He returned to his room and slammed the door.

He had to raise some money before tomorrow. For a long time he stood thinking, then his face brightened. Of course! Gilda Dorman! He should have thought of her before. She might part with a few bucks if he called on her. She would probably be interested to know her old lover, Maurice Yarde, was in town. She might be still sentimental about him. She might also be interested to know that Lieutenant Adams thought her brother had killed Fay. The possibilities were endless!

Sweeting glanced at the clock on the overmantel. It was a quarter past eleven. These nightclub singers kept late hours. He might catch her if he hurried.

He went over to the pile of directories, flicked through the pages of one of them and found what he wanted.

"45 Maddox Court," he muttered. "That's only five minutes from here."

He took his hat from the cupboard, placed it at an angle on his head so as to hide his bruised eye, picked up Leo, turned off the lights and hurriedly left his apartment.

III

The Washington Hotel had an unsavoury reputation. It was a-room-by-the-hour-and-no-questions-asked joint, sandwiched between an amusement arcade and a beer shop, facing the river. In its basement, hidden away behind a cleverly constructed sliding panel, was a big room where you could enjoy a pipe of opium if you wanted it and if you could pay for it.

On the top floor were a number of well-furnished rooms which were occupied by the hotel's residents: mostly men just just out of prison who were feeling their feet, taking a look around and getting used to their new-found freedom.

The hotel was owned by Séan O'Brien, and Police Captain Motley had taken care that his men didn't worry the management or the residents.

The manager, Seth Cutler, short, thick-set and as hard as granite, was startled when he saw Lieutenant Adams coming across the dimly lit lobby. He leaned his elbows on the desk and waited, his eyes watchful.

"Evening, Lieutenant," he said, when Adams came to rest opposite him. "Long time no see."

"Yeah," Adams said. "Let me take a look at your register."

Cutler raised his eyebrows, poked his little finger into his right ear, wiggled it about and then withdrew it and examined his nail to see what he had found.

"Snap it up!" Adams barked, his voice suddenly harsh.

Cutler said, "Excuse me, Lieutenant, but haven't you come to the wrong joint? This is the Washington. We've got protection."

"Give me the book!" Adams said.

Cutler raised his shoulders, produced a well-worn, leather-bound book, blew dust off it and laid it on the desk.

The last entry in the book was dated June 19th, 1941.

"It's a wonder you keep in business," Adams said in disgust. He shoved the book back. "I'm looking for Maurice Yarde."

Cutler shook his head.

"Never heard of him, Lieutenant. Sorry. Help you if I could."

Adams nodded.

"That's too bad. Then I'll have to go from room to room until I find him."

"I wouldn't do that, Lieutenant."

Adams stared steadily at Cutler.

"That's what I'm going to do unless you tell me where I can find him."

"The Captain wouldn't like it."

"You have your lines snarled up," Adams said. "The Captain told me to talk to Yarde. This isn't a pinch. I just want information."

Cutler hesitated.

"I don't like my best clients bothered, Lieutenant. I'd rather get it straight from the Captain."

"Okay, if that's the way you feel about it," Adams said, shrugging. "I'll start in on the ground floor and work up, and I'd like to see you stop me! Don't blame me if your other clients get annoyed with you."

"He's on the top floor, No. 10," Cutler snarled, his face turning red.

"Thanks."

Adams wandered over to the ancient elevator, got in, closed the gate and hauled on the rope that raised the evil-smelling cage up the equally evil-smelling shaft.

He was thankful when the elevator creaked to a standstill on the top floor. All the way up he had been expecting the rope to snap or the bottom of the cage to drop out.

Facing him was a long passage with doors every few yards. He walked to room 10, listened outside, then hearing no sound in the room, he rapped on the door. Nothing happened, and he rapped again.

The door opposite abruptly opened.

A girl in a blue-and-red silk wrap, her auburn hair about her shoulders, leaned against the door-post and showed him a long white leg and a well-rounded thigh through the opening in her wrap.

"He's out," she said. "If you want to wait, there's a chair in my room."

"You're talking to a police officer," Adams said mildly.

The girl wrinkled her nose, then lifted her shoulders.

"I can't afford to be fussy. The offer still stands."

Adams joined her at the door.

"When did Yarde go out?"

"Last night. Is he in trouble?"

"Not that I know of. What time last night?"

"About eight. Are you coming in or are you just wasting my time?"

"I told you I was a police officer," Adams said patiently. "You are giving me evidence for an arrest."

The girl giggled.

"Funny man! Didn't anyone tell you this joint's got protection?" She made a face at him and closed the door.

Adams scratched his chin thoughtfully, then moved back to room 10, turned the handle of the door and pushed speculatively. To his surprise the door swung open. He put his hand on the inside wall and groped for the light switch, found it and turned it down.

The disorder that met his eyes made him step quickly into the room and close the door.

The room looked as if it had been hit by a cyclone. Drawers were pulled out and their contents strewn over the floor. The bedding had been ripped: the mattress stuffing and the pillow feathers were all over the room. The two easy chairs had been ripped to pieces. Pictures had been taken down, and now lay on the floor, their backs torn off. The wardrobe door stood open: suits, shoes, shirts and underwear lay in a disordered heap before the wardrobe.

Someone had obviously been searching the room for something pretty important, Adams thought, and the search had been as thorough as it had been destructive.

He walked over to the telephone, lifted the receiver and, when he heard Cutler's voice, he said, "I want you. Come up."

While he waited, he examined the room, but found nothing to interest him.

Cutler came in hurriedly. From the way he was breathing, Adams guessed he had run up the stairs.

When Cutler saw the disorder, he came to an abrupt standstill.

"For crying out loud!" he exclaimed.

"Why didn't you tell me Yarde was out?" Adams asked acidly.

"I didn't know he was," Cutler said. "What the hell's been going on here?"

"How do I know? I found it like this. Have you another way out beside the main lobby?"

"Yeah. At the end of the passage and down the fire escape."

"So whoever did this could have come up that way?"

"I guess so."

Adams grunted.

"There's a girl in the opposite room. She might have seen something. Bring her here."

Cutler hesitated, but the cold, hard light in Adams' eyes warned him this wasn't the time to be unco-operative.

He crossed the passage, opened the opposite door.

"Hey, Milly, come here a moment."

The girl appeared, looked across the passage at the disordered room and her eyes lit up.

"Gee! Did someone lose something?"

"Did Yarde go out by the escape last night?" Adams asked.

"Do I answer this copper's questions?" she asked Cutler.

He nodded.

"Okay, if you say so," she said, "but I thought this joint had protection."

"Did Yarde go out by the escape last night?" Adams snapped.

"Yes. Everyone uses the escape."

"This mess couldn't have been made without a lot of noise. Didn't you hear anything?"

"I had the radio on, but I did hear furniture being pushed around. I didn't think anything of it."

"What time last night?"

"About half-past ten."

"You didn't see any stranger in the passage?"

"If I had I would have called Seth."

"You said just now that Yarde was out. Didn't you think it was odd to hear noises in his room after he had gone out?"

"How was I to know it was in his room? I just heard noises. Why should I care?"

"How do you know Yarde went out at eight last night? Did you see him?"

"Yes."

"Did he say where he was going?"

"He said he was going to raise some money."

"Did he tell you that?"

159

"Yes. He had borrowed ten bucks off me and I wanted it. He said he hadn't got it on him, but he would give it to me when he got back." She looked around the room. "Doesn't look as if he is coming back now, does it?"

"Did he say how he was going to raise the money?"

"I didn't ask him."

"Okay," Adams said, waving her to the door. "You can go."

"Thanks copper for nothing," she said, and flounced back to her room.

"Got any ideas about this?" Adams asked Cutler.

Cutler shook his head.

"If Yarde shows up tell him I want to talk to him. I want information. He isn't in trouble, but he will be if he doesn't get in touch with me."

"I'll tell him. Want to go out by the escape?"

"Anything's better than your elevator."

They walked along the passage to a door at the far end. Cutler opened it and Adams stepped out on to an iron platform. From where he stood, he had a good view of the waterfront and the surrounding buildings. Immediately below him was a dark alley that ran by the side of the hotel and led out on to the waterfront.

"So long, Lieutenant," Cutler said.

Adams wasn't paying attention. He was watching two men standing in the shadows. Facing them was a cop. The taller of the two men suddenly stepped back.

There was something about the cop's cautious attitude that held Adams' attention. He saw the taller one move slightly around to the back of the cop. He made a sudden movement and then the quiet night was shattered by the sound of gunfire.

The cop took a step forward and fell on his knees. The man who had fired grabbed his companion by the arm and dragged him down the alley immediately below where Adams was standing.

Adams' hand slid inside his coat and he jerked out his .38 police special. He took a snap-shot at the taller of the two men and had the satisfaction of seeing him stagger. He raised the gun to fire again, but Culter appeared to slip and cannoned into him, spoiling his aim.

The two men had now disappeared down the alley.

Shoving Cutler aside, Adams raced down the escape, three steps at a time.

CHAPTER VIII

I

WHILE Ken rowed across the dark, oily water of the estuary, he tried to think how he was going to get Johnny into Adams' hands without raising Johnny's suspicions, but the problem defeated him.

Johnny had a gun. He sat in the stern of the boat, watching the outline of the *Willow Point* as it slowly faded into the darkness, holding the gun in his hand.

"I should have killed that punk," he said suddenly. "He'll come after us. I was a mug not to settle him while I had the chance." He peered at Ken in the dim light of the moon. "Who the hell are you? How did you appear exactly at the right time?"

"My name's Holland," Ken said. "I had been told Tux was a good man if you were in trouble. I wanted somewhere safe to hide. As I came alongside the cruiser I heard two men talking. They were arranging to murder you. I thought you might want help, so I horned in."

"Well, I'll be damned! You certainly turned up at the right time, but you don't know what you've let yourself in for. Tux won't forget you. I'm getting out of town. You'd better come with me."

"Where are you going?"

"I know a guy who'll lend me a car. We'll go to Los Angeles. I have friends there."

"I wouldn't get far," Ken said. "The police are looking for me."

"I'll get you out of town," Johnny said. "You leave it to me. You helped me; I'll help you. The cops in this town are a dumb lot." He shoved the gun in his hip pocket. "Here, move over. Let me handle one of the oars."

It took them twenty minutes to reach a lonely stretch of the shore. As Ken got stiffly out of the boat he heard the distant engine of a motorboat. Johnny heard it too, and he looked across the dark street.

"That's Solly going back. We'll have to get under cover fast.

Those two guys will come after us, and they're a damn sight more dangerous than the cops."

Leaving the boat, they walked quickly along the path that led towards the waterfront.

"If we run into a cop, let me handle him," Johnny said.

It took them ten minutes to reach the line of shops and cafés that had been Ken's starting-point.

The waterfront appeared deserted. The amusement arcade was in darkness. The only light that showed was the electric sign that flashed on and off above the hotel, spelling out the word WASHINGTON.

Then suddenly a cop appeared out of the darkness.

Both Johnny and Ken stopped short.

"Hey you!" the cop said, pointing his night stick at Ken. "I want a word with you."

"What is it?" Ken said, his heart sinking.

Johnny stepped back.

"You answer to the description of Kenway Holland, wanted for questioning at headquarters. Are you Holland?"

Ken saw Johnny move slightly behind the cop, his hand flash to his hip pocket.

"No!" Ken exclaimed. "Don't . . . !"

The cop spun around, but he was too late.

The crash of gunfire shattered the silence. Horrified, Ken saw the cop drop to his knees and then roll over. He made to bend over him, but Johnny grabbed his arm and dragged him down a dark alley.

"Run!" Johnny said thickly. "Come on, you fool! They'll be after us!"

Immediately above them a gun barked. Ken heard the slug zip past his face and saw Johnny stagger.

"Run!" Johnny snarled, recovering his balance.

Panic-stricken, Ken bolted down the dark alley after Johnny as a police whistle shrilled in the darkness.

They hadn't run more than fifty yards when Johnny suddenly staggered, lost his balance and fell on hands and knees.

Ken pulled up and bent over him.

"Were you hit?" he panted.

"Got it in the arm," Johnny gasped. "I'm bleeding like hell."

Ken looked frantically to right and left. He could hear some-one running down an iron staircase not far off. He could hear distant shouts and more police whistles. He caught hold of Johnny and hauled him to his feet. Johnny leaned against him.

"Where's this alley lead to?" Ken asked.

"I don't know. Leave me! They'll be on to us in a moment."

"No!"

Ken wanted to run, but he knew he had to stick with Johnny. Adams had said he wanted Johnny, and Ken was determined he should have Johnny.

He pulled Johnny back against the wall. Nearby was a door, leading to a tall, shabby house. Suddenly the door jerked open and a shadowy figure of a girl appeared in the doorway.

"Hey! Come inside quick!" she said in an urgent whisper.

Ken could hear the thud of running feet coming from the end of the alley. He didn't hesitate. Dragging Johnny over to the door, he bundled him into the darkness beyond and heard the girl hurriedly shut and lock the door. Almost immediately he heard someone run by.

"Is he hurt?" the girl asked.

"He's shot in the arm."

"Stay here. I'll get a light."

"Aren't women wonderful?" Johnny muttered. "Everytime I get into a jam there's a woman to help me out." He leaned more heavily against Ken. "I feel like hell. I think I'm going to pass out..."

He slumped suddenly nearly pulling Ken over, then he slid to the ground.

The girl came quickly down the steep flight of stairs, holding a flickering candle above her head.

"I think he's fainted," Ken said.

"Can you carry him up? I have a room at the head of the stairs."

Ken managed to get Johnny across his shoulder and he staggered up the stairs after the girl, who lit the way.

He got Johnny into a small room, lit only by an oil lamp. "Put him on the bed."

When he had lowered Johnny on to the bed, he turned to look at the girl and he saw with a sense of shock it was the girl he had met in the amusement arcade.

"Hello, handsome," she said, smiling at him. "So you're still in trouble." She handed him the oil lamp. "Hold it so I can take a look at him."

Too surprised to say anything, Ken held the oil lamp while

she quickly cut away Johnny's coat sleeve and shirt. The sight of the blood and the torn flesh sickened him.

"It could be worse, but I've to stop that bleeding," she said calmly. She moved quickly across the room, filled a basin of water, went to a cupboard and pulled out a couple of towels and came back to the bed.

In an astonishingly short time she had got the bleeding under control and had bandaged Johnny's arm.

"That's fixed it," she said as she began to clear away the blood-stained rags. "He'll be okay now."

Ken set down the lamp on the table. While she had been working on Johnny he had been uneasily listening to the noises going on outside. He heard police whistles, distant shouting and sirens, and he guessed the alley and the surrounding buildings were being cordoned off.

He had to get in touch with Adams.

As soon as the girl had finished clearing up, he said, "I must use the telephone. Have you got one?"

"Does it look like it?" she said impatiently. "There's a pay booth at the end of the alley, but you'd better not use that."

"I must get him away from here. If they found him here you'd get into trouble," Ken said anxiously.

The girl laughed.

"Be your age, handsome," she said. "What do I care? I'm never out of trouble."

"But you don't understand. He shot a policeman. He probably killed him."

"So what? My brother killed two cops," the girl said indifferently. "They're fair game, aren't they?"

Ken looked helplessly at her.

"I must get him away from here!"

"Relax. You can't go yet. They're out there like a swarm of bees. Sit down. I'll make some coffee." She bent over Johnny. "He's lost a lot of blood. He won't be able to move yet."

Ken sat down. He suddenly felt exhausted. While she made coffee he listened to the uproar going on outside.

"They're certain to come here," he said uneasily. "They'll search every building."

"Oh, forget it!" she said impatiently. "They're not here yet."

Standing in the shadows, Raphael Sweeting watched the night clerk at the reception desk as he idly turned the pages of the evening newspaper.

Sweeting hadn't expected to find a night clerk on duty at Maddox Court. He was sure the clerk wouldn't let him upstairs if he saw him, and he thought it unwise to walk in boldly and ask for Gilda at this hour.

But he had infinite patience. He waited, holding Leo close to him, while he leaned his fat shoulders against the pillar. He had to wait twenty minutes before the opportunity he was hoping for came.

The clerk suddenly glanced at his wrist-watch, dropped the paper on the desk, and went into a room immediately behind the desk.

Sweeting was through the revolving doors in a flash. He scuttled across the thick pile carpet that covered the lobby floor and darted up the stairs and around the bend as the clerk came out of the room.

Sweeting waited, listening; then, hearing nothing to alarm him, he went on up the stairs.

It took him some moments to work out where apartment 45 was located in this vast building, and eventually found to his dismay that it was on the top floor.

He was tempted to use the elevator, but decided against the risk. There would be an indicator on the ground floor, and the clerk might wonder who was using the elevator. So Sweeting toiled up the stairs. By the time he had reached the sixth floor, he was sweating and puffing.

The time was now ten minutes to twelve. What a flop it would be, he thought , as he stood outside Gilda's front door, if she were out. He dug his grimy thumb into the bell-push and held it there.

After a slight delay he heard someone coming, and a moment later the door opened.

Gilda stared blankly at him. She was wearing a pale blue *négligé*, trimmed with blue mink. Her bare feet were thrust into blue-quilted slippers. She made a quick movement to shut the door, but Sweeting had had too many doors slammed in his face in the past not to be ready for such a move. His foot was already against the bottom of the door.

"Don't be alarmed, Miss Dorman," he said, with his oily smile. "I've come about Maurice Yarde and your brother."

With satisfaction he watched her turn pale. Frightened women were always easy to handle.

"Who are you?" she said, still pressing the door against his foot.

"My name is Raphael Sweeting. I am a friend of your brother. He may have mentioned me." Sweeting said. "Perhaps I might step inside? I have had a most tiring day and I would be glad to sit down."

"You can't come in. I can't see you now. Please go away!"

Sweeting smiled.

"I don't want to make myself objectionable, Miss Dorman, but I assure you it is to your advantage to hear what I have to say. I have some interesting information for you."

The big green eyes swept over him, taking in his soiled creased suit, the three large grease stains on his tie, and the swollen, bloodshot eye the hat brim didn't quite conceal.

"What information?"

"It's about your brother."

She hesitated, then, stepping aside, motioned him to come in.

Sweeting entered the hall happily. He followed her into a big, luxuriously furnished sitting-room that immediately told him she had much more money than he had imagined. It was possible, he thought as he looked around, that she was the mistress of some wealthy man. But that wasn't his affair. The point was she was living in style and must have money.

He took off his hat and settled himself in the most comfortable chair in the room, holding Leo on his lap.

"You'll excuse my eye. I had an unfortunate accident," he said. "Are you fond of dogs, Miss Dorman? This little fellow is a remarkable specimen." He gently stroked Leo's silky coat. "Such a companion. Do you have a dog?"

Gilda stood facing him. Her face hard.

"What do you want?" she said curtly. "What have you got to tell me?"

Sweeting lifted his shoulders.

"Would it be inexcusable of me if I asked for a whisky and soda?" he asked hopefully.

"You're getting nothing here!" Gilda snapped. "What have you to tell me?"

166

Sweeting's fat face hardened. There was no reason to be polite to women unless they were exceptionally polite to him. When dealing with men he had to be more careful. Some of them, like that Holland fellow, could be violent, but there was no fear of that with a woman.

"My information is for sale," he said. "I have information concerning your brother that you will be anxious to buy."

"Shall I?"

She moved away from him, opened a silver cigarette box and lit a cigarette.

"Are you attempting to blackmail me?" she asked.

"I would scarcely call it blackmail. Valuable information is always worth paying for. The price is five hundred dollars."

"You don't imagine I have such a sum in this apartment, do you?" she asked contemptuously.

"Why not? You are obviously well off. It's not a vast sum, but if you haven't, I would consider taking some jewellery as security to be reclaimed for cash tomorrow."

"And what is this information?"

Sweeting smirked.

"Surely you don't expect me to tell you that without the money or the jewellery, Miss Dorman? From experience I find women have no sense of honour."

She looked at him for a long moment. There was something cat-like in her stillness that made Sweeting feel a little uneasy.

"Then I suppose I'll have to see what I have. Will you wait?"

She went into another room.

Sweeting took out his handkerchief and dabbed at his aching eye.

Perhaps his technique wasn't as good as it used to be, he thought uneasily. He had never had so much trouble before. First, Holland had been violent and had thrown him out, and now this girl was being suspiciously difficult.

The first indication he had that he had lost control of the situation came from Leo, who suddenly bolted off his lap and dived under the couch.

Sweeting hurriedly looked over his shoulder.

Gilda was standing in her bedroom doorway, a .38 automatic in her hand, its blue nose pointing at Sweeting's head.

Sweeting froze at the sight of the gun. If he had a horror of violence, guns terrified him. His heart seemed to turn over, and he shrank back in his chair, his fat face turning grey.

Gilda came over and stood over him.

"What's your information?" she said. "You'd better talk, you little rat, or I'll shoot you in the leg and tell the night clerk you broke in here."

Sweeting nearly fainted with fright.

"Take care," he quavered. "That gun might go off. Please put it down. I'll be only too glad to tell you what I know."

"Talk!" Her voice cracked like a whiplash. "What do you know about my brother?"

"Lieutenant Adams came to see me tonight," Sweeting said, trying to shrink even further back in the chair as she came closer, holding the gun not more than a foot from his flinching eyes. "He's sure Johnny killed Fay Carson. I told him he was wrong. I told him Maurice Yarde probably killed him."

Gilda stiffened.

"Why did you tell him that?"

"Yarde saw Fay Carson the night before last. They quarrelled. I heard him tell her he would cut her throat."

"You told Adams that?"

"Yes. I didn't want Johnny to get into trouble. I'm an old friend of his. I'm sure he wouldn't hurt Fay. I like to look after my friends."

She stepped back, lowering the gun.

"Is that all?"

"Isn't it enough? If it hadn't been for me, the Lieutenant would still be thinking Johnny did it. I saved Johnny."

"Do you imagine that was worth five hundred dollars?"

Sweeting licked his lips.

"That depends on you," he said cautiously. "Johnny's your brother. I saved his life."

She looked at him in disgust.

"Are they still looking for him?"

"I don't know. I do know Adams is looking for Yarde. He has gone to the Washington Hotel. He thinks he'll find him there."

To his relief she moved away from him.

"I thought you might be interested to know that Yarde is in town again," he ventured. "Or perhaps you know already?"

She looked at him, her eyes dark and mysterious.

"I didn't know and I'm not interested." She opened a drawer in the desk, took out a packet of bills, from which she took four five-dollar bills. "Here take them! That's all your information is worth to me. Now, get out!"

Sweeting got unsteadily to his feet and took the money with a shaking hand.

"You couldn't spare a little more?" he whined. "I appreciate your kindness, but I am entirely without funds."

"Get out!" she repeated.

As he moved to the front door with Leo slinking at his heels, the door-bell rang sharply.

Sweeting stopped in his tracks and looked swiftly at Gilda. She stared beyond him at the door.

"Come with me!" she said sharply, and again the gun came up, threatening him. "Quickly!"

Terrified the gun might go off accidentally, Sweeting snatched up Leo and dived through the door she had opened and into the passage beyond.

"That takes you down to the street," she said pointing to another door at the far end of the passage. "Get out and stay away from me!"

Sweeting scuttled down the passage, opened the door as the front-door bell rang again. He glanced back over his shoulder. He wasn't too frightened to wonder who her late visitor could be. She waved impatiently at him.

As he opened the door he looked at the lock and saw it was the type he had handled before. He stepped into the passage that led to the back stairs and shut the door sharply behind him.

He waited a moment or so, his ear against the door, then hearing the passage door close, he felt quickly in his trousers pocket for a pick-lock, and inserted it into the keyhole. It took him only a few seconds to turn the lock, and opening the door a few inches, he cautiously peered into the passage.

He looked back and signed to Leo to wait for him. Leaving the dog outside, Sweeting closed the door and went silently down the passage. He paused outside the door that led into the sitting-room and placed his ear against the panel.

III

As O'Brien walked into the big sitting-room he thought Gilda was tense and even a little frightened. He looked sharply at her.

"What's the matter, kid? Worried?"

"Of course I am," Gilda said, a little impatiently. She sat down on the couch. "Johnny's disappeared. Have you any news?"

"Yes; that's why I came over. He was waiting for me at the house when I got back."

Gilda stared at him.

"At your place?"

"Yes. I was surprised to find him there." O'Brien sat beside her. "He made terms."

"What do you mean?"

"He was quite frank. He told me he realized he was a nuisance. He is aware, too, that he could be suspected of Fay's murder. So he made me a proposition."

Gilda continued to tare at him.

"What proposition?"

O'Brien laughed.

"Do I have to tell you? You know Johnny. His main interest is money. He suggested I should finance him and he'd go on a trip around Europe."

"Did you?"

"Of course. It was cheap at the price."

"Oh, Séan you shouldn't have. I can't have him taking money from you."

"It's done now. It's the best thing that could happen. Now we're both rid of him."

"You don't mean he's gone already?"

"Yes. I've just come from the airport," O'Brien lied glibly. "There was a hell of a scramble to get him on the plane."

"He went without saying good-bye to me?" Gilda said, looking searchingly at O'Brien.

"There wasn't time, but he scribbled a note." O'Brien took an envelope from his billfold and gave it to her. "He tried to call you, but every telephone booth was engaged. You know what it's like at an airport. So he wrote instead."

She ripped open the envelope, read the note and then laid it down.

"Was it necessary for him to leave so quickly, Séan?"

"I think so," he returned quietly. "He wanted to go, and I didn't want him snarled up with the police."

"I wish I had seen him off."

"There just wasn't time. Get him out of your mind, Gilda. I know you're fond of him, but you've got to forget him now.

He won't be back for some time. Anyway, until after we're married; and talking about marriage, let's go ahead and make it quick now. How about the end of the week?"

Her face brightened.

"Yes. Whenever you like, Séan."

He got up.

"Fine. Leave it to me. I'll get things fixed. Now go to bed and don't worry any more. It's getting late. I'll call you to-morrow and let you know what I've fixed."

Sweeting listened to all this with growing interest. So Johnny had skipped to France. And she was planning to get married. Who was this guy she called Séan? Could it be Séan O'Brien? He wished he had the nerve to open the door a crack so he could get a glimpse of Gilda's visitor, but, remembering Gilda's gun, he decided against the risk.

He heard them talking on the landing; then, a few moments later, the front door shut.

He heard Gilda cross the sitting-room, turn off the lights and go into her bedroom. The door shut.

Sweeting relaxed.

He had better go. At least he now had twenty dollars. That would meet his rent, but it wouldn't leave him anything in hand. He suddenly realized how hungry he was. He hadn't had anything to eat all day, and Leo must be starving too.

No harm in seeing what she had in her ice-box, he thought. A chicken or a ham would be acceptable.

Softly he tiptoed across the passage to the kitchen door, gently turned the handle, found the light switch and turned it on.

Facing him was a massive refrigerator, and his eyes lit up with eager anticipation. He paused to listen, but heard nothing. Sneaking across the polished floor he took hold of the refrigerator handle, gently lifted it and pulled.

The door of the refrigerator swung back.

A thin, frightened scream came out of his mouth before he could stop it, and he jumped back, shuddering.

Sitting, hunched up on the floor of the refrigerator, his face a bloody mask, his lips drawn off his teeth in a snarl of death, was Maurice Yarde.

CHAPTER IX

I

THE motorboat swept inshore, its prow clear of the water. A long white wash from the churning screws marked its passage from the *Willow Point*.

Tux sat in the bucket seat while Solly had charge of the wheel.

For the first time in years, Tux was scared. He had fallen down on an order, and he knew what was ahead of him. O'Brien would pass the word around. Tux would be shut out, and to be shut out of O'Brien's world meant going back to small-time heists, not having police protection and scratching for a living. It wouldn't be long before he would get himself involved in a gun battle with a cop. It wouldn't be long, either, before he was on a slab in the police mortuary.

Tux ran his tongue along his dry lips at the thought. There was still a chance to rectify his mistake. If he could find Johnny, wipe him out and get rid of his body there would be no need for O'Brien ever to know Johnny had escaped from the cruiser.

But where was he to find Johnny? Would Johnny go to his sister's apartment or would he leave town? The chances were he'd leave town. Johnny was no fool. He would know Tux wouldn't rest until he found him.

The lighted waterfront was now well in view, and Tux suddenly leaned forward.

"What's going on over there?" he shouted above the noise of the engine.

Sooly turned his great pear-shaped head and stared.

"Looks like cops," he said. "That's a cop car."

"Better take her to Sam's jetty," Tux said. "We don't want to get snarled up with those boys."

Solly altered course, and in a few minutes he brought the motorboat alongside the jetty.

Both men scrambled up the ladder, and then hurried down the jetty to the waterfront.

Police whistles were blowing and they could hear the sound of distant sirens.

"This ain't healthy," Tux said. "Come on; let's get the hell out of here."

"Think they're after Johnny?" Solly asked, looking along the waterfront at the distant police car and the four cops who were standing in a group, their backs turned to them.

"How do I know?" Tux snarled. "Goddamn it! He could get away in this shindig." He had a sudden idea. "Maybe Seth knows what it's all about."

He set off down an alley, followed by Solly.

Tux knew all the short cuts and the back alleys of the waterfront as well as he knew the geography of his cruiser. But he was surprised to find a number of the alleys were already guarded by cops.

It was only the darkness and his knowledge that prevented them from being seen. By climbing over walls and passing through back yards, they managed to reach the rear entrance of the Washington Hotel.

"Stick around," Tux said to Solly and, leaving him to wait in the basement passage, he went on up the stairs to the main hall.

Cutler had returned to the reception desk. He was smoking and staring out of the window that overlooked the waterfront.

He started when he saw Tux.

"What the hell's going on?" Tux demanded.

"You'd better get out of here," Cutler said. "Right now, it's hotter than a red-hot stove."

"What's going on?" Tux snarled.

"Johnny Dorman's just shot a cop."

Tux recoiled.

"What?" His voice shot up.

"Yeah. I saw him do it."

"Did he kill him?"

"Can you imagine Johnny making a good job of anything?" Cutler sneered. "Naw, the cop's okay, unless, of course, he dies of fright."

"How do you know it was Johnny?"

"I saw the lug. Adams was here after Yarde. We were up on the top platform of the escape when I spotted Johnny with another guy down on the waterfront. A cop spotted this other guy. Johnny threw an iron on him and shot him."

"Have they got him?" Tux asked anxiously.

"Not yet, but they will. You know what Adams is like. He

pulled a gun on Johnny and knicked him. I jogged his arm or he would have had him with his second."

"I want Johnny," Tux said. "Where did he go?"

Cutler grinned.

"You ain't the only one. The place is swarming with cops. I didn't know they had so many."

"Where did he go?" Tux snarled.

"He's holed up with Rose Little."

"Who's the hell's she?"

"Oh, just a twist. She works in the amusement arcade next door during the day and flashes a leg along the waterfront at night. You remember her. Her brother's Ted Little, the guy who knocked off a couple of cops last year."

"How do you know he's with her?"

"I saw her take them in. If Adams hadn't been in such a hurry to get down the stairs, he would have seen them too."

"Can I get in there?"

Cutler shook his head.

"Not a hope. The whole district's sewn up tight by now."

"I'll be right back," Tux said grimly, and ran across the hall to the stairs. He whistled for Solly, who came up quickly and silently.

"I know where he is," Tux said. "Now we've got to get at him."

Solly's great black eyes blinked and he nodded. Together they returned to the desk.

"We'll go up and take a look," Tux said to Cutler. "Come on. Show us."

Cutler shrugged.

"Suit yourself. It won't get you anywhere. The cops have really got this organized."

The three entered the elevator which took them slowly and creakingly to the top floor.

"About time you got a new elevator," Tux said as they all stepped out. "That thing doesn't feel safe."

"It isn't," Cutler said cheerfully, "but I'd rather die than walk up all those damn stairs twice in a night."

He turned off the passage light, then opened the door that led on to the outside escape.

"Watch yourself. These cops may be trigger happy."

Tux went down on hands and knees and crawled out on to

the platform. He flattened out and Cutler, also crawling, came and lay by his side.

"That's the joint; down there," he said, pointing to a dark building across the alley and to their right.

"Okay," Tux said. "You take care of the desk. Me and Solly can handle this."

Cutler retreated and Solly crawled up to take his place.

"That's it," Tux said, keeping his voice down. He pointed. "We've got to get in there somehow."

They lay looking down into the dark alley. Every now and then they saw a movement as a cop walked slowly along the alley, turn and retrace his steps, passing the door of the building they were watching.

"Maybe I could get down there and knock that lug on the head," Solly said hopefully. "Then you could get in."

"No." Tux said. "That's not the way to play it. If we are going to get in, we'll get in by the roof."

He studied the lay-out of the district as far as he could see it.

"We'll have to get to the other side of the alley first," he said finally. "We'll have to go down the way we came up, cut around the back and get to Dave's place. We can use his roof. It'll take time, but it'll be safe."

Solly edged backwards. He was essentially a man of action. Show him what to do and he did it.

Tux followed him, and together they went down the stairs, two at a time.

II

Johnny opened his eyes, blinked and lifted his head. He looked across the dimly lighted room as Ken got quickly to his feet.

"I guess I threw an ing-bing," Johnny said, and half-sat up, grimacing. "Hell! My arm hurts. How long have we been here?"

"Twenty minutes," Ken said, coming over.

"Where's the girl?"

"She's downstairs getting some milk."

Johnny lay back with a little grunt of pain.

"I feel as weak as a rat. What's happening outside?"

"I don't know. From the sounds going on, they're surrounding the place."

"I don't think I'm going to get far. Think we're safe here?"

"I guess not. They may search each house. They must know we're hidden in one of the buildings."

"Yes." Johnny shut his eyes. "Think you can get away on your own?"

"Not yet anyway."

"Put the lamp out and take a look out of the window."

Ken turned down the wick, blew out the flickering flame and groped his way across the room to the heavily curtained window.

"Be careful," Johnny muttered.

Cautiously Ken lifted the edge of the curtain and peered out into the dark night. At first he could see nothing, then he spotted two shadowy figures almost under the window. He hurriedly lowered the curtain and stepped back.

"Two of them are right outside."

He heard the door open.

"What's happened to the light?" Rose asked out of the darkness.

"I'll light it again," Ken said, struck a match and lit the lamp. "I was looking out of the window. The police are right outside."

She noticed Johnny was staring at her.

"Well, how do you feel?" she asked, going over to him.

"Lousy," Johnny said, and forced a grin. "Thanks for fixing my arm. I guess I must have bled a lot."

"What do you expect?" she turned to Ken. "If you want to skip, handsome, you can get away over the roof. I'll look after this guy."

Ken didn't hesitate. If he could get clear and telephone Adams and tell him where Johnny was holed up, he would solve a problem that had been nagging at him ever since he and Johnny had left *Willow Point*.

He looked over at Johnny.

"What do you say?"

"Sure," Johnny said. "You skip."

"What about you?"

"There's something I want you to do for me," Johnny said. "Come here."

Ken went over to him.

"I don't know if you have anywhere to go," Johnny went on. "Every road will be watched, and you may have to hole up somewhere. Go to my sister. Her place is 45 Maddox Court.

176

She'll let you stay with her until the heat cools off. Tell her what's happened to me. Tell her O'Brien tricked me into writing her a letter so she should think I was going to Paris. Tell her about the barrel. I want her to know the kind of guy she's marrying. Will you do that for me?"

Ken hesitated.

"You'll do yourself some good," Johnny urged. "She'll give you money. She'll get you out of town."

"All right," Ken said reluctantly. "I'll get to her if I can."

"Maybe she can think of some way to get me out of this jam. She's full of ideas. Don't let anyone see you. There's a night clerk in the lobby. You'll have to get past him without him seeing you." He pointed to his coat, lying on a chair. "Get me my billfold."

Ken took the leather billfold from the inside pocket of the coat and handed it to him.

Johnny found an old envelope addressed to himself in the billfold.

"Got a pencil?" he asked.

Ken gave him his pen.

Johnny scribbled on the back of the envelope.

"Give her that. She'll know you've come from me."

Ken took the envelope and put it in his pocket.

"Good luck," Johnny said. "I'll keep the gun. I may need it more than you."

"So long," Ken said, anxious to get away. He was uneasy about leaving Johnny. If the police found him before Adams got to him, and if Johnny were killed in a gun battle, he would be stuck with Fay's murder. But he had to go. He had to get in touch with Adams.

"Come on, handsome, if you're going," Rose said impatiently. "They may get around to watching the roof before long."

Ken followed her into the passage. At the far end was a skylight.

"Go ahead," she said. "It's not too bad. Make for the Paramount movie house. You can't miss it. That's the way my brother used to go when he was in trouble. There's an escape on the movie house that'll bring you down to their parking lot. Get over the wall and you'll find an alley that'll take you to Lennox Street. The rest is up to you."

"Thanks," Ken said awkwardly. "I owe you something. If I

get out of this mess I won't forget you."

"I bet you do, handsome. Go on, beat it! I'll look after your pal."

"But I won't forget you," Ken said obstinately.

"Okay, then you won't forget me," she said carelessly. "Go on, beat it."

"I'm very grateful for your help," he said, and held out his hand.

She giggled, looking at him.

"You're a nut, handsome," she said, moved close, slid her arms around his neck and pressed her lips against his. Then she pushed him away. "Get going, Romeo. You're wasting time."

He reached up, slid the skylight back, caught hold of the wooden surround and hauled himself up.

He hung for a moment, looking over the dark roof; then, seeing no movement, he pulled himself up until he was on the roof. He looked down at the dim white shape of Rose's face, waved to her, replaced the skylight, and, crouching down, began to move silently across the roof to the shelter of a chimney stack.

When he reached the stack, he paused to study the geography of the roofs. Away in the distance he could see the blaze of neon lights on the walls of the movie house. They looked some way from him. The sounds below of men's voices and the tramping of feet unnerved him. It was some moments before he could steady himself to concentrate on his way of secape.

Roof after roof stretched away into the darkness; some of them flat, some sloping, some ridged. Having decided the way to go, he cautiously set off, climbing a six-foot wall to haul himself up on the next roof. This sloped gently into a gutter, then rose steeply to the next roof.

Half-way up the steep roof, his foot slipped, and he slithered back into the gutter, making a noise that brought him out in a cold sweat. He tried again, and this time managed to hook his fingers over the ridge of the roof. He hung for a moment, then hauled himself up, trying to keep as flat as possible against the skyline.

He climbed down on to another roof, crossed it, and as he was peering down at the roof below, he heard an excited shout away to his right.

He looked quickly over his shoulder, his heart pounding.

Across the alley, standing on a balcony, he could just make out a man and a woman looking in his direction. The man waved at him, then he bawled at the top of his voice: "Hey! A guy's up on the roof. Over there!"

Ken swung his legs over the edge of the roof and dropped, landing with a thud. He staggered, regained his balance, as police whistles shrilled in the darkness below.

He bolted across the roof, then came to an abrupt stop when he found himself face to face with a twelve-foot brick wall.

Below, he could hear running feet, and then someone began to hammer on a door that seemed immediately below him.

He moved hurriedly along the wall until he came upon an iron ladder.

"Hey! You!" a voice shouted.

Ken didn't pause. He went up the ladder, scraping his hands and knees, and as he reached the top of the wall, a gun banged and splinters of brickwork sprayed dangerously near his face.

He let himself drop into the darkness and landed on another roof.

"There's only one of them," a man shouted. "He's heading to your right."

Ken looked back over his shoulder, his heart hammering. A cop had joined the man and woman on the balcony. Ken ducked down just in time. The cop fired at him, and the slug whizzed within a foot of Ken's head.

Keeping in the shadows, he ran desperately for the shelter of a long line of chimneys. He reached them as the cop fired again, but his aim was wild, and Ken didn't even hear the slug. He dodged around the stack, paused for a second to take a quick look to right and left.

The movie house was still far off. He couldn't hope to reach it now. He had to get down somehow and take his chance in the mass of alleys below.

He heard noises behind him, and he peered between the chimneys.

Outlined against the skyline, he could see four figures moving cautiously towards him. They were still four roofs away from him, but they were coming fast.

Crouching, he bolted across the roof, came upon another ladder that led down to a lower roof. He went down it.

"Can you see him, Jack?" a voice bawled.

"Naw," the cop on the balcony shouted. "More to your right. He's behind that big stack."

Ken spotted a skylight not far from him, and he ran over to it and lifted it. He bent to peer into darkness, trying to see what lay below, then, as the sounds of pursuit grew louder, he swung his legs over the wooden surround, hung with one hand while he lowered the skylight down on top of him. He released his hold and dropped quietly on to floor boards.

As he regained his balance, he heard gunfire, followed by three cracks from a heavier gun. He heard a yell, and then more gunfire. It sounded to him as if the police were shooting at each other.

He leaned against the wall, panting and scared, while he listened.

"There are two of them by the big stack," a voice yelled. "I can see them."

Again the heavier gun barked.

Bewildered, Ken struck a match and looked quickly around him. He found himself in a dusty attic, full of old junk. He went quickly to the door, opened it, and stepped cautiously out into a dark passage.

III

Tux and Solly made their way over the roofs towards Rose's skylight. They had had several narrow escapes in getting up on to the roofs, but once there, they felt free to move quickly.

Suddenly Solly grabbed Tux's arm and pulled him down.

"Look! Over there," he muttered, and pointed.

Tux stared into the darkness. For some seconds he couldn't see anything, then he thought he saw something moving ahead of him.

"Someone up here," Solly whispered.

Tux's hand slid behind him and he jerked out his .45. They lay still and watched.

The figure ahead of them began to climb up the steep slope of a roof, three roofs away from them. He got halfway up and then slithered back.

"Think it's Johnny?" Solly whispered.

"Johnny was hit. Must be the other guy," Tux said. "To hell with him. I want Johnny."

They watched the figure climb the roof and slide over. Then they heard a man shout.

Tux cursed under his breath.

"The cops will be here in a moment. Come on! I've got to get Johnny."

Bending low, he moved hurriedly across the roof, dropped down on another roof, followed by Solly.

A shot rang out.

Four roofs away, Tux could see Rose's skylight.

"Cops!" Solly muttered, and slid like a shadow towards a line of chimneys.

Tux hesitated, then followed him.

As they crouched in the shadows, Tux caught sight of four cops climbing through a nearby skylight. They spread out and began to move cautiously forward.

"They'll walk right into us!" Tux snarled.

Solly pulled a .38 from inside his coat.

"Yeah," Tux said. "Get them before they get us. I'll take the outside guy. You take the one on the left."

They both fired.

Two cops dropped. The remaining two threw themselves flat, and opened up with their guns.

The cop on the balcony across the alley yelled excitedly, "There are two of them by the big stack. I can see them."

Tux swung around, lifted his gun and fired.

The cop on the balcony staggered, his legs banged against the rail of the balcony, and he pitched forward into the alley below.

Tux felt a violent blow on his arm, then a searing pain. The bang of a gun followed immediately.

Cursing, he dropped the gun and clutched at his wrist. Solly fired calmly, and one of the cops who was lying flat heaved up and rolled over.

"Get the other lug," Tux snarled, groping for his gun with his left hand.

Both Solly and the cop fired simultaneously. The cop jumped up, ran a few yards, then dropped.

Tux felt Solly recoil as the cop's slug slammed into his thick body. Solly gave a little coughing grunt and dropped his gun.

Tux didn't wait to see if he were badly hurt. He had to get Johnny. He was losing blood, and every second wasted made his task more difficult.

He moved forward, his damaged arm hanging uselessly at his side, slithered down one roof, lost his balance and fell heavily on the roof below. For a moment he blacked out, then shaking off his faintness he got up and staggered across the roof and paused to look down at Rose's skylight.

He didn't see a cop come quietly around the stack. Moving silently, the cop crept up to him.

"Stick your hands up!" the cop barked suddenly.

Tux swung around, firing from the hip.

The cop staggered, dropped on one knee and shot at Tux.

Tux took the slug in the belly. He tottered, fired again, saw the cop drop on his face, then Tux bent double, took a step back, overbalanced, and went crashing through the skylight to the passage below.

IV

Johnny and Rose had been listening to the shooting.

Rose leaned against the wall, her face white and her eyes large. Johnny sat on the edge of the bed, holding his gun in his lap, his face twitching.

"He shouldn't have tried to get away," Rose said fearfully. "It was my fault. He'll be killed."

"Shut up!" Johnny snarled. "Let me listen."

More gunfire rolled above them.

"I didn't know he had a gun," Johnny muttered. "He's shooting it out with them!"

"But aren't there two guns firing at them? Listen!"

"Yes, you're right."

Two guns! Johnny immediately thought of Tux and Solly. Were they up on the roof? Had they somehow found out where he was and in coming after him had run into the cops?

He pushed himself off the bed and slowly stood up. It was as much as he could do to stand upright, and he had to hang on to the bedpost to steady himself.

"I've got to get out of here," he said thickly.

"You can't go now – listen!" Rose said.

From the noise going on outside in the alley, it sounded as if the police were right under the window.

A voice shouted, "Get some more men up there! What the hell are you playing at?"

More gunfire crashed above their heads, and Rose flinched, crouching down.

Johnny moved slowly over to the door.

"Don't be a fool!" Rose cried. "Stay where you are!"

Suddenly there was a tremendous crash of breaking glass and a thud of a heavy weight just outside the door.

Johnny recoiled, staggered, and sprawled on the floor.

"What's that?" Rose whispered, her hand over her mouth.

"Someone's got in!" Johnny gasped. "Put out the lamp!"

Rose ran over to the lamp, turned down the wick and blew out the flame. She stood in the darkness, her heart hammering, while she listened to a slow dragging sound outside as if someone were crawling along the passage.

"Lock the door!" Johnny panted.

She blundered to the door. As she groped for the key, she felt the door open, and she caught her breath in a sharp scream.

She threw her weight against the door in an endeavour to shut it, jut it jammed.

Leaning against the door, she groped down into the darkness. Cold fingers suddenly closed over her wrist; fingers that gripped into her flesh like a vice.

She screamed wildly, tried to wrench free, but the grip didn't slacken.

Hearing her scream, Johnny crawled up on hands and knees. He remained crouched in the darkness, cold sweat on his face.

Rose felt the door moving against her, and opening. She struck downwards with her free hand, and her fist encountered a face.

She heard a man curse, then she was jerked savagely forward and she fell across a body that lay on the floor.

Terrified and desperate, Rose struck out while she screamed wildly.

Tux let go of her wrist and hooked her close to him. He had only one hand, but that was enough. He scarcely felt her fists beating against his face; his hand reached for her throat. He held her while she scratched at his face. Her finger-nails cut one of his eyes and he cursed. Then he tightened his grip on her savagely. Her hands scratched and tore at his fingers; then he felt the girl go suddenly limp against him. He threw her off, reached inside his coat for his gun and lay panting while he tried to locate where Johnny was.

Johnny had remained still, listening in terror to the sounds coming out of the darkness.

Now he could hear Tux's heavy breathing. He knew Tux was no more than a few feet from him, but he was too frightened to fire, knowing if he missed the gunflash would give away his position.

Tux felt as if red-hot wires were being drawn across his belly. He didn't think he could hang on much longer.

"Are you there, Johnny?" he whispered, the .45 thrust forward while he strained his ears for the slightest sound.

Johnny held his breath. Cold sweat ran into his eyes; his heart hammered so violently he thought he was going to faint.

Then he heard a heavy thud in the passage, followed by two more thuds, and he knew the police had broken in.

He knew what the police would do. They would take no chances. They would kick the door open and spray the room with riot guns. Nothing living in the room would survive.

He lost his nerve.

"Keep out!" he screamed wildly. "Don't shoot!"

Tux's .45 went off with a deafening roar. The slug caught Johnny in the centre of his forehead, scattering his brains.

Tux flopped back, tried to lift his gun again as the door kicked open.

He couldn't find the strength to raise the gun, and a blast of machine-gun fire ripped open his chest.

CHAPTER X

I

KEN stood in the dark passage and listened. All he could hear was the gun battle overhead raging more violently. The house was silent, and no lights showed.

He made for the stairs, and, moving as quietly as he could, he went down into the darkness, holding on to the banister rail. He reached the bottom of the stairs, and, before moving on, he struck a match to see where he was going. Ahead of him was the street door. He eased the bolt, blew out the match and very cautiously opened the door.

He looked out on to an alley that led to a side street. He listened, hearing shouting away to his right, and then more gunfire.

He had no idea what was happening up on the roofs, but he realized the attention of the police was focused up there and not where he was, and this was too good a chance to miss.

He moved into the alley, ran to the end of it and paused to peer into the side street.

The street appeared deserted, and keeping in the shadows he began to walk quickly to the main street he could see ahead of him. He hadn't walked more than thirty paces or so when a police car came around the corner and headed towards him.

He had no time to duck for cover. The car was coming fast, and with his heart hammering, Ken kept moving. The car swept past him. He caught a glimpse of four cops in the car; none of them looked in his direction, and when the car pulled up at the end of the street, the cops jumped out and ran into one of the side alleys.

Ken kept on until he reached the main street. He paused to peer cautiously around the corner before showing himself. Some way up the street a line of cops formed a barrier, holding back a dense crowd that were staring expectantly towards the water-front.

Ken stepped quickly back.

A narrow alley between two houses offered a way of escape, and he went down the alley which ran parallel to the main street. By climbing over several walls and crossing several backyards, he came eventually out into the main street again, but this time well behind the crowd and the police cordon.

His one thought now was to find a telephone booth and get into touch with Adams. Further up the street he spotted a lighted drug store, and he made his way towards it.

The drug store was deserted. The white-coated clerk stood on the kerb, staring down the street at the police cordon. He was too absorbed in what was going on to notice Ken, and Ken entered the store and shut himself in the telephone booth by the door.

He called police headquarters.

"Lieutenant Adams," he said when he got his connection.

"The Lieutenant's not here," a voice told him. "Who is it?"

"This is an urgent personal call," Ken said. "Can you give me his home number please?"

"You'll find it in the book," the voice growled, and the line went dead.

Ken flicked through the pages of the telephone book and found Adams' private number. After some delay the operator told him there was no answer.

Ken hung up and stood hesitating, wondering what he had best do. The chances were Adams was down by the waterfront, supervising operations there.

Ken knew he had to get off the streets. He had promised Johnny to see his sister, and Johnny had said he would be safe there. He decided to go to Maddox Court right away. From there he might be able to get into touch with Adams.

He called police headquarters again.

The desk sergeant sounded impatient.

"I don't know when he'll be in. Do you want to leave a message?"

Ken thought for a moment.

"Yes. Tell him the man who stayed at his apartment is now at 45 Maddox Court. He'll know all about it."

"Okay," the sergeant said indifferently, and he hung up.

As Ken came out of the drug store, the white-coated clerk said, "What's all the shooting about?"

"I don't know," Ken said, without pausing.

"No one ever knows anything in this street," the clerk said bitterly.

But Ken was already out of earshot. He walked fast. It took him under ten minutes to reach Maddox Court.

Several times he had to dodge down a side street and wait until a cop passed. He was in a bad state of nerves as he walked up the drive to the imposing entrance to the building.

He remembered Johnny's warning about the night clerk, and he peered through the revolving door into the big hall. He couldn't see a sign of any clerk, but behind the reception desk, a half-open door led into an inner office. He guessed the clerk was in there.

He quietly pushed past the revolving door and stepped into the hall. Then swiftly and silently he ran across the hall to the cover of the stairs and went up them.

It took him some minutes to locate Gilda's apartment and even longer to climb the stairs to the top floor. As he paused outside her front door he glanced at his wristwatch. The time was twenty minutes to one.

He wondered if she were still up. He wondered, too, if she would call the night clerk instead of answering the door. He had to risk that.

He pressed the bell and waited. After a short delay, he heard sounds on the other side of the door, then a girl's voice called sharply: "Who is it?"

"I have a message from your brother," Ken said. He took the envelope Johnny had given him from his pocket and, bending, he slid it under the door.

There was a pause, then the door jerked open. He found himself staring at the tall, willowy blonde he had seen at the Blue Rose nightclub. She had on a magenta coloured silk shirt and a pair of black slacks. Her face was pale and her great green eyes glittered.

"What is it?" she said. "What has happened to Johnny?"

"He is in trouble," Ken said. "He asked me to come and see you."

He wasn't sure if she had recognized him or not. Her face was expressionless as she stood aside.

"You'd better come in."

He followed her into the luxuriously furnished sitting-room.

"Sit down," she said curtly. "Now what is all this?"

"The police are looking for your brother. He shot a policeman," Ken said, sitting down.

"Shot a policeman?" Gilda repeated, her face tightening. "He – he hasn't killed him?"

"I don't know. Your brother was hurt. He was shot in the arm."

"For heaven's sake!" Gilda said impatiently. "Can't you tell me what happened?"

"I'm trying to. Perhaps I'd better begin at the beginning . . ."

While he was speaking, she was staring at him, her eyes puzzled.

"You say my brother shot a policeman and he is hurt?" she said. "When did this happen?"

"About a couple of hours ago."

"Oh, I see." She looked at the creased envelope that Johnny had given Ken. "How did you get hold of this?"

"Your brother gave it to me. He said you would know I came from him."

"He just says I should help you. He doesn't say anything about being hurt."

"He couldn't write well. His arm hurt him."

She studied him, her eyes angry and suspicious.

187

"Would you be surprised to know that my brother is at this moment flying to Paris?"

"He isn't! It was a trick. O'Brien planned to murder him. He persuaded your brother to write a note to you so you should believe he had gone to Paris."

"This gets more and more complicated as we go along, doesn't it?" she said, moving over to the sideboard. "Are you telling me that Séan O'Brien was planning to murder Johnny?"

"I know it sounds fantastic," Ken said, worried by her obvious suspicion, "but if I told you the whole story . . ."

"That won't be necessary," she said, jerking open a drawer in the sideboard. She dipped into it, turned to face him, an automatic in her hand. "Don't move! You're lying! I know who you are! You're the man the police are looking for! You killed Fay Carson!"

II

The telephone began to ring as O'Brien entered the lounge.

"Get it," he said impatiently to Sullivan, and crossed the room to the liquor cabinet.

Sullivan picked up the receiver, listened, grimaced and looked over at O'Brien, who was mixing himself a highball.

"Police Captain Motley," Sullivan said. "Want to talk to him, boss?"

O'Brien drank half the highball, lit a cigarette and took the receiver.

"What is it?" he snapped.

"A report's just come in that's going to start something," Motley said, his voice shaking with excitement. "Johnny Dorman's been shot dead."

O'Brien stiffened; his face changed colour.

"What the hell are you talking about?" he snarled.

"One of my men was on the waterfront keeping a lookout for this guy Holland. He spotted him with Johnny Dorman . . ."

"With Johnny? He's lying!" O'Brien broke in violently. "He couldn't have been with Johnny . . ." He stopped abruptly, realizing what he was saying.

"He was with Dorman," Motley said. "There's no mistake about it. My man started to question Holland, and Dorman shot him."

Certain that Tux had carried out his orders and had wiped out Johnny, O'Brien wondered if Motley was drunk, but he realized he had to be careful. He couldn't tell Motley he knew Johnny was in a barrel of cement at the bottom of the river.

"The two of them bolted," Motley went on, "but they were seen by Adams who happened to be in the neighbourhood. He took a shot at Johnny and hit him in the arm. They got away and holed up in a house off the waterfront. Adams had the place surrounded. Holland got away over the roofs. He was spotted, and Adams sent men up after him. They ran into Tux and Solly who were up there."

O'Brien nearly dropped the receiver.

"What?"

"Don't ask me what they were doing up there," Motley said. "The fools started a shooting match. They killed five of my men. Tux got into the house where Dorman was hiding and shot him before our men could get at him."

O'Brien turned cold.

"What happened to Tux?"

"My men blew him to bits," Motley said.

So Tux had made a mess of it! O'Brien thought. Somehow Johnny must have escaped from *Willow Point*. What was Gilda going to say when she read the morning papers? He realized he would have to see her immediately and get a convincing lie in first. Damn Tux! He was lucky to be dead.

"Holland got away," Motley went on. "We're still looking for him. We've got the press on our backs."

"Get Holland! Do you hear?" O'Brien snarled. "That's an order!"

He slammed down the receiver, went quickly across the room to the hall where Sullivan stood waiting.

"I'm going out," O'Brien said. "Wait up for me!"

He hurried to the garage, got the Cadillac out again and drove fast to Maddox Court.

It took him a little under ten minutes to get there, and by that time he had his story ready. He had to convince Gilda that he had nothing to do with Johnny's death. He had told her he had seen him off in a plane for Paris. Very well then: the plane had returned with engine trouble and Johnny had left it. That's the best he could do. She would be too upset by Johnny's death to question the story.

The night clerk, who knew O'Brien well, hurried to open the elevator doors as O'Brien crossed the lobby.

"Miss Dorman is in, sir," he said.

O'Brien grunted, got into the elevator and was whisked to the top floor.

The poor kid would be in bed and asleep, he thought as he crossed the passage to her front door. This was going to be a hell of a shock for her.

He rang the bell.

There was a pause, then Gilda called through the door, "Who is it?"

"Séan. Let me in, kid."

She opened the door.

He was startled to see she had her back turned to him and she was facing the open door of the sitting-room. He saw she had a gun in her hand.

"What's happening . . . ?"

He looked into the sitting-room at the tense, white-faced man sitting in a chair who stared at him with frightened eyes.

"A burglar . . . or what?" O'Brien asked. "Here, give me the gun." He took it from Gilda and walked into the sitting-room. "What's all this about?"

"It's the man who killed Fay Carson," Gilda said, breathlessly. "He broke in here."

O'Brien stiffened.

"Are you Holland?" he demanded.

"Yes," Ken said, "but I didn't kill her."

"Yeah?" O'Brien said. "Well, tell that to the jury." He looked at Gilda. "What's he doing here?"

"He must be crazy. He came here expecting me to hide him. He says Johnny shot a policeman and is wounded. He says you planned to murder Johnny and he rescued him."

"That's a laugh," O'Brien said. "Get police headquarters." He waved to the telephone. "They'll be glad to see him."

"Wait!" Ken said. "You must listen to me." He was looking at Gilda. "I heard this man . . ."

"Shut up!" O'Brien said, threatening him with the gun. "Open your mouth again and you'll get shot!" To Gilda he went on, "Get Motley. He'll handle this."

As she moved over to the telephone, the front-door bell rang. She looked quickly at O'Brien, her hand hovering over the telephone.

"Are you expecting anyone?" he asked, as the bell rang again. "No."

"Here, take the gun and watch this guy. I'll see who it is."

He gave her the gun, walked into the hall and opened the front door.

Lieutenant Adams stood in the passage, his hands in his pockets. His face didn't betray his surprise at seeing O'Brien, but he was surprised.

"What the hell are you doing here?" O'Brien rasped.

"Holland's here, isn't he?" Adams said mildly.

"How do you know?"

"I got a message."

O'Brien stood aside.

"You'd better come in and take charge of him."

Adams walked into the sitting-room, looked at the gun in Gilda's hand, then at Ken. He gave Ken a sly wink.

"This is the man who killed Fay Carson," O'Brien said. "Charge him and take him away."

Adams shook his head.

"He didn't kill her," he said.

"I'm telling you he did!" O'Brien snapped. "The Commissioner has all the evidence he needs for a conviction. Don't argue with me! Charge him and take him away."

"The Commissioner got his information from Sergeant Donovan, who is invariably inaccurate," Adams said, watching Gilda as she laid the gun down on the sideboard.

"If Howard is satisfied, I am. I told you to arrest this man!"

"But he didn't do it. I had instructions to carry out an independent investigation. I've done so and I've cracked the case. This isn't the man."

"I suppose you are going to tell me Dorman killed her?" O'Brien said angrily.

"No, he didn't, either."

O'Brien made an impatient gesture.

"Don't be so damned mysterious! Who killed her, then?"

"It's quite a story. The facts . . ."

"I don't want to listen to this," Gilda said. "Séan, can't he take this man away? This has been a shock to me. I want to go to bed."

"You'll be interested, Miss Dorman," Adams said before O'Brien could say anything. "Fay Carson was murdered because you married Maurice Yarde. You can't fail to be interested."

Gilda stiffened, her mouth tightened into a thin line.

"What did you say?" O'Brien's face flushed. "Married to Yarde? What the hell do you mean?"

Gilda turned to him.

"He's lying! Don't listen to him, Séan. Get them out of here!"

"You can't deny it, Miss Dorman," Adams said. He sat down in a chair near Ken. "I had confirmation from Los Angeles not ten minutes ago. You married Maurice Yarde thirteen months ago. You lived with him for four months, then you left him. It's on record."

Gilda appeared to make an effort to control herself. She shrugged and turned away.

"All right," she said, her voice harsh. "So it's on record. It's no business of yours."

"Yes, it is," Adams said, crossing one leg over the other. "Your marriage supplies the motive for Fay Carson's murder."

Gilda looked at O'Brien, who was standing motionless, his eyes glittering.

"Don't believe him, Séan. He's either mad or drunk!"

"You'd better be careful what you are saying," O'Brien said to Adams.

"I can produce evidence of her marriage by tomorrow morning," Adams said indifferently. "She's wasting time denying it."

O'Brien went to Gilda, took her arm and looked intently at her.

"Are you married to Yarde, kid?"

She hesitated, then gave a despairing little shrug.

"Yes. I'm sorry, Séan. I should have told you. I'm getting a divorce. I was a fool to have married him, and I've paid for it. I didn't live with him for more than a month before I found out what he was. I was too ashamed to tell you."

O'Brien gave her a crooked little smile.

"Forget it. We all make mistakes." He patted her arm. "It's okay, kid." Then he turned to Adams. "You've poked your goddamn nose into too much of this. Take that guy out of here, charge him with the murder of Fay Carson and make it stick! If I have any more bleating from you, I'll have you thrown off the force!"

Adams stroked the tip of his thin nose as he met O'Brien's furious eyes.

"It can't be done. He didn't kill her."

"Then who did?" O'Brien snarled.

Adams nodded at Gilda.

"She did, of course."

"My God!" O'Brien exploded. "I'll make you pay for that!

I'll . . ." He broke off as he caught sight of Gilda's face.

She was now as white as a fresh fall of snow. Her eyes stared past O'Brien, her hand at her throat. He followed the direction of her staring eyes.

In her bedroom doorway, looking up at her, was a fawn Pekinese dog.

III

Deliberately, the dog crossed the room and stopped outside the door leading to the kitchen. It scratched at the paintwork, whined, then scratched at the door again.

Gilda screamed, "Get it out of here! Get it out!"

"Gilda!" O'Brien exclaimed, shaken by her terror. "What is it?"

Adams left his chair, crossed the room with two strides, turned the door handle and threw the door open.

The dog darted into the kitchen.

Adams watched it run to where Sweeting lay face down on the floor. There was a puddle of blood at his side; an ice-pick was embedded between his fat shoulder-blades.

The dog paused beside him, sniffed at his face, then backed away, whimpering, and crept under the kitchen table.

Adams looked swiftly at Ken, then towards the door leading into the hall. His eyes were expressive.

Ken got up, went over to the door and set his back against it. He was watching Gilda, who abruptly sat down, her face ashen.

"You might like to take a look," Adams said to O'Brien.

O'Brien walked into the kitchen, kicked Sweeting over on his back and stared down at the dead face.

"Who's this?" he asked, and Adams could see he was badly shaken.

"Raphael Sweeting, a blackmailer," Adams said. He was watching the Pekinese, which had come out from under the table and was now sniffing excitedly at the refrigerator. It stood up, whined and scratched at the door. "It can't be that easy," Adams went on, under his breath. "He can't be here too."

"What the hell are you muttering about?" O'Brien snapped.

Adams took hold of the handle of the refrigerator, lifted it and let the door swing open.

O'Brien caught his breath sharply when he saw the crumpled body of Maurice Yarde in the refrigerator.

"For God's sake!" he exclaimed. "Who's this?"

"Her husband – Maurice Yarde. I wondered where she had hidden him," Adams said.

O'Brien pulled himself together with an effort. He walked into the sitting-room.

Gilda stared at him.

"I didn't do it, Séan! You've got to believe me!" she gasped. "I found him there. I swear I did!"

He touched her shoulder lightly.

"Take it easy, kid. I'm on your side," he said, then, looking at Adams who was leaning against the kitchen door-post, he said, a rasp in his voice, "Let's get this thing straightened out."

"I'm charging Miss Dorman with the murders of Fay Carson, Yarde and Sweeting," Adams said. "We'll sort it out at headquarters."

"We'll sort it out right here!" O'Brien said curtly. "Miss Dorman denies the charge. You have no evidence that she did it, or have you?"

"I've got enough evidence to make Carson's killing stick," Adams said.

"What is the evidence?"

"It's a matter of motive. The key to Carson's murder was something I nearly missed. At first I liked Dorman for the job. He was unbalanced and he had threatened to kill her, but I found out he couldn't have done it. He was seen outside the Blue Rose club when Carson and Holland left the club. He didn't know where she lived. He couldn't have gone ahead and got into her apartment, so I had to rule him out. I got a tip that Maurice Yarde had quarrelled with Carson. I thought maybe he had done it. I went to his hotel. He was missing, but his room had been ransacked. From the way the search had been conducted, it looked like the searcher was after a document of some kind. I had a hunch. That's why I'm a good cop. I get these hunches. Was the searcher a woman, and could the paper be a marriage certificate? I didn't think it was likely. It was a blind guess, but I called Los Angeles and checked up on Yarde. I found he married Miss Dorman thirteen months ago." Adams pushed himself away from the door-post and came into the room. He began to pace slowly up and down, his hands in his pockets, while O'Brien watched him, a hard glitter in his eyes. "I had heard Miss Dorman was going to marry you. So far as she was concerned it was a pretty good match. I wondered if Fay Carson

194

had found out from Yarde that he was married to Miss Dorman. Carson had a score to settle with Miss Dorman. She was in a position to blackmail her if she knew Miss Dorman was married to Yarde. Just ideas, you see, but ideas that established a motive. So I started checking on Miss Dorman. I found out she was at the Blue Rose club last night, and left half an hour before Carson and Holland did. That would give her time to get to Carson's apartment. She had once shared an apartment with Carson, and knew of Carson's habit of leaving a key under the mat. Whoever was hiding in the bedroom had to have a key as the door was undamaged. I began to like Miss Dorman for the job. The night clerk downstairs tells me she came home last night at two o'clock. The killer left Carson's apartment at twenty minutes to two. It is a twenty-minute drive from Carson's apartment to here. Work it out for yourself. I learned, too, from the night clerk that Maurice Yarde called on her last night after nine o'clock, and the night clerk didn't see him leave. Yarde probably tried to get money out of Miss Dorman. He probably told her Carson knew, too. She killed him, put him in the refrigerator until the opportunity came for her to get rid of his body. She went to his hotel, searched for the marriage certificate, found and destroyed it. She then went to the Blue Rose, spotted Carson with Holland. She went to Carson's apartment, sure that Carson would bring Holland back, and he'd make a fine fall guy. She killed her, fused the lights and got back here."

O'Brien got to his feet, took a cigarette from his case, and wandered over to the sideboard for the cigarette lighter.

"You haven't told me anything that a good attorney can't blow to hell," he said, as he lit a cigarette. "Now, I'll tell you something: Johnny told me he killed her."

Adams shook his head.

"He told you because he wasn't going to marry you," he said quietly. "You might have hesitated to marry Miss Dorman if you knew she had a murder on her hands. Dorman was financially interested in your marriage, wasn't he?"

"You can't make this charge stick," O'Brien said, his face tightening. "You're going to drop it!"

"In a week I'll have a case no attorney can upset, and I'm not dropping it."

O'Brien set the lighter down. His hand jumped to the gun, whipped it up, and, turning, he covered Adams.

"Don't make a move unless you want a slug in you!" he

rasped. He looked at Ken, who still stood against the door. "Get over there with him!"

Ken obeyed.

Adams appeared completely unruffled.

"This won't get you anywhere, O'Brien," he said. "She can't beat the rap: not with those two stiffs in her kitchen. Maybe she might have wriggled out of the Carson killing, but those two in there fixes it."

"That's what you think," O'Brien said. "But you haven't my talent for organization. You may be a smart cop, but you've still got a hell of a lot to learn."

Gilda had got unsteadily to her feet.

"Get Whitey here," O'Brien said to her, without taking his eyes off Adams. "Speedwell 56778. Tell him to bring four of the mob with him, and to step on it."

She crossed to the telephone.

"I wouldn't do it," Adams said softly. "It won't get you anywhere."

"Won't it? Let me explain what's going to happen," O'Brien said, his eyes gleaming. "You and Holland are going to get knocked off. The night clerk is also going to get knocked off. The boys will walk those two stiffs out of here and plant them somewhere safe. You will be found in the lobby downstairs, shot by Holland's gun. He'll be found on the stairs, shot by your gun. The clerk got shot accidentally, getting in the way. That'll take care of it, won't it?"

"It could do," Adams said.

"It will. Carson's killing will be blamed on Holland. That's what I call organizing, Adams," O'Brien said, showing his teeth in a fixed grin.

Gilda was shaking so badly she couldn't hold the receiver.

"I can't do it, Séan," she moaned.

"Leave it!" he said sharply. "I'll handle it. Go into your bedroom. Don't worry, kid. You're in the clear."

Gilda turned, stumbled across the room, opened her bedroom door, went inside and shut the door.

O'Brien looked at Adams.

"So long, smart cop," he said.

He didn't see Leo come out of the kitchen. The dog trotted up to him and stood up, its paws against O'Brien's knee.

Startled, O'Brien, looked down, then kicked the dog away.

Adams' hand flew inside his coat, yanked out his gun.

O'Brien fired a shade late.

Adams' gun barked and a red splash of blood appeared under O'Brien's right eye. He dropped his gun, staggered back as Adams fired again.

O'Brien slammed against the wall, heeled over and spread out on his face.

"The punk had me sweating," Adams said softly. He blew out his cheeks, wriggled his shoulders inside his coat, and grinned at Ken. "Did he make you sweat, too?"

Ken didn't say anything. He went unsteadily to a chair, sat down, holding his head in his hands.

Adams looked at him, shrugged, and went quietly to the bedroom door, turned the handle and pushed open the door.

Gilda was standing in the middle of the room, her hands to her ears, her face drawn. When she saw him, she gave a sharp scream.

"It didn't work," Adams said. "You're right out on your own now, sister. Come on. We'll go down to headquarters and talk this thing out."

Gilda backed away.

"The dog foxed him," Adams went on, moving slowly towards her. "He hadn't got the dog organized. I got him before he got me. Come on, sister, don't play it the hard way."

"Keep away from me!"

Her voice was a croak. Her face was ugly with terror.

"The jury will love your legs," Adams said comfortingly. "You'll only get twenty years. You'll be out of all the misery that's coming when they drop the H-bomb. You don't know it yet, but you're a lucky girl."

Gilda turned and ran. She took five swift steps before she reached the big, curtained window. She didn't stop. She went through the curtains, through the glass and out of the window.

Adams heard her thin wailing scream as she went down into the darkness, and the thud of her body as it struck the sidewalk, sixteen stories below.

He lifted his shoulders, walked quickly back into the sitting-room, ignoring Ken, who still sat with his head in his hands, and called headquarters on the telephone.

"Get an ambulance and a squad to 45 Maddox Court, fast," he said into the mouthpiece, "and when I say fast, I mean fast!"

He dropped the receiver back on to its cradle, went over to Ken and jerked him to his feet.

"Get the hell out of here! Don't you want to go home?"

Ken stared blankly at him.

"Go on, beat it!" Adams said. "You're in the clear. Keep your mouth shut and you won't hear anything more about it. Go on, get the hell out of it!"

Too shocked to speak, Ken went unsteadily to the door.

"Hey!" Adams said, pointing to the Pekinese who had taken refuge under the sideboard. "How about this dog? Wouldn't you like to give it a home?"

Ken looked at the dog in horror.

"No!" he said, his voice shaking. "It's all right with me if I never see another Pekinese again in my life."

He went down the stairs at a stumbling run.

IV

A few minutes to half-past eight the next morning, Ken stopped his car at the corner of Marshall Avenue where he could see down the road. He waited a few minutes, then he saw Parker open his gate and come towards him.

The usual spritely snap had gone out of Parker's walk. He came towards Ken as if it were an effort to drag one foot after the other. He looked pale, haggard and depressed.

Ken got out of the car.

"I thought I'd give you a lift to the bank," he said awkwardly.

Parker started and stared at him.

"Of all the damn nerve!" he said angrily. "You can't go to the bank! The police are looking for you. Now look here, Holland, you've got to give yourself up. I can't have you with me all day, not knowing when the police are coming to arrest you. I won't have it!"

"Keep your shirt on," Ken said. "I've been to the police and explained. They caught the killer last night, and I'm in the clear."

Parker gaped.

"They got the killer? Then you didn't do it?"

"Of course not, you dope!"

"Oh! Well, I don't want anything more to do with you. You're a damned dangerous influence. You've ruined my home."

Ken asked the question that had been torturing him for the past few hours: "Did you tell your wife I went to see Fay?"

"Tell her?" Parker's voice shot up. "Of course not! You

198

don't think I'd tell her I gave you an introduction to a tart, do you? It's bad enough now, but she would never have forgiven me."

Ken drew in a deep breath of relief. He suddenly grinned, and clumped Parker on his back.

"Then this lets me out!" he said. "You'll keep quiet about this to Ann, won't you?"

Parker scowled at him.

"I don't see why both of us should be in the soup. It'd serve you damn well right if I did tell her, but I won't."

"Honest?" Ken said, looking at him.

"Yes," Parker growled. "No need for the two of us to be in the dog-house."

"That's swell. Brother! I've been sweating it out since I had her letter. I heard this morning. She's coming back in five days' time. Her mother's going into a home. She should have gone weeks ago, and now Ann's persuaded her. She's coming back next Monday."

Parker grunted.

"It's all right for you, but I'm in a hell of a fix."

"How's Maisie this morning?"

Parker shook his head.

"She's looking like a saint with indigestion. She's horribly quiet and polite and distant. I'll be in the dog-house for months before she gets over it."

"Buy her an expensive present: a fur coat for the winter," Ken suggested.

"That's right: spend my money for me. How can I afford a fur coat?"

"You were a mug to have told her, anyway. You needn't have. If you had used your head you could have cooked up some yarn."

Parker nodded gloomily.

"I know. I've been thinking about that. I was a mug, but that sergeant rattled me."

"We can't stand here all day. Get in if you want to."

"Well, all right," Parker said, and got into the car. "But don't think it'll ever be the same between us, because it won't."

"Oh, shut up!" Ken said shortly. "You started the mess and you got what was coming to you."

Parker gave him a surprised glance. He noticed Ken appeared to have acquired more character overnight. He looked tougher, more confident, and not the kind of man you'd push around.

"Who killed her?" Parker asked. "What happened?"

"I know as much as you do," Ken lied. "I went to the police station, told the Lieutenant that I had been with Fay last night and waited to be arrested. He told me to go home as they had the killer. I didn't wait for a second invitation. I went."

"I thought you had a good story for me," Parker said, disappointed. "That's damn dull."

"I guess it is," Ken said, his face expressionless.

As they drove into the parking lot behind the bank, Parker said, "Are you going to tell Ann what happened?"

Ken shook his head.

"You may be a mug," he said as he got out of the car, "but I'm not."

V

Five days later, Ken stood on the platform waiting for the train that was bringing Ann home.

He was feeling particularly virtuous. For the past four evenings he had worked ceaselessly in the bungalow and in the garden. All the various jobs that Ann had been asking him to do for the past months, and which he had put off, had been done. The garden had never looked better. The kitchen had been decorated. The windows had been cleaned. The broken hinge on the gate had been repaired; even the car had been polished.

The newspapers had been full of the shootings. The City's Administration had come under fire, and several prominent members had resigned, among them Captain Joe Motley, who felt that his work was becoming too arduous for his easy-going methods. Lindsay Burt's name kept cropping up in the papers as the next likely political leader, and the *Herald* was prophesying that Lieutenant Adams would shortly be elected Captain of Police.

For the first time since Ken had found Fay's dead body, he felt safe. With a feeling of intense excitement, he watched the train come slowly along the track.

He caught sight of Ann's blonde head as she leaned out of the window. They waved frantically to each other. A few moments later he had her in his arms.

"Oh Ken!"

"Darling, I've missed you!"

There was a babble of talk, both too happy to listen to what the other was saying.

"Have you been all right?" Ann asked, when eventually they calmed down. She looked up at him and was puzzled by his thinness, the sterner look about his mouth that gave him character and which she found attractive.

"Of course I've been fine," Ken said, grinning at her.

"But, darling, you look different. There's something about you . . ."

"Nonsense!" Ken said. "Come on. Let's get your luggage organized."

Later as they drove out of the railway depot in the shabby green Lincoln, Ann said, "Have you been lonely, Ken? Did you go out – do any shows?"

"My dear girl, I haven't had time for shows," Ken said virtuously. "I've been busy in the bungalow. I've decorated the kitchen, looked after the garden and generally worked my fingers to the bone."

Ann looked at him, her eyes suddenly thoughtful.

"It sounds very much as if you had been up to mischief. It's nothing serious, is it?"

"The trouble with you is you have a suspicious mind," Ken said, avoiding her eyes. "Besides, is it likely I would tell you if I had been into mischief? I admit I did think of going off with some woman, but I just didn't have the time."

Ann leaned forward and kissed him.

"You've had your chance, Ken. I'm not leaving you again."

"That's no way to behave when I'm driving. Wait until we get home." He put his hands on hers and squeezed it. "I don't want you ever to go away again. Now tell me what's been happening to you."

He listened while she talked, and he felt at peace with the world. She need never know, he told himself. It would never happen again. He had had a narrow escape, and he had learned his lesson.

"Well, here we are," he said, as he pulled up outside the bungalow. "Take a look at the garden. How's that for hard work? And don't miss the gate. It works now."

"Darling. I think I'd better go away again after all," Ann said, standing at the gate and looking at the weedless garden, the close-cut lawn and the clean-cut edges. "It looks wonderful, and the windows have been cleaned."

"Just part of the service," Ken said, as he struggled with her luggage getting it out of the car.

Ann gave a sudden exclamation.

"Oh, Ken, you darling! Is this your big surprise? How lovely!"

Ken followed the direction of her pointing finger.

On the doorstep, its bulging eyes looking fixedly at Ken, was a fawn Pekinese.

CRIME FICTION – NOW AVAILABLE IN GRANADA PAPERBACKS

James Hadley Chase

One Bright Summer Morning	75p ☐
Coffin from Hong Kong	65p ☐
Mission to Venice	75p ☐
Mission to Siena	65p ☐
Strictly for Cash	65p ☐
What's Better Than Money?	75p ☐
He Won't Need it Now	75p ☐
Just the Way It Is	65p ☐
A Whiff of Money	65p ☐
An Ear to the Ground	60p ☐
You're Dead Without Money	65p ☐
Believed Violent	75p ☐
Like a Hole in the Head	65p ☐
There's a Hippie on the Highway	75p ☐
Want to Stay Alive?	75p ☐
The Vulture is a Patient Bird	65p ☐
This Way for a Shroud	75p ☐
Just a Matter of Time	75p ☐

CRIME FICTION – NOW AVAILABLE IN GRANADA PAPERBACKS

Georgette Heyer

Penhallow	95p	☐
Duplicate Death	75p	☐
Envious Casca	95p	☐
Death in the Stocks	95p	☐
Behold, Here's Poison	85p	☐
They Found Him Dead	95p	☐
The Unfinished Clue	60p	☐
Detection Unlimited	95p	☐
Why Shoot a Butler?	60p	☐
A Blunt Instrument	60p	☐
No Wind of Blame	60p	☐

MYSTERY AND SUSPENSE FROM COLIN WILSON

Ritual in the Dark	£1.25 ☐
The Philosopher's Stone	95p ☐
The Schoolgirl Murder Case	75p ☐
Order of Assassins	95p ☐
The God of the Labyrinth	75p ☐
The Occult	£2.50 ☐
The Killer	60p ☐
The Mind Parasites	95p ☐
The Space Vampires	75p ☐
Rasputin and the Fall of the Romanovs	75p ☐
Origins of the Sexual Impulse	95p ☐

TRUE CRIME – NOW AVAILABLE IN GRANADA PAPERBACKS

Ludovic Kennedy
A Presumption of Innocence £1.25 ☐
10 Rillington Place 95p ☐

Stephen Knight
Jack the Ripper: The Final Solution £1.25 ☐

Peter Maas
The Valachi Papers 95p ☐

John Pearson
The Profession of Violence £1.25 ☐

Ed Sanders
The Family 95p ☐

Vincent Teresa
My Life in the Mafia 95p ☐

Colin Wilson
Order of Assassins 95p ☐
The Killer 60p ☐

Leslie Waller
Hide in Plain Sight £1.25 ☐

AGATHA CHRISTIE – QUEEN OF DETECTIVE FICTION

The Secret Adversary   95p ☐
The Murder on the Links   95p ☐
The Mysterious Affair at Styles   85p ☐
The Man in the Brown Suit   85p ☐
The Secret of Chimneys   80p ☐

C S FORESTER

Plain Murder   85p ☐
Payment Deferred   80p ☐

All these books are available at your local bookshop or newsagent, or can be ordered direct from the publisher. Just tick the titles you want and fill in the form below.

Name ....

Address ....

Write to Granada Cash Sales, PO Box 11, Falmouth, Cornwall TR10 9EN.
Please enclose remittance to the value of the cover price plus:
UK: 30p for the first book, 15p for the second book plus 12p per copy for each additional book ordered to a maximum charge of £1.29
BFPO and EIRE: 30p for the first book, 15p for the second book plus 12p per copy for the next 7 books, thereafter 6p per book.
OVERSEAS: 50p for the first book and 15p for each additional book.
Granada Publishing reserve the right to show new retail prices on covers, which may differ from those previously advertised in the text or elsewhere.